Monet Talks

Monet Talks

A Den of Antiquity Mystery

Tamar Myers

LARGE PRINT

This large print edition published in 2005 by
RB Large Print
A division of Recorded Books
A Haights Cross Communications Company
270 Skipjack Road
Prince Frederick, MD 20678

Published by arrangement with HarperCollins Publishers, Inc.

Publisher's Cataloging In Publication Data
(Prepared by Donohue Group, Inc.)

Myers, Tamar.
Monet talks : a Den of Antiquity mystery / Tamar Myers.

p. (large print) ; cm. — (Den of Antiquity mysteries)

ISBN-13: 978-1-4193-5723-7
ISBN-10: 1-4193-5723-9

1. Timberlake, Abigail (Fictitious character)—Fiction. 2. Antique dealers—Fiction.
3. Large type books. 4. Mystery fiction. I. Title. II. Series: Myers, Tamar. Den of
Antiquity mysteries.

PS3563.Y475 M66 2005b
813/.6

Printed in the United States of America

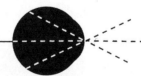

This Large Print Book carries the
Seal of Approval of N.A.V.H.

For
Selina McLemore

CHAPTER 1

I bought the Taj Mahal for ten thousand dollars at an estate auction. A slew of people bid against me, but I kept my cool, and when the auctioneer's gavel pounded, closing the sale, I was the proud owner of India's most identifiable landmark. The crowd applauded.

Afterward, a number of people came over to congratulate me. "Way to go, Abby," they said, "way to go," but every single one of them sounded jealous. All in all, it was a very good day, even though I had one heck of a time fitting the Taj into the back of my Volvo station wagon.

It wasn't the real Taj Mahal, of course, but a handmade wire and sheet-metal replica that was actually a birdcage. The bit of information that came with it claimed that this piece had been commissioned by a British officer's wife back in the days of the Raj. The strange black bird that came with the cage was a more recent addition. Other than that the bird's name was Monet, and what he liked to eat, there was no further information.

My name is Abigail Washburn, by the way. I'm

an antiques dealer, the proud owner of the Den of Antiquity, on lower King Street in downtown Charleston, South Carolina. My assistant is C.J.—a.k.a. Jane Cox—which stands for Calamity Jane. She has a genius level IQ, is a brilliant businesswoman and a dear friend, but she is one beer short of a six-pack, if you get my drift.

When I arrived at my shop with the Taj Mahal in tow, C.J. was all atwitter. "Ooh, Abby, he's beautiful," she said referring to the bird. "Where did you get him?"

"He came with the cage. The auctioneer called him a, uh—well, I've forgotten. Sorry, but I'm not up on my birds."

"He's a *Gracula religiosa intermedia.*"

"Excuse me?"

"A Greater Indian Hill Mynah. They're a member of the starling family. What are you going to do with him?"

"I haven't really thought about that. I was just so interested in buying this cage. Don't you think this cage is beautiful, C.J.?"

"I've seen prettier."

"But look at all that work. Whoever made this had to bend all these wires to create these filigree bars, and just look at all the bezel-set semiprecious stones on these sheet-metal domes. It must have taken hundreds of man-hours to make, and I'll bet some of these larger stones—like that amethyst, for example—are worth something by themselves.

I hope to double money on this with the right buyer."

C.J. shrugged. "The amethyst looks cloudy to me. Abby, can I have the bird?"

"Well—"

"This species of mynah is about the best talker in the whole world, Abby. They can sound just like a human, or a cat, or a fire engine, whatever they want to imitate."

"Is that so? He hasn't said a word yet."

"Then I can have him?"

There is nothing like someone else lusting after your property to make it suddenly seem desirable. I gave the bundle of feathers a second glance. He wasn't much to look at; mostly black, with dark orange-brown shadings. There were featherless patches on his neck—wattles I'd guess you'd call them—that were bright yellow, but I certainly wouldn't call them attractive. A mockingbird might have made a prettier pet, a blue jay surely.

At any rate, neither C.J. nor I heard the man sneaking up behind us, which is why we both jumped when he spoke.

"Whatcha looking at?" he demanded.

We whirled. There was nobody there.

"You looking to pick a fight, buddy?"

"C.J., this is freaking me out." The voice reminded me of my long-dead daddy's, only without his Upstate drawl.

"Maybe it's a ghost, Abby. Have you ever had your shop exorcised?"

"They prefer to be called Apparition Americans these days, and no, I haven't had it exorcised. I've never had any problem with ghost—Apparition Americans."

"Dennis, Dennis," a woman shrieked, *"bring me a fresh pot of tea."*

I'm four feet nine. C.J. is five feet ten. The thing that kept me from leaping into her arms was the look on her face.

"C.J., what is it? Besides the fact that this shop suddenly has more spirits than the state liquor store."

Much to my horror, the big gal started laughing maniacally. I wouldn't have been surprised to see her horse-size head start spinning à la Linda Blair. Between guffaws she tried to speak, but wasn't getting anywhere.

"If you don't stop laughing this minute, I'm going to have *you* exorcised."

C.J. sobered pronto. "Abby, it's not one of them that's your culprit. It's him!" She pointed at the mynah.

"Say what?"

"I told you they were good talkers, didn't I?"

"Didn't I? Didn't I?"

If I hadn't been staring at the bird, if I hadn't seen its throat bob up and down, I wouldn't have believed my ears. It sounded exactly like C.J.

"Now do you believe me?"

"Yes, I—"

4

"Betty bleaches her toe hair?" The new voice was high and sweet, with a breathy quality. *"Get out of town!"*

"Ooh, Abby, you gotta let me have him. Please, pretty please."

I was about to say I would give her the bird when the bells hanging from my shop door jangled, and in walked two of Charleston's grand dames. I won't mention names, but they both wore wrinkled linen suits and chunky jewelry. Their shoes came to roach-killer points and their handbags came from Moo-Roos. Yes, I know, that description fits half the women living South of Broad, and a good number of Junior Leaguers everywhere. Mama calls them Linen Ladies.

"Will you look at that!"

"Ladies, I apologize!" I cried, absolutely mortified.

"That's one hot mama, guys."

Linen Lady One walked straight to the Taj Mahal. "What a clever bird."

Linen Lady Two followed suit. "Dahlin', I believe it was referring to me."

"You want to hear a dirty joke?" The bird used a child's voice this time.

The Linen Ladies twittered.

"Jimmy fell in the mud!"

The grand dames threw back their heads and laughed uproariously, an eerie sight given the limitations imposed on them by Botox.

The mocking mynah threw back its head as well. *"Ha ha ha ha ha."*

5

"Dahlin'," Linen Lady Two gasped, "have you ever heard anything so precious in your life?"

"Dahlin', have you ever heard—who wants a second helping of pie? Pie? Pie?"

I watched spellbound as two pillars of Charleston society fell in love with a starling from India. They were all over that bird like white on rice. They said everything they could think of to Monet, who obligingly parroted it right back— pardon the cross-species reference. But what really delighted the doyennes were things Monet had picked up prior to coming into my possession. The fact that some of his blather was on the bawdy side was icing on their cake.

Had I contemplated such a scenario in advance, I would have surmised that a distraction like Monet would be bad for business. *Au contraire.* The ladies dropped a wad of money, and then immediately called all their friends, who, when they popped in to see Monet, were all too happy to push their plastic on me. The only loser was C.J.

"Abby, are you sure I can't have him?" C.J. was still whining a week after Monet's auspicious debut. "His cage stinks, you know. You don't want a stinky cage in your shop, do you?"

"C.J., his cage stinks because you don't clean it every day like you're supposed to."

"C.J., his cage stinks. Okeydokey, senhora. Now they won't find it."

"Shut up, will you please?"

6

"Abby!"

"I meant the bird. Look, C.J., why don't you take off early today and go visit the pet stores. Maybe they have mynahs for sale, or know how to get one for you."

C.J. actually stomped one of her enormous feet. "It won't be the same," she whined.

I'd never seen the woman so upset about anything. Not even when her great-uncle Horace Ledbetter vanished into the great blue yonder, after having tied all eighty-nine of his birthday balloons to the arms of his lawn chair.

"I'm sorry, dear, but I'm not willing to give him up. But I tell you what, from now on I'll clean his cage."

"Clean his cage, clean his cage. Did you call the dentist? Fights powerful odors with just one application."

My friend and assistant was not amused. She stomped off to dust some highboys, while I fetched an old newspaper from under the counter and got to work on cleaning Monet's elaborate abode.

Engrossed as we were, neither of us really heard the bells ring for the umpteenth time that day. That's why I nearly jumped out of my pumps when someone poked me in the ribs. Folks who sneak up on one like that deserve lumps in their grits for at least a week.

"Mama!"

"Sorry, Abby, but you saw me coming."

"I most certainly did not."

"You were looking this way," one said.

"Maybe I was, but I didn't see you. I was distracted. C.J. won't take no for an answer and—"

"Little people have little problems, dear, and big people have big problems."

"You're not that much taller than me, Mama."

"Four inches," she replied. "But I wasn't referring to height. Like I said, dear, I have a serious problem."

I led Mama to my storeroom behind the shop, and then, to make sure C.J. couldn't eavesdrop, I turned on a small radio I keep in there for company while I'm checking inventory. "Okay, Mama, spill it."

CHAPTER 2

Mama patted her pearls. They are a gift from Daddy, the last thing he gave her before he died in a freak accident that involved a seagull with a brain tumor the size of a walnut. That was going on twenty years ago. My minimadre has worn these mollusk secretions around the clock since then. That they still have nacre is a tribute to the high standards of Mikimoto. At any rate, Mama pats the pearls when she's agitated. She twirls them when she reaches her breaking point. If you see her necklace spin, you best hightail it out of there.

"Abby, it's about the St. Necrophilia Society."

"Excuse me?" Mama only sometimes shocks me, but she never ceases to surprise me.

"You know, that exclusive club to which only blue bloods can belong. I think your family has to have lived in Charleston three hundred years in order to join. Of course we aren't eligible since we moved here only three years ago—"

"Mama, that's the St. *Ophelia* Society!"

"Are you sure?"

"Just a minute." I tiptoed over to the door and

9

pounded on it with my fist. I heard a muffled "ow" and the scraping of feet. "Yes, I'm sure. Look, I already know where you're going with this. Why do you want to join a club that doesn't want you as a member?"

"But they don't know me. If they did, I'm sure they would invite me."

"Mama, they aren't going to change their rules just because you want them to."

"I know that, dear. I may be old, but I'm not stupid."

I made her wait until the count of ten. "You're not old."

The telltale gems began a slow rotation. "Abby, you know how you're always saying that your only wish is for my happiness."

"You say that, Mama, not me."

"Let's not quibble over facts, dear. The point is, you want me to be happy here in Charleston, don't you?"

My husband Greg and I moved down to the coast when he retired as a detective on the Charlotte police force. Greg started a new life here as a shrimp boat captain. We invited Mama, who lived up in Rock Hill, South Carolina, to join us, which she did in a heartbeat. Greg and I were both amazed at how quickly she adapted to her new surroundings. She immediately joined Grace Episcopal Church—although she was not allowed to join the choir—and took advantage of their myriad activities. She also belongs to an eccentric circle of friends who call themselves the Heavenly Hustlers. To my knowledge, she was as happy as a body had a right to be.

"Mama, I don't have all day. Can you cut to the chase? What is it you want from me?"

"Why I never, Abby! In my day—"

"It's still your day. Last time I checked you were very much alive."

"Well!" The pearls gained speed.

"Theatrics aren't going to help, Mama. If we're through here, I'm going back out to work." I started for the door.

"I'm going to crash their ball."

I whirled as the pearls twirled. "The St. Ophelia Ball?"

"Maybe 'crash' was the wrong word. You see, dear, Betty Lou Crustopper has two tickets again this year, and she's not planning to go. In fact, she never goes. She hasn't gone since her husband, Cotton Crustopper, died in 1947."

"How do you know Mrs. Crustopper, and what do her tickets have to do with you?"

"Abby, if you went to church, you'd know her, too. Every Sunday they wheel her into the sanctuary and park her up next to the organ. She likes to watch Scott Bennett tickle those keys. She used to teach piano. Didn't retire until she was eighty."

"How old is she now?"

Mama's sigh was meant as a comment on my poor church attendance. "She turned a hundred

11

and two in June. The entire parish was there—well, except for you and Greg. You should have seen Betty Lou try to blow out her candles. Some of the children tried to help—"

"The tickets, Mama!"

"I was getting there. Honestly, Abby, I don't know where you get your impatience from." She sighed again. "Anyway, as I was about to say, Betty Lou gave me tickets to the ball, and I plan to use them. There is no point in letting perfectly good tickets go to waste, is there, dear?"

"She *gave* you her tickets?"

"Essentially." As Mama backpedaled, her pearls slowed to a crawl and then reversed directions.

"Define 'essentially.'"

"I might have traded them for a basket of muffins. But they were homemade muffins, and I chopped the dates myself. And it was a very nice basket, Abby, and I tied a pretty pink bow on the handle. Everyone in the nursing home was ogling it."

It was my turn to sigh. "Let me get this straight. You talked a centenarian into trading two tickets to the St. Ophelia Ball for a batch of baked goods?"

"Let's not quibble over details, dear. The only reason I'm here is to ask you if you're coming with me, or not."

"So that's where I come in! Mama, from what I've heard, they have guards posted at the door, checking everyone's identification."

"They check only the tickets, dear."

"Even so, we could never pass for Mr. and Mrs. Cotton Crustopper. Mr. Crustopper has been pushing up daisies for over half a century."

"But that's the good part. No one has to pretend to be Mr. Crustopper. The tickets read 'Mrs. Cotton Crustopper and *guest*.' I'll dress up as Betty Lou— of course we'll have to rent a wheelchair—and you can be my guest. The only restriction is that the guest has to be male. They still don't allow same-sex couples. They don't allow divorcées, either, for that matter. They check on that. Divorced men, yes, but not divorced women. At any rate, we'll hit one of the costume shops and get you a fake mustache and a little boy's tux—no offense, dear."

I must admit that for a millisecond I was tempted to participate in Mama's shenanigan. The St. Ophelia Ball is *the* event of the season. That's all folks talk about for two months prior and two months post. The talk is, of course, all speculation. No one really knows what happens at that ball except for the attendees, and their thin patrician lips are sealed. But it was absurd to think we could pull it off, and even if we did, would we dare tell anyone? I, for one, would bust a gut trying to keep all that juicy gossip to myself.

"Mama, my answer is no."

"Then I'll ask C.J. She'll do anything."

Boy, wasn't that the truth. If my assistant accompanied my mother to the ball, Charleston society would never recover. And since Charleston is un-disputedly the manners capital of the country, its decline would signal the end of Western civilization. Therefore, I had no choice but to accompany Mama and save the world as we know it.

"Okay, Mama, I'll be your date. But you've got to promise me you won't do anything that Mrs. Crustopper wouldn't do."

"But she's confined to a wheelchair, and I want to dance."

"Mama!"

"All right, dear. I promise."

Just for the record, I didn't expect her to keep her word; Mama's promises are meant to be broken. But at least I'd be along to handle damage control. The South might teeter as a result of our charade, but it wouldn't topple.

To be absolutely honest, by the time I got home that evening I was brimming with anticipation. The St. Ophelia Ball is held in the Daughters of Fine Lineage building. If you reside in Charleston and don't know where that building is, chances are your lineage does not meet their standards. The Daughters of Fine Lineage are every bit as secret as the St. Ophelia Society, and it was only by accident that I stumbled onto this building on lower Meeting Street. I mean that literally. I'd gotten a pebble in my pump and was hopping about on one foot, and lost my balance. The next thing I knew, I was sitting on some steps, and when I looked up I saw a row of tiny brass letters above a door. THIS IS IT, they spelled. Then several weeks later I was eavesdropping on some customers, Linen Ladies all, and I heard the word IT bandied about. I put two and two together and got three hundred—three hundred years of blood so blue, members of this exclusive group are forbidden to donate their periwinkle plasma, lest it cause the nurses to panic.

At any rate, both Mama and I had to work very hard to keep from spilling the beans over dinner. Just because Greg is no longer employed as a detective doesn't mean he's stopped detecting.

"I smell a rat," he said as he passed the roast.

"I don't smell anything," Mama said, and wiggled her nose like Samantha on *Bewitched*. The woman prides herself on her olfactory powers.

Greg turned to me. "Abby, what kind of nefarious plot are you two hatching?"

"Nothing, darling. Would you like the gravy?"

"What I'd like is to know how much trouble I have to prepare for. Will I need to bail you out?"

"Gracious no," Mama said. "This isn't one of C.J.'s schemes."

"Mama!"

"Aha," Greg said, trying to mask a smile, "so you *are* up to something."

"But it isn't illegal, darling. At least I don't think it is."

"It's definitely not," Mama said. "Unless we resist when they try to throw us out."

Greg pressed his hands to his ears. "Okay, that's enough. I don't want to know the rest. Just

15

remember that if I'm out shrimping, it may take a couple of hours for me to get back. Can you two stand to share a toilet in the holding cell with a dozen other women?"

"No problem," Mama said, without skipping a beat. She carries paper liners in her purse wherever she goes.

I cut an extra large piece of pecan pie for my dearly beloved that evening. And behind closed doors he was the recipient of even more sugar.

Tuesday is C.J.'s turn to open the shop. Because the big gal is so competent, I am used to sleeping in late, with nary a care in the world—that is, if my grown children, Susan and Charlie, are not going through some crisis, and Mama is behaving, and my cat, Dmitri, is not out to convince me that I should have gotten a dog instead.

Dmitri can't get enough of Greg's fishy smell, so he spends the night curled up on my husband's back. Greg leaves to go to work before five in the morning; thereafter the pussy with the passion for *poisson* usually seeks out the next best thing: *moi.* The trouble is, I am a back sleeper, and Dmitri weighs ten pounds and counting. Some mornings I wake up unable to breathe.

That morning, however, Dmitri had resumed sleeping on Greg's side, so I was running about la-la land with a naked Tom Cruise and a fully clothed Jack Nicholson when the bedside phone rang. At first I refused to answer, but when Tom threatened to put his clothes on—and Jack threatened to remove his—unless I picked up, I struggled back to the land of the sentient.

My eyes were too bleary to read the caller ID. "Hello?"

"Abby, I didn't take him. I swear."

"C.J.?"

"Please don't be mad, Abby. I've looked everywhere. Even in the armoires and the highboy drawers. Not that he could have gotten in those by himself, mind you, but he could have had accomplices."

"C.J., please—"

"Granny Ledbetter had a goat back in Shelby, North Carolina, that was an escape artist. Yes, I know, goats are famous for being able to escape from just about anything, but this one—we called him Homer—not only got out of his pen on a regular basis, but the next morning we'd find him locked up in Cousin Arvin's closet. It happened about a billion times. Granny Ledbetter said it was trolls who did that, but Abby, I don't think we have trolls in downtown Charleston. Although some of the tourists dress like that."

I shook my head to clear it of cobwebs. It was an exercise in futility.

"*What* is missing, C.J.? Your granny's goat?"

"Don't be silly, Abby. It's Monet."

The cobwebs disappeared. "The mynah?"

"Abby, are you hard of hearing?"

I hung up, threw on yesterday's clothes, and

broke a few traffic laws getting to the store. Imagine the mixture of relief and irritation I felt upon discovering that verbose bird sitting safe and sound on one of his perches.

"C.J.! That wasn't the least bit funny. I could have killed someone driving over here."

"Frankly, Abby, your bad driving habits aren't my fault. And this isn't what you think. That's not Monet in there. That's a common starling—*Sturnus vulgaris*. They were imported from England, you know. In 1890 about a hundred of them were released in Central Park by a group that wanted to have every bird mentioned in Shakespeare flying loose on this continent. Well, they got their wish, because there's about two hundred million starlings in this country now."

"What?"

"It's one thing to be hard of hearing, Abby, but not to listen is just plain rude."

"I'm listening, I'm listening." I was also giving the so-called missing mynah a closer look. "Well, I'll be! That *is* a regular old starling. How did that happen? I mean, a fancy starling like a mynah couldn't have turned into a regular one, could it?" I knew that was stupid of me, but seeing is supposed to be believing, and I was trying my darnedest to believe.

To her credit, the big gal chuckled only briefly. "That's a stuffed bird, Abby. Like the kind taxidermists make."

"I'm calling the police."

"I already did that. They should be here any minute."

"Good. I know I'm going to regret saying this, but I was getting used to Monet. It's going to seem very quiet around here until we get him back."

"Shouldn't that be *if* we get him back? Somebody obviously went to a lot of trouble to do this. This wouldn't have happened, Abby, if you'd given him to me."

Mercifully, the shop phone rang. I ran to get it.

"Hello?" I said, hoping it was the police, telling me they were just seconds away.

"Is this Mrs. Timberlake?"

"It's Washburn now, but yes, this is the place that was burgled. I know it was just a bird, but I feel violated—"

"Do you want Monet back?"

"Excuse me?" I stared at the caller ID box. The number was blocked.

"If you want him back, Mrs. Timberlake, then you have to give me the real Monet."

"Who is this?"

I got a dial tone in reply.

CHAPTER 3

The Charleston police force has officers who number among the finest in the world, but none of them were on duty that day. Officers Tweedledee and Tweedledum could not get it into pumpkin heads why I should be so upset over the loss of a bird. A real bird pooped, they bothered to inform me. At least a stuffed starling couldn't spread disease. Nevertheless, they dusted for prints between calls on the loudest walkie-talkies on the planet. The only way I could get the cops to leave was to toss a box of day-old Krispy Kremes into the street.

After I locked the door behind them, I tried calling Greg, but by then he was well out into the ocean and couldn't be reached. I needed comfort then, not harebrained schemes, so the next person I called was my best friend, Wynnell Crawford (I have several best friends, by the way). Wynnell is also an antiques dealer, although her shop, Wooden Wonders, is in West Ashley, not on the peninsula.

"That's terrible," she said, after I explained what had happened. "Abby, you must feel so violated, having your shop broken into like that."

"That's exactly what I feel. But the police didn't seem to care about that. All they wanted to do was flirt with C.J."

"Let me guess . . . Officers Tweedledee and Tweedledum?"

"You got it. Wynnell, it makes me sick to my stomach to think that someone not only has the key to my shop, but knows my security code."

"Abby, do you know that for sure?"

"The lock wasn't forced. And it was locked again when C.J. arrived this morning. I guess it's possible I forgot to set the alarm last night, but you know how I am."

"One check short of obsessive-compulsive?"

"And that phone call—it didn't make a lick of sense. The *real* Monet. I've never had a Monet painting in my shop, and I've certainly never owned one. And that creepy stuffed starling." I shuddered. "Wynnell, what kind of demented person would do such a thing?"

"Is that a question, Abby, or do you just want to be heard?"

"Both!"

"Well, I hear you. I'm also afraid you're not going to like what I'm about to say."

I sighed. "You're not going to blame it on a Yankee, are you?"

"They're a strange bunch, Abby. Just yesterday a group of Yankee tourists came into my shop. They were headed out toward Middleton Plantation but had gotten lost. Of course I gave them directions,

21

but do you think they bought anything? All they did was use my bathroom."

"To be fair, Wynnell, you only sell furniture. And you don't ship. What did you expect them to buy?"

"Just the same, never trust a Yankee, my daddy always said, and he was right. I bet you dollars to doughnuts it was a Yankee who stole your bird."

"As long as we're being fair, Wynnell, your daddy's mama was a Yankee."

"You don't need to be insulting," she said, and hung up.

I waited by the phone while I counted the seconds. It rang precisely at ten.

"Hello."

"Sorry about that, Abby. I know I'm kinda touchy on the subject, seeing as how I'm not a purebred Southerner like you. But back to your problem. You need to change the locks, of course, and your security code. Also, I don't think you or C.J. should work alone until you learn what kind of kook you're dealing with."

"Good advice. Maybe I'll just close the shop altogether for a few days. Mama's been wanting me to spend some time with her, and C.J. has been asking for some beach days."

"It must be nice," Wynnell said pointedly.

When we both lived in Charlotte, North Carolina, we were more or less on equal footing. But now I'm an S.O.B. and Wynnell is a W.O.T.A. That is to say, I live South of Broad Street on Charleston's coveted lower peninsula, and my buddy lives West of the Ashley River. There is nothing wrong with being a W.O.T.A.—some of the best people are—but the area South of Broad is said to contain the fifth highest concentration of wealth in the nation. Sure, I would lose money by closing my shop, but it wasn't going to make much of a dent in my personal finances.

"Business has been slow," I said, lying through recently capped teeth.

"Whatever. Abby, promise you'll call if you need me?"

"I promise."

"I gotta go. Some customers just walked in."

Before I hung up I heard her talk in the high-pitched voice she uses when she's pretending to talk to customers. Before I locked the doors to my shop for the next few days, I would put a sign in the window directing my customers to Wynnell's shop, Wooden Wonders, well West of the Ashley.

I was still upset when lunch rolled around, so some of my other best friends, the Rob-Bobs, insisted on taking me out to eat. Their shop, The Finer Things, is doing so well that they now have an assistant, Simone Dupree. The girl speaks perfect English, but can put on a French accent at the drop of a syllable. If she tilts her nose skyward, the Rob-Bobs' sales head that way, too. FYI, the lunch offer was just for me, which was just as well, because C.J. was already out on Folly Beach, searching for skin cancer.

I suggested Sticky Fingers on Meeting Street as our lunch spot. You can get just about any style of ribs there, but the very best, in my opinion, are the Memphis Dry. They are so good your tongue will reach out and slap your face silly. The meat is served with side orders of baked beans and cole slaw. Perhaps it was not their intention, but the owners of Sticky Fingers have hit upon a formula that ensures their delicious meals will be remembered for the rest of the day.

At any rate, the Rob-Bobs' real names are Rob Goldburg and Bob Steuben, respectively. Rob is tall, handsome, and in his early fifties. Bob is—well, he's still in his thirties. Rob, who hails originally from Charlotte, is the epitome of a Southern gentleman. Bob is from Toledo, Ohio. Rob is *the* antiques expert in Charleston. Bob fancies himself a gourmand.

After we'd ordered our drinks—sweet tea all around—Bob complained, as usual, that we weren't eating lunch at their place.

"It wouldn't have been any trouble, Abby. You know how I love to cook."

Knowing what was coming next, whether I invited it or not, I humored him. "What would have been on your menu?"

"Poached quail eggs on toast points with hollandaise sauce, chilled asparagus aspic, and a piping hot sweetbread soufflé."

"He means thymus glands," Rob growled. "From calves. We had them last night."

"From calves? Aren't you afraid of getting mad cow disease?"

"Moo-ve over," Rob said, and poked his partner good-naturedly. "You're taking up too much table space."

"I don't get my sweetbreads just anywhere," Bob said. "I special order them from a ranch in Argentina, where mad cow disease has never been found."

"He also orders rhea meat from that ranch."

"What kind of meat?"

"Rhea," Bob said. "It's a large, flightless bird, kind of like an emu or an ostrich. In fact, it's the largest bird in the Americas. Gets up to five feet tall. I've been ordering just the steaks so far, but I'm thinking of ordering a whole one for Thanksgiving. Yes, I know, the air freight will be a killer, and I'll have to hunt around for an oven to fit it—maybe a bakery, or someplace like that—but just think, I'll be able to invite everyone I know over to dinner."

"For their last meal," Rob quipped. "Remember what happened when you made the eel flambé?"

"That was a fluke."

"No, that's when you served whale. Maybe you should order a live rhea, and Abby can ride it to dinner."

"Guys, I appreciate your attempts to distract me, but I can't stop thinking about the break-in. It gives me the heebie-jeebies when I think of how I might have been in the storeroom at the time. And that horrible stuffed starling. This is a sick person."

"Or a student from the College of Charleston."

"You're kidding—aren't you?"

Rob shook his head. "It could have been an initiation prank. School's just starting. This city is flooded with kids. And then there are the Citadel cadets. If I was thirty years younger—"

"Which you're not," Bob said.

"But it couldn't be kids," I protested. "How would they know my alarm code?"

"Are you positive you set it?"

"Of course I am. You know that I make a ritual out of it every night, unless, of course, it's C.J.'s turn to close. And last night was mine—oh my gosh!"

"Abby, you're pale as a sheet. What is it?"

"Mama came in right before closing. We got to talking in the storeroom, and I remember thinking about closing—intending to close—but then I walked Mama out to her car, and then I got in mine, because I was so distracted by the thought of crashing—uh, never mind. I guess maybe I didn't. Set the alarm, I mean."

"Whoa," Rob said, and waved the waiter away. "Back up a bit there, girl. What were you so distracted about?"

"Do you have to know?"

"Absolutely," they said in unison.

"Mama wants us to crash the St. Ophelia Ball."

Rob whistled in admiration. "She's something else, that Mozella."

"We have a friend who crashed the St. Ophelia

26

Ball," Bob brayed. The man has a bass voice that is the envy of bullfrogs everywhere. "He said it's a cinch if you smell like mothballs and don't move too fast."

"Did he crash it by himself?" I asked. "I thought only couples were allowed."

"Maynard's a ventriloquist. He took a mannequin. He had it—he calls it Sheila—strapped to his shoes."

"Very funny."

"Bob's not joking, Abby. They won a trophy for best-looking couple. They would have won another one for best dancing, but one of Sheila's feet came loose and dragged around the dance floor. At a very slow pace, of course."

"I don't believe you guys, but thanks for trying to cheer me up."

"That's what friends are for, Abby. And quit worrying so much about that stupid prank— because I'm sure that's what it was. When I was in college, we went into town and borrowed a toilet from a plumbing store, which we then put in a fountain in the middle of campus. But first we stuck an effigy of the college president on the john."

"When he says 'borrowed,' he means swiped," Bob boomed, which got the entire room's attention.

Rob frowned at his partner. "Anyway, you shouldn't worry about your alarm, either. It wouldn't hurt to get the number changed, but I bet anything it was a simple case of forgetfulness. It happens to me all the time."

"Amen to that," Bob said, at only slightly diminished decibels.

"Yeah?" Rob said. "Well, I'm still trying to forget what you served me for supper last night."

I waved the waiter back over.

One might think it would be hard to plan such an elaborate charade with a live husband in the house, but Mama and I managed to pull it off. It definitely helped that Greg works hard outdoors all day and generally isn't interested in going out unless I drag him. We told him we were going to an opera at the Gaillard, and when he politely asked the name of the production, I told him "The Man from La Mannequin." He told us to have a good time and went back to watching a taped baseball game.

We're not stupid; we changed into our ball clothes at the Rob-Bobs'. Rob has acted in community theater from time to time, and he fancies himself an expert at stage makeup. When he was through trying to turn Mama into a 102-year-old woman, she looked like the victim of a hit-and-run graffiti artist.

"Don't you think those lines on her face are a little wide?" I asked gently.

"Maynard said they use only candlelight, because it makes everyone look good. If I made Mozella's lines any thinner, they wouldn't show up."

"Maybe if she was on a stage," Bob whispered in my ear. He was in charge of plastering my short but very thick hair to my head. He'd run out of mousse halfway through and switched to Vick's VapoRub. At least my sinuses weren't going to bother me.

"I heard that," Rob said. He turned and gave me the once-over. "Abby, your hair isn't the only thing that needs flattening."

"I'll take that as a compliment. But I'm sure that when I put the tux jacket on, you won't even notice."

Bob sighed. "My two favorite people—all dressed up and ready to knock Charleston dead."

"Careful," Rob said. "Some of those people there tonight might be closer to death than you think. Some of them played with God as a child, and from what Maynard says, some of them are richer. Are you good at mouth-to-mouth, Abby?"

"Only with Greg."

The doorbell rang. Bob ran to get it and returned a moment later with C.J. loping along behind him. To my astonishment, the big galoot was wearing a purple ball gown and matching high heels.

"So I was thinking," she said, as she teetered into the master bedroom, "that we could all chip in and buy Abby another mynah. It wouldn't have to be a *Gracula religiosa*, of course, but Abby's not very observant and she'd never notice—" She lumbered to a stop. "Oh, I'm sorry, I didn't know you had company."

"We don't," Bob said. "It's only—"

"Mrs. Cotton Crustopper," Rob said, bowing to Mama, "I would like to present Jane Cox— C.J., this is Mrs. Crustopper and her escort for the evening, Reginald Stiles."

C.J. offered Mama a mitt the size of New Jersey. "I remember you. We sat beside each other at the Daughters of Fine Lineage Hat and Chat Luncheon last summer."

Mama looked stunned. We both knew that C.J., despite her country-bumpkin persona, had relatives as inbred as the best of them. But I'm sure neither of us dreamed that she belonged to the Daughters of Fine Lineage and was a member of the St. Ophelia Society to boot. She'd never talked about any of it.

Rob came to Mama's rescue. "Miss Cox, I'm afraid Mrs. Crustopper has a touch of laryngitis tonight."

C.J. scratched her chin. "Granny Ledbetter has this surefire treatment for laryngitis, but it involves a possum, and I don't know where to find a possum in Charleston on such short notice. But Cousin Orville swears that a big rat will work just as well—if you add a little extra sugar—and I know where to find plenty of big rats."

Mama opened her mouth to say something, but Rob shook his head ever so slightly before laughing a bit too loud. "Ha! Ha! Please forgive Miss Cox. Always joking, this one."

"But I'm not joking. If you don't have time for me to bring back a big rat, two little rats might do. I saw some in the alley when I parked my car. It will only take me a minute to catch—"

"Rats?" Bob barked. "In our alley?"

But C.J. was looking at me. "You look awfully familiar, Mr. Stiles."

I smiled and shrugged.

"Ooh, I remember now. I dated your brother, Stacy. We only went out a couple of times, then the cousins came to town and we all went to see a 3-D movie at the Imax, and then, just because Cousin Orville and Cousin Alvin had to be carried out on stretchers, your brother dumped me." She sighed. "But you don't look like that type, Mr. Stiles. I mean, to dump a girl for no good reason."

I shook my head.

"And you're certainly cuter than your brother."

I smiled wanly.

"Ooh, I had an idea. If Mrs. Crustopper isn't feeling very well—no offense, Mrs. Crustopper, but you usually talk up a storm—maybe we could go to the ball by ourselves, Mr. Stiles." She had the audacity to wink at me.

I couldn't stand it a second longer. "C.J., it's me, Abby!"

C.J. blinked. "Huh?"

"Abby Washburn—your boss and best friend."

"Good one, Mr. Stiles. But Abby has a squeakier voice, and she isn't as tall."

That did it. That hiked my hackles so high, I was even taller than Stacy Stiles.

31

"For your information, missy—"

But Rob had grabbed me with a lobsterlike pinch on the elbow and was steering me into the bathroom. "Keep your cool, Abby," he whispered. "If C.J. doesn't recognize you, then y'all are a cinch for getting into the ball."

"Yes, but she's hitting on me."

"Take that as a compliment, Abby. I certainly do. Who knew I was so good at stage makeup? Although frankly, I'm still not attracted to you. No offense intended."

"None taken. But Rob, Mama will never agree to stay behind, and you can bet your rococo she isn't going swallow any rat potion—sugar or not."

"Don't worry, darling. Just play along." He dragged me back into the bedroom. "Hey folks, sorry about the interruption. I had some urgent business to discuss with Reginald here." He slapped me on the back so hard that I appeared to leap forward. Right at C.J.

"Ooh, Mr. Stiles," she said, rubbing her hands together in anticipation, "have you agreed to be my date?"

"Shame on you, C.J.," Rob said, surprising me with his sharpness. "You're engaged to Abby's brother, or did you forget?"

She looked Rob right in the eye. "Of course I didn't forget, silly. But Toy had to stay up in Sewannee this weekend. Seminary students have to do a lot of studying you know."

"In that case," Rob said, before I had a chance

to speak, "Mr. Stiles will be glad to include you in his party."

"Party? Does that mean Mrs. Crustopper will be coming with us?"

Mama's eyes gleamed. "You're darn tooting," she in a voice I'd never heard before.

And so the fatal die was cast.

CHAPTER 4

It was a fine summer evening, appropriate for Charleston's finest to strut their stuff. And strut C.J. did. Meanwhile Mama bumped gamely along while I, of course, pushed. I had no objections to being a gay man, even one taller than myself, but you would think C.J. could have at least given me a hand at the curbs. She is, after all, nearly twice my size.

By the time we got to the hall I was perspiring so profusely I worried that my mustache might fall off. All this sweating was a new experience, I assure you. As a Southern woman, I had hitherto only glistened, or, at the very most, dewed.

I will confess to being a mite disappointed when the couple taking tickets at the door barely gave ours a glance. "Be careful on the stairs," the man said. "Someone spilled a glass of punch."

"I'll be taking the elevator," Mama said in that strange, nasal voice she'd adopted.

"There's punch in that, too. And you'll have to mash the 'close door' symbol twice."

"And pray that it doesn't get stuck," the woman said.

"It better not," Mama said. "I'd hate to be stuck in an elevator with these two."

We were a touch on the late side, even by Charleston standards, and as soon as we got inside, the sounds of a mediocre orchestra could be heard wafting up the stairwell along with the smell of spilled punch. Immediately C.J. began tapping one of her monstrous purple pumps.

"That's 'Begin the Beguine,'" she wailed. "It's my favorite song."

"Then I think you two should dance to it," Mama said, still vocally a stranger.

"But we have to take you down in the elevator and—"

"Nonsense, dear. You run along with Mr. Stiles—who, by the way, looks to have quite the dancer's body—and trip the light fantastic. I don't mind taking the elevator alone."

"Are you sure?"

"Quite certain. Now off with the two of you," Mama said, dropping the nasal tones as she adopted a pseudo-English accent. "Cheerio, hip-hip-hooray, and all that sort of rot."

C.J. needed no further encouragement. She grabbed my hand and literally pulled me down the stairs. Thank heavens we missed all the wet spots. Without asking my permission she dragged me out into the crowded dance floor, propped me up against her bosom, and began to sway in countertime.

"Isn't this so romantic?" she cooed.

I turned my face so I could see around her breasts. The room was filled with dancing couples, the men holding the women at a discreet arm's length, but my senior prom was more romantic. There had been nothing done to disguise the fact that we were in the basement. The walls were beige, the floor was covered in black-and-white-checkered linoleum, and the only decorations I could spot—if indeed that's what they were—were a pair of silk ficus trees badly in need of dusting. Despite all the people, the room gave the impression of bareness. Even the orchestra had been sequestered behind a plain white screen, lest they gaze upon the faces of the socially privileged and have to be put to death.

My clueless employee has an insatiable appetite, and it wasn't long before she maneuvered me over to the refreshment table. It was yet another disappointment. Instead of a cloth, the table was covered with paper that had been ripped, not cut. A plastic punch bowl in a faux cut-glass pattern served as the centerpiece, but it was almost empty. The sandwich plates looked like they'd been picked over by a flock of buzzards, and there were less nuts in the nut tray than there were on the dance floor.

C.J. grunted. "I knew I should have come straight here. No offense, Mr. Stiles."

I grunted as well. It seemed like a manly thing to do, and unless I'm sorely mistaken, a good grunt is supposed to be worth a hundred words.

C.J. pressed my head deeper into her bosom. "Ooh, I've always loved a man who could grunt like that. Do you scratch as well, Mr. Stiles?"

"Argh?"

"Absolutely." She sighed deeply. "If only my fiancé, Toy, would grunt and scratch himself. But oh no, just because he's studying to be an Episcopal priest, he thinks he has to have decorum. Who's he trying to kid? That's what I want to know. You ought to see his family. His mother is locked in a 1950s time warp, a real head case, if you ask me. Wears a mountain of crinolines under her full-circle skirts, just like Donna Reed, and never, ever goes without her pearls. I bet she showers in them. And then there's Toy's sister. Whew—now there's a whack job!"

I pushed free of her bosoms and ripped off my fake mustache. "That is enough, C.J.!"

She had the gall to grin. "Yeah, maybe I did get carried away. Sorry for calling your mama a head case, Abby. You know how much I like her."

"You *knew* it was me all along?"

"Of course, silly. You said so yourself back at the Rob-Bobs."

"But you acted like you didn't believe me."

"I was getting back at you, Abby. You and Mozella really hurt my feelings, you know. How come you didn't tell me you were coming here tonight?"

"Well, because, uh—we didn't want you to get in trouble."

At twenty-four, she's half my age, but that didn't stop her from regarding me sternly. "You didn't want me *causing* the trouble, isn't that it?"

"Yes, but coming here wasn't my idea, I swear. Mama—oh my gosh, where is Mama? I haven't seen her since we left her upstairs by the elevator. C.J., you're a head taller than anyone else, can you see her?"

"I'm afraid I don't, Abby."

I slapped the fake mustache back on. "Keeping looking, C.J., while I run back upstairs."

"Try the elevator," C.J. hollered as I vaulted up the stairs one step at a time.

But Mama was nowhere to be found in that building. We even checked the shrubbery outside. In desperation we called the Rob-Bobs, who said they hadn't heard from her since we left for the ball. It was with a sinking heart that I called Greg.

He picked up just before the answering machine would have switched on. "Hey, hon," he said, "can you make this quick? The score is tied and the bases are loaded."

"Mama's missing."

"That's nice. I'm glad you're enjoying the opera. Talk to you later." He hung up to the distant sound of cheering.

"Well?" C.J. demanded,

"He's in a sports fog. Unless it involves beer and pork rinds, he's beyond reaching."

"Cousin Oglethorpe is like that. Once he got

into football fog and didn't move for days. His wife hooked him up to a long plastic hose—she attached it to his you-know-what—and put vitamin pills in his beer, which she fed him through a tube—"

"C.J., this is not the time for Shelby stories!"

"Sorry, Abby. Do you think she walked home?"

"Rolled, maybe. Mama doesn't walk unless she has to. But if we split up—I'll walk—we'll spot her on the way to my house."

"Will do, Abby."

But Mama was nowhere to be seen, even though we covered every possible route. Finally, with mounting dread, I grabbed one of C.J.'s oversized mitts and dragged her into the house. My dearly beloved didn't even bat one of his enviably long lashes. It wasn't until I shut off the TV that he stirred. Even then it took a second or two for him to withdraw from his sports-induced coma. (Funny how this type of coma does not prevent the ones experiencing it from jumping up and down and hollering from time to time.)

"Is the opera over already?" he asked.

"We obviously didn't go to the opera, Greg. Is Mama home?"

He shrugged. "Hon, do you know if we have any more pork rinds?"

"I don't know. What day is it?"

"Saturday."

"In that case, we don't. The pork rind fairy doesn't come again until Monday."

"You're kidding, right?"

"I'm sure she isn't," C.J. said. "Back home the pork rind fairy comes on Sunday, but down here . . ."

C.J. may have been dead serious for all I know. But while she fed my husband one of her infamous Shelby stories, I checked every room in the house. No Mama. I also checked the phone for messages.

"Greg," I called, running back into the den, "she's really missing."

"Cute, Abby, but don't you think you and C.J. are running this pork rind fairy bit into the ground?"

"I'm talking about Mama!"

"Mozella?"

"She was supposed to take the elevator, and we were going to meet her in the basement, but she never showed up. And there's no sign of her wheelchair, either."

"Mozella?"

"Greg, look at me."

"I'm looking."

"What do you see?"

"Uh—a beautiful, sexy woman?"

"With a mustache?"

"I didn't want to say anything, hon, in case it was a hormonal thing."

"Greg! It's a obviously a fake." I ripped it off for the second time that night. Any semblance of a real mustache I might have had was pulled out by the roots.

My husband stared at me, taking in my tux and plastered locks for the first time. He seemed at a loss for words.

If only C.J. could be rendered speechless. "Granny Ledbetter had a handlebar mustache," she said. "Once it got caught in her spinning wheel—"

"C.J.!" Perhaps my tone was too harsh, but it brought Greg fully to his senses.

"Hon," he said, jumping to his feet, "why are you wearing a tux? Do I want to know?"

I spilled my guts. Fortunately, being a small person, it wasn't messy. When I was through, Greg read me the riot act, but since he's a kind and generous man, that too was tolerable. Well into the night we called everyone Mama knew, even her friends back in Rock Hill. But no one had a clue as to her whereabouts.

Finally, about two A.M., my dear sweet husband, the ex-cop, coaxed me into breaking the law by taking one of Mama's prescription Xanax. Just as it was taking effect the phone by our bed rang.

"Hello?" I said.

"Mrs. Washburn, Mrs. Washburn—if you ever want—more fruit—more fruit—see your mother again. Again. Fork over the Monet."

The caller hung up.

I have a vague recollection of Greg pressing another Xanax on me. Shortly after that, I hung up on reality.

41

When I awoke, sun was streaming through the windows and my darling husband was sitting next to me on the bed holding a breakfast tray in his lap.

"Good morning, sleepyhead," he said. "What perfect timing. You've got orange juice, scrambled eggs, bacon, and cinnamon toast. And of course, grits."

Greg does take off work on Sunday mornings, but he never brings me breakfast in bed. He tried that once with an ulterior motive, but there are certain things that shouldn't be done on a full stomach. The sloshing around of juice and several cups of coffee was distracting.

I scooted up and stuffed my pillow behind the small of my back. "Thanks, dear, you shouldn't have." I snatched a piece of bacon from the tray. "You wouldn't believe the crazy dream I had—oh my God! Is it true? Is Mama missing?"

"I'm afraid so."

"Greg, in my dream the phone rang—"

I dropped the bacon as the real phone rang.

"Abby, darling," Greg said gently, "wait until the fifth ring and then answer."

"But what's going on? Is she—"

Greg reached over me, picked up the receiver, and held it against my ear. "Speak slowly. Try and keep the caller on the line as long as possible."

"Hello," I said, instead of my usual "Hey."

"Mrs. Washburn, Mrs. Washburn, is that you?"

"Yes, it is me, Abby Washburn. But my maiden name was—"

"No police, Mrs. Washburn, Mrs. Washburn. No police. We have a wardrobe malfunction. Malfunction, malfunction. Police, Mrs. Washburn?" The caller hung up.

Greg's head pressed against mine. I'm sure he heard every word.

"You did good, Abby."

"Oh Greg," I wailed, "Mama's been kidnapped by a lunatic, and it's all my fault."

My dearly beloved took the breakfast tray from my lap, sat on the bed next to me, and cradled me in his arms. "No one—even the Man Upstairs— could have stopped Mozella from going to that dance. If scientists could harness her strength and determination, she'd be a national treasure."

"But I shouldn't have let her out of my sight!"

"Again, Abby, that couldn't have been prevented. You have got to stop blaming yourself for something that was out of your hands, and start focusing on what you can do to bring Mozella back."

"Like what? Greg, you know I'm not all that religious—"

He laid a finger—which smelled of fish—gently against my lips. "Prayer is always appropriate, but I was thinking of something a bit more concrete."

"Such as?"

"Hon, how would you describe the voice on the phone?"

"Well, it was a man's—you heard it, too. What gives?"

"Humor me."

I sighed. "As I was saying, it was a man's voice. I couldn't place the accent—it seemed to be all over the board, like when Yankees try to sound Southern. And the phrasing was weird."

"Like it had been patched together, maybe on a tape?"

"Exactly."

"Could it have been a bird's voice?"

"What?" I shook my head as my sedated brain resumed thinking. "Monet! That was a montage of Monet's vocalizations. That means—Greg, it isn't college boys, is it?"

He squeezed my shoulders. "Probably not. Don't worry, hon, the Feds are working hard on it—"

"The *Feds*?"

"You know that kidnapping is a federal crime."

"But that's on TV and in the movies. It's not supposed to happen with Mama."

"And don't believe everything you see in the movies, Abby. The overwhelming majority of kidnapping victims are returned unharmed."

"That's because the overwhelming majority are kidnapped by a parent. You said so yourself, once. Greg, this is a whole different—"

The phone rang again. This time I lunged for it.

"Remember," Greg whispered, "keep them on the line."

"I want to speak to Mama," I yelled.

Having been made stupid by fear, I missed the first part of the recording. ". . . Pineapple Fountain. More fruit—from its frame—roll up—you're one hot number, kiddo—tube in the fountain—top tier, top tier—do you understand, Mrs. Parker," the mynah asked, suddenly switching to a woman's voice. "Will be shot, will be shot—Golconda fruit." The conversation ended with a dial tone.

"Good job," Greg said.

"Good job? I didn't do anything, except almost blow it."

A soft tap on the bedroom door made me jump, smacking Greg on the chin with the crown of my head. Fortunately, we're both heavy milk drinkers and have strong bones and teeth.

"Come in," Greg called without missing a beat.

The door opened and in stepped a pair of agents from the Bureau of Information. I could tell that even before they introduced themselves, because they were brimming with authority. Frankly, I'm surprised they knocked.

"She needs to remain calm," the female agent said, as if I wasn't in the room. Since she was scowling, I decided to call her Scowler—to myself, of course.

"We almost didn't hear the drop-off time," her companion said. His suit was rumpled, and he looked like he hadn't bathed in days—perhaps he was English—so I decided to call him Moldy.

Greg squeezed me tighter. "But of course you taped the conversation," he said.

I pushed free from his embrace. "Drop off what? That was a bird on the phone, and it was demanding itself as a ransom."

Scowler and Moldy exchanged glances.

"Is she under a doctor's care?" Scowler asked.

"*She's* right here," I said through clenched teeth.

"Monet was the name of a bird my wife bought at an auction," Greg explained. "It was stolen from her shop a few days ago. And my wife is right: that was Monet on the phone demanding my mother-in-law's ransom."

The Feds conferred briefly.

"Sir," Scowler said, addressing Greg, "I'm afraid this matter is out of our jurisdiction."

"Kidnapping is in your jurisdiction," Greg snapped. I had never seen him so angry.

"Yes," Moldy said, "but practical jokes aren't."

"My mother-in-law is missing—that's not a practical joke."

"Perhaps she ran away."

I never knew that Greg had a vein on his right temple, much less one that could throb. "Mozella Wiggins did not run away."

"We'll have to turn this matter over to your local police," Scowler said.

Moldy was, hands down, the more compassionate of the pair. "It's already been almost twenty-four hours, so you only have one more day to wait until they'll act on the missing person's report."

I nudged Greg. "But it hasn't been anywhere near twenty-four hours," I whispered.

"Darling," he whispered back, "it's Sunday afternoon."

"What?"

"You needed your sleep, hon."

46

"Holy guacamole!" I broke free of Greg's embrace and sat up. Too late I remembered that I normally sleep au natural. I slid back down until the covers came up to my eyes.

"My wife never sleeps this late," my dear husband said on my behalf.

"Harrumph," Scowler said, using the actual word.

"My wife works," Moldy said.

"So does Abby," Greg said.

I slipped an arm out and waved it. "I'm right here, y'all."

The three of them stared at me.

"And if you don't mind," I continued, "I'd appreciate it if everyone would adjourn to the living room while I make myself presentable."

They continued to stare, like I was a talking pillow. I had no recourse but to flip the covers back altogether.

CHAPTER 5

"You didn't!" Rob gasped, properly aghast.

"I did."

"Then what?"

"They left the room, of course."

"Abby, I can't believe you bared it all for the Feds," Bob boomed.

"I didn't. Greg put me to bed, so I was still wearing a bra and panties. We've been married two years and he still can't—never mind. Mama's missing, and we have to wait another day to do anything."

Bob draped a brotherly arm around my shoulder. "We feel your pain, Abby. Mozella is a special woman."

"Who's been kidnapped by a lunatic who uses a bird's voice to deliver his messages."

"Or her messages," Rob said gently. "I mean, the kidnapper could be a woman."

"Whatever. But this nutcase is demanding we fork over Monet, which he or she already has."

"I'll have to admit it's weird," Bob said.

"Can you repeat the phone call word for word?" Rob asked.

I took a long sip of my beverage before obliging him. We were standing in the Rob-Bobs' kitchen, which was disgustingly clean and smelled of baking bread. I'd been immediately invited to stay for Sunday night supper, but upon hearing that the main course was octopus aspic, I'd declined. But that didn't mean I couldn't partake of the "house wine," which, like in every good Southern household, is really sweetened ice tea.

"Very interesting," Rob said when I was done imitating the stupid bird that had brought so much trouble into my life. "The Feds may have missed something."

"Like what?"

Rob hoisted me atop a bar stool so we could see eye-to-eye. "That bit about Pineapple Fountain and the tube, it sort of makes sense."

"Huh?"

Pineapple Fountain, by the way, is a Charleston landmark. Shaped like a pineapple—of course—the fountain is located in Waterfront Park near the cruise boat passenger terminal on Charleston harbor.

"The fountain is being cleaned," Rob said, gathering momentum. "It's dry as a bone right now. Bob and I saw it yesterday on our walk. If you were to leave something in a tube on the top tier, it might be out of sight, and it certainly wouldn't get wet."

"You mean like a test tube?"

Rob chuckled. "No, Abby, I'm thinking of a cardboard tube."

49

"I get it!" Bob bellowed, sounding very much like a moose in heat I'd seen on Animal Planet.

"Well, I don't," I wailed. "Would somebody please explain?"

Bob clapped his hands with excitement. "Let me tell her."

"Go ahead," Rob said, his eyes twinkling.

"Abby, they—I mean he or she—wants you to roll the Monet up in a tube and hide it in the top tier of the fountain."

"But that's silly, I can't roll a bird up in a tube. Especially one that I don't have."

"Not the bird, Abby, but the *real* Monet."

"I beg your pardon?"

"Someone thinks that you own a real Monet—you know, a painting by Claude Monet."

"The impressionist?"

"Is there any other?"

"But that's impossible. You know I don't own a Monet, and even if I did, his paintings are huge. You could never hide one in the top tier of Pineapple Fountain."

"Not necessarily," Bob said, his voice at reasonable decibels. "Every painter goes through periods. Old Claude might have had a tiny phase."

"I'm sure he did," Rob said, "but it had nothing to do with his paintings. Abby's right; Monet liked things on the grand scale. His painting *Women in the Garden* was almost eight feet high. He had a trench dug in his garden so he could raise or lower the canvas to the level he needed to paint on."

"But he started out as a caricaturist," Bob said, and crossed his arms in defiance.

I was already out of my field of expertise. The sad truth be known, I don't even have a field of expertise. I just love old things, and get a kick out of it whenever someone else falls in love with something I've collected. I believe the enthusiasm I have for my merchandise is what has made the Den of Antiquity a success.

"Look, guys," I said, "I don't own even a minute Monet. There has got to be a better explanation."

Rob refreshed my tea glass. "Abby, what do you know about the bird? How did it get its name?"

I shrugged. "A piece of paper came with the sale. It just told his name and what he ate. But you would have thought that his cage was made of gold, the way folks were bidding on it."

"Hmm. How many bidders were there?"

"I don't know—maybe a dozen at first, but five that hung in there until the ridiculous end. I think they only dropped out because they were afraid of being committed if they paid that much for a birdcage."

"But you weren't?"

"If I was going to be committed, it would have happened long ago. After all, I hang around with you, don't I?"

Bob snorted. "You tell him, Abby."

Rob smiled while simultaneously shooting his partner the evil eye. "Did you know any of the other bidders?"

"As a matter of fact, I know three of them. And all three of them could benefit from a good therapist."

"Do tell," Rob said, and pulled up a stool for himself.

But I refused to gossip—for the moment, at least. Instead I made them promise to meet me for the lunch the next day at Chez Fez, a new Moroccan restaurant that had opened on Meeting Street, just up the block from Jestine's. That was every bit as hard as pulling teeth from a lockjawed hen. Chez Fez had garnered rave reviews in the *Post and Courier,* which proclaimed its chef as the best cook to set foot in Charleston in the last three years (our city has a plethora of fine eateries). At any rate, Bob somehow interpreted the article as a put-down of his culinary skills, even though he's never cooked professionally. He agreed to go to Chez Fez only after I suggested he write a review of his own and submit it to *Southern Living,* which, of course, has a far wider circulation.

I barely slept a wink that night, which was to be expected. But neither did I toss and turn. As I lay in the dark, listening to my husband and Dmitri vie for loudest snore, I comforted myself by mentally reliving some of Mama's wildest escapades. The woman was resourceful and, despite her eccentric appearance, as sharp as a brand-new tack. *If* indeed she'd been kidnapped, her captor would soon be sorry. I could just see her offering to knit him or her a sweater, and then knitting a straitjacket instead. The next time I saw her she'd be sitting on the set of *Good Morning America,* describing her great escape to Diane Sawyer.

And it was quite possible that my minimadre wasn't even the victim of foul play. Although she's still a virgin, I've long suspected that Mama has a secret spicy side. I would be properly shocked, but not surprised, to learn that she'd gone home from the ball with whichever bachelor codger had the strength to push her wheelchair back to his pad. They wouldn't actually have sex, mind you (she would have stayed in his guest room—after giving it a thorough cleaning), but she would have cooked him meals loaded with both carbs and cholesterol, and in a wild and impetuous moment she might even have done his laundry without first separating the whites from the coloreds.

Of course I wasn't about to quit worrying about my mother, but neither would I obsess. When Greg roused at the crack of dawn, as he normally does on a shrimping day, I got up with him. I'm telling the truth when I say I felt curiously refreshed.

"Oh hon," he said, when he remembered he'd decided not to go in to work that day, "I'm sorry. I just forgot."

"There's no need to be sorry, Greg, and there's no need to stay home from work."

"You need me, babe. Besides, I want to stay

and—oh shoot, Abby, you're not going to put on your gumshoes again?"

"They're from Bob Ellis, and they're ostrich leather."

He sighed deeply. "I don't have a snowball's chance in Charleston of stopping you, do I?"

"Not even a snowball's chance in Columbia." Our state capital has colder winters than Charleston, but fiercely hot summers. Some wags claim it was built over Hell.

"Promise me you'll carry your cell phone at all times, and will not do anything that is overtly illegal or extraordinarily dangerous." A little danger was to be expected from me.

"I promise."

He sighed again and then folded me into a long, hard embrace. "Hon, if anything happened to you—well, it better not. Why, oh why, did I marry such a headstrong woman?"

"Because you love me, including my strong head. Just don't forget that I love you, too, and I want to spend your golden years with you, and not among strangers, pushing up daisies."

That earned me a passionate kiss, another brief lecture, and a peck on the forehead.

Deephouse Designs, on Broad Street, is a Charleston phenomenon. It is the au courant place for interior design, in an historic city where there are more houses being refurbished than there are cobblestones. The powerhouse behind this successful

54

business is Catherine Deephouse herself, or Cat, as she is known in the biz.

In the 1970s, venerable, but often cash-strapped, citizens of the peninsula began selling off their moldy mansions and moving to the suburbs, where property taxes were significantly lower. This began an influx of people from "off," as Charlestonians refer to anyone other than themselves. What had once been a shabby-chic city underwent a transformation as the new owners, a few of whom had more money than God, began to vie for their shot at appearing in *Architectural Digest*. It didn't matter that they viewed their Charleston homes as vacation getaways. What mattered was status, which often involved things, and the mistress of things was Cat Deephouse.

I'm not jealous, mind you, because Cat frequents my shop in her search for things. We get along as colleagues, but shy away from each other in social settings. It is probably my fault. I prefer quieter moments, surrounded by a few close friends. Cat, on the other hand, is an expert at the shouted sound-bite conversations that are inevitable at large cocktail parties.

Although I consider myself to be a neat dresser, I always feel a bit dowdy in the designer's presence. A stout woman in her middle years, Cat dresses with a flair that borders on theatrical. On this particular day she was wearing a fire-engine-red sleeveless sheath that had been cut low in front to emphasize her deeply tanned and somewhat wrinkled bosoms. Lavender eye shadow neither complemented nor accentuated dark brown eyes and bottle-brown hair. From sagging earlobes dangled chandelier earrings that were rumored to contain three carats of flawless diamonds—*each*.

I was greeted by an assistant, who then scurried to the back room to fetch Cat. She appeared seconds later, proceeded by a cloud of perfume.

"Abby," she said, unable to arrange her Botoxed brow into a suitable frown, "you've been a very naughty woman."

"I have?"

"Don't play coy, dear. You knew how much I wanted that fabulous birdhouse. But ten thousand dollars—well, even the nouveaus aren't going to pay that retail."

The nouveau riche, or just nouveaus, as Cat called them, are the legions of doctors, lawyers, and real estate agents that have supplanted the planters of historic Charleston. Although we sometimes joke about them to ourselves, we take their money very seriously.

"I'm not planning on reselling the birdcage."

One brow struggled in vain to rise. "You're not?"

"It speaks to me," I said, resenting the fact that I felt I had to explain myself.

"Funny *and* naughty," she said, and shook her head just enough to make the diamonds dance. "Tell you what, I'll give you fifteen thousand, but only because you've always been fair to me."

"No, what I meant was that the cage itself

speaks to me—well, not literally. But I've always wanted to travel to India and see the real Taj Mahal. I'm afraid this is as close as I'm going to get."

"I was there last winter. It was a disappointment."

"Then I should be glad I haven't spent the money to visit the real thing."

"A tomb's a tomb, I always say. Okay, Abby, you drive a hard bargain. Sixteen five, and we'll call it a day."

I smiled. The view from the catbird's seat can be fabulous, especially for someone as vertically challenged as myself.

"Cat, if you didn't like the Taj Mahal, why would you want to pay so much for a birdcage replica?"

Her scarlet lips came together in a soft smack, and I could see the wheels in her head pick up speed. "Actually, it's for a very wealthy client. Fell in love with it at the auction—said he must have it for his new home on Legare Street."

"Then why didn't you snag it on Saturday? If he's that rich, I mean."

"Well, you seemed so determined, and like I said, you've always been fair to me. It wasn't until I saw the look on his face—when the gavel fell— that I realized how much he wanted it."

"Who is this client—if you don't mind me asking?"

"He wants to remain anonymous. I'm sure you understand that, dear."

"I see." I slipped a business card from my purse

and held it out. "Give this to him, would you, please? Tell him to check in from time to time. Who knows, I could tire of that thing tomorrow and slap a price tag on it."

There are limits to expressing shock when one's muscles are frozen by toxic mold. "But you wouldn't just put it on the market like that, would you? Not without telling me."

A very wise person once told me that silence is the most powerful weapon there is, mightier even than the pen. Unfortunately, it is hard for my lips to stay sealed, unless there is a piece of candy behind them.

"Sure, I'll give you a call."

She nodded. "Abby, you still haven't told me why you came here this morning."

"Oh, that. Well, I just got this shipment in from Aiken, South Carolina, most of which is to die for. Although a few appear to have been died in— but that's part of the charm of old things, isn't it? Gives them that certain patina, don't you think? For instance, there's a grandfather clock, which C.J. swears used to belong to her Granny Ledbetter—oh, my gracious! I totally forgot about C.J. She woke up with a nasty toothache and I promised to spell her so she could go to the dentist."

With that I turned and fled. I'm not very good at lying, unless it involves my age, and even then I don't see the point. Why pretend to be younger than you are, and have people think time has treated you badly? Better to add a few years, and leave them with the impression that genetics have been kind to you.

At any rate, it was because I tend to flub fibbing that I headed straight from the frying pan and into the fire.

CHAPTER 6

Martin Gibble fancies himself the most knowledgeable antique dealer in Charleston. I won't argue with this, but surely Rob Goldburg comes in a close second. I, on the other hand, would fly completely under Martin's radar were it not for the fact that last year I outbid him on an unprepossessing little table that turned out to have been made right here in Charleston in the early eighteenth century, and which I resold for ninety thousand dollars. I suppose there would be no good reason for me to further rub it into Mr. Gibble's face and mention that I paid a mere fifty bucks for this piece of history.

So it was with mixed feelings that I rang the bell beside the door of Encore on King Street. Through the glass I could see Martin wrinkle his patrician nose before buzzing me in. He turned his back to me as I approached.

"Hello, Martin."

"Abby."

"It's going to be another hot one." Weather talk may be trite, but it's seldom controversial.

"Yes, I suppose where you come from this could be considered hot."

Martin Gibble is a native Charlestonian, born in one of the mansions that fronts the Battery. It is a fact that he trots out within minutes of meeting a new person. If he dislikes you, he trots it out in every conversation thereafter as well.

"Martin, one doesn't get credit for where one is born. Or to whom, for that matter."

He turned. "Excuse me?"

"Unless, of course, before conception, one is offered a choice. If that's the case, and I chose not to be born in Charleston, I must have had good reasons."

Patrician nose aside, Martin has the messy hair and facial stubble currently popular with celebrities. He looks more like he's been on a three-day bender than he does stylish. At any rate, he scratched his chin with nails that had been lacquered a transparent pink.

"Are you just here to taunt me, Abby?"

"It's about the birdcage."

"Aha, so you are here to taunt."

"Martin, I didn't realize what I was getting when I outbid you on that table last year. We both thought it was a knockoff until *Antiques Road Show* came to town. I was going to use it in my potting shed and—"

"So you say."

I bit my tongue while I counted to ten in

Portuguese. It is a language of which I have only a tourist's knowledge, so Martin got an extra second of grace when I made a false start.

"Back to the birdcage, Martin. I wanted to tell you that I have no plans to resell it."

"Your point in telling me this?"

"I didn't want you to think I was going to make a huge profit from it." There was no need to add "like last time."

He snorted and started to turn, but stopped abruptly. "What about the bird?"

"What about him?"

"Surely you're not going to continue to let that bird crap in a ten thousand dollar replica of the Taj Mahal."

"Well—"

"Abby, I know we don't get along—never have—but I'm asking you a favor, as one connoisseur of beautiful things to another. Please," he said, almost imploringly, "don't let that stupid bird crap one more time in that exquisite piece of art."

I don't know which surprised me the most: his strange, and somewhat moving, request, or his assertion that we'd never gotten along. To the best of my memory, we'd gotten along quite well until the Keeno brothers came to town.

"Don't worry," I said, trying to appear unruffled. "Monet will not be crapping in that cage today."

He tugged on his right earlobe, home to a sizable diamond stud. "Am I supposed to believe you capitulated this easily?"

"Believe what you want," I said, and flashed him what I hoped was an enigmatic smile.

"Okay, I'll bite. What gives, Abby?"

"Monet's missing."

"What the—" The diamond stud popped loose from his ear, pinged off the inlaid surface of a Louis IV commode, and disappeared under a row of French high chests.

"Oh gosh, I'm sorry!" I cried and dropped to my knees.

"That can wait," Martin said with astonishing sharpness.

"I beg your pardon?"

"It's only a CZ. I mean, why wear the real thing to work, right?"

I hopped to my feet. "Right. And I promise not to tell anyone."

"Good one, Abby. So fast with the quips. Perhaps I misjudged you."

"Most likely you didn't." I started for the door.

"The bird!" he shouted. "Did you say it was stolen?"

I pivoted slowly. "Stolen? Oh no, I think you heard wrong. Monet isn't stolen; he's simply misplaced."

"Misplaced?"

"Well, you know C.J. She was cleaning his cage over the weekend, and put him in a drawer in for safekeeping. Now she can't remember which one."

"Drawer? Like a dresser drawer?"

"Yup, or maybe it was a cupboard. I just hope we can find the poor thing before he starves."

He stared at me for what seemed like an eternity, but I refused to look away or add to my story. Do you see what I mean about silence being a powerful weapon?

"I think you're both nuts," he finally said.

"And with you, we'd make a nice bridge mix," I said, and bolted for the second time that morning.

When the going gets tough, the tough get going, and the weak ones, like myself, head right for food. I had several hours to kill before lunch, so I headed across the street to my shop, where I keep a stash of chocolate bars in case of an emergency. It's anybody's guess when the next big earthquake will hit Charleston, but if it's anything like the killer quake of 1889, at the very least the roof will collapse and I could be buried in the rubble for days. Much better to be buried with Mounds bars than without.

C.J. must have seen me coming, because she flung open the door to the Den of Antiquity just as I was about to push. As a result, I went sailing through the air as if I'd leapt off a bridge while bungee-jumping, but of course I didn't have as far to fall. And a floor is much less forgiving than an elastic cord.

Two pairs of hands helped me to my feet. "Abby, are you all okay?"

"Wynnell! What are you doing here?"

"I heard about Mozella. I came to help."

"How did you hear about Mama?"

"Bob called me, and then I called C.J., but she didn't know where you were—"

"Abby," C.J. said, her big gray eyes brimming with tears, "I thought we were friends."

"We are!"

She shook her leonine head. "Friends confide in each other. Besides, Abby, Mozella was my best friend. You should have told me."

"She's right," Wynnell said, as the hedgerows above her eyes met.

"Okay, okay, I'm sorry. But I didn't want to worry y'all, and anyway, it's not like there is any proof she's been kidnapped. I haven't even told the children yet. For all we really know, Mama's off discovering herself again."

Susan and Charlie are my college-age offspring. The man who supplied the ingredient necessary for their conception was my first husband, Buford Timberlake. I used to hate Buford, but after he finally apologized for his mistreatment of me, and having learned that there is nothing to be gained by hate—except for a sour stomach—I let go of that crippling emotion.

"Your mama does do some strange things from time to time," Wynnell agreed, "like that time she ran off to Cincinnati to join a convent."

"And got kicked out for wearing curlers under her wimple and singing on the stairs."

"Cousin Sister Leviticus Ledbetter had a pimple under her wimple," C.J. said, absolutely deadpan.

Wynnell and I both sighed, a fact that the big galoot must have interpreted as encouragement. "And it wasn't just an ordinary pimple, either. It looked exactly like St. John the Baptist—before he lost his head, of course. It even had his dimples."

"Hold it right there," I said. "Nobody knows what John the Baptist looked like."

The enormous gray eyes, now dry of tears, held me in a steady gaze. "Are you calling the Vatican a liar?"

"No. And just so you know, C.J., the Vatican isn't a person, but an institution."

Her gaze shifted as those eyes executed a quarter turn. "I know that, silly. Now, where was I? Oh yeah, so anyway, folks for miles around came to see Cousin Sister's pimply pate—she had to keep her head shaved, you see—but it got to itching really bad, so the convent doctor gave her this prescription cream to use on it, which she did, but the next morning St. John the Baptist was gone, and it was back to being just an ordinary zit. Except for one of the dimples. It still had one of those, so it looked like a Smiley face without the eyes, but nobody was willing to pay to see that."

"A simple dimpled pimple under a wimple," I said. "What a moving story."

"Abby, are you making fun of me?"

"Maybe just a tad. Look y'all, I'd love to stay and chat, but I've got work to do."

"You mean sleuthing work," Wynnell said. "Give us assignments, Abby."

"Ooh, Abby, please," C.J. begged. "Cousin Agatha Ledbetter, up in Shelby, was a private eye. So maybe it runs in the family."

"Was her last name Christie?"

"You're being mean again."

"Sorry, C.J."

"That's okay. So Abby, are you going to give us our assignments now?"

Silence may be the world's most powerful weapon, but guilt comes in a close second. "Sure," I heard myself saying. "Wynnell, let's start with you. I would very much appreciate it if you went to see John Norman—you know, the owner of the Lowcountry Auction Barn up on Rivers Avenue. There was a beautiful blonde who was bidding furiously against me, and a black man—mmm—maybe in his sixties."

"You mean African-American."

"Yes. The blonde, by the way, is European-American. At any rate, see if you can get their names and phone numbers from John. You may need to sweet-talk him a little, which is why it's best to do it in person. But a good-looking woman like you should find it a piece of cake."

Wynnell grinned so wide I was afraid her dentures might fall out. "Sure thing, Abby. I'll get right to it. Do you want me to call you on your cell with the information?"

"That would be super. And just so y'all know, I'm meeting the Rob-Bobs at Chez Fez for lunch today."

"And me?" C.J. was bouncing around like a nine-year-old on Christmas morning. "What's my job?"

"C.J., yours is the most important job of all. I'm putting you in charge of the command center. I need you to answer the phone, coordinate shipments and arrivals, maintain the economic status quo, and, of course, monitor the comings and goings of suspicious people."

"In other words, Abby, you want me to stay right here and sell your merchandise."

"That's putting it harshly."

"Why does Wynnell get to have all the fun? Why don't I get a real assignment?"

"Because you have a job," I said gently. "Besides, I wasn't exaggerating when I said yours was the most important job. What if Mama calls here—this *is* where she'd expect me to be on a normal day—and no one is here to answer? What if that was the only call she was allowed to make?"

C.J. hung her head. "If anything happened to Mozella, and it was my fault, I'd never forgive myself. I'd have to do what Cousin Exodus did."

"I thought her name was Leviticus."

"That's his sister. Cousin Exodus is a boy, silly. Whoever heard of a girl named Exodus? And anyway, he ran off to Vegas, not a convent. You see, he wanted to be a bouncer, on account of he was a big guy—well, most of him was." She paused to giggle. "He had the tiniest—"

I ran to my desk, unlocked the middle left drawer, and waved a Mounds bar above my head. The delicious combination of dark chocolate and chewy coconut brought C.J. and Wynnell over at a fast trot. C.J. had already switched off her storytelling mode and was gearing up for a sugar high. Like I said, I keep those bars around for emergencies.

Chez Fez is currently Charleston's most talked-about eatery. A lot of rednecks, as well as a few reasonable people, disliked the idea of an "Arab" restaurant. Never mind that "the Fez," as it is called now by its regulars, is all about good food and fabulous entertainment, and has absolutely nothing to do with politics.

From the second one steps in off the street, one is transported to the land of Aladdin and Scheherazade, but with a pseudo-Moroccan spin. The interior of the restaurant is entirely filled by one large white tent. Maroon velvet draperies tied back with gold tassels form the private eating areas. Diners sit cross-legged on genuine faux Oriental carpets, or recline against brightly colored rayon pillows brought all the way from Pier One Imports. The food is served on beaten brass platters, laid on tables of simulated mother-of-pearl inlay.

In the center of the room is a circular stage topped with a white plastic garden gazebo from Home Depot. Inside a trio of musicians—two flutists and a drummer—plays haunting desert melodies. About every twenty minutes the tempo picks up and from the direction of the kitchen a bevy of bovine beauties bounce in and proceed to shake their stuff. There is one dancer for every table, and they position themselves so close to the diners that even if you close your eyes against the sight of rolls of jiggling fat, the smell of cheap perfume, fanned by the fluttering of polyester veils, still assaults the senses. Even the most parochial guest soon realizes that these are not professional belly dancers, but bored housewives bused down from North Charleston and Hanahan.

For all its tackiness, Chez Fez exudes a certain charm, and the man responsible for this is the very charming Blackmond Dupree. He is a slight man with dark brown eyes and hair, but a black handlebar mustache that appears to have been dyed. His costume consists of white pants, a white V-neck shirt with gold embroidery around the collar, and an ill-fitting red fez that has to be kept in place with bobby pins. His red slippers curl up at the toes, like those of Santa's elves. Monsieur Dupree claims to have been born in Casablanca of French parents, and his unconvincing accent aside, we all want to believe that this is so.

"Ah, Madame Washburn," he said, greeting me with a limp handshake, "your friends, they are already seeting at zer table."

"Splendid—but I was hoping to speak with you for a few minutes. In private."

"Zat would be very nice, madame, but zees eez zee lunch hour, no?"

"But zees eez—I mean, this is rather important. It's about the birdcage."

"Birdcage?" His eyes darted about like minnows in a pond, never quite making contact with mine.

"The one shaped like the Taj Mahal."

"Ah, zat one." Monsieur Dupree snapped his fingers and a waiter, dressed in a similar costume, appeared at his side. The owner mumbled something into his employee's ear, then beckoned me to follow him through a pair of moth-eaten green drapes I couldn't recall seeing before.

I hesitated only a second.

CHAPTER 7

Monsieur Dupree's office was a wallboard box, perhaps not unlike hundreds of other work cubicles in greater Charleston. It was piled high with papers, clipboards, and what appeared to be cookbooks. Hanging from a nail behind the desk was a calendar of Morocco, displaying a breathtaking scene of the Atlas Mountains covered in snow; a photograph of a beautiful young woman, who seemed oddly familiar; and a shadow box containing about a dozen bent forks. He caught me staring at the last item.

"Zose are ferks zat my customers have make bend."

"Excuse me?"

"Een zer teez."

"Y'all must serve some mighty strong tea."

"No, no, not zee tea, zee teez." He held a pinkie in front of his mouth and mimed chomping on it.

"Ah, their teeth! Gotcha. Well, in that case, they must have some mighty strong teeth."

He nodded vigorously. "I sink zees happen only in America—zees very strong teez. Eet eez zee fleride zat eez to blame, *n'est-ce pas?*"

"Nescafé all the way," I said, trying to be agreeable. "Is the beautiful woman in that picture your wife?"

His dark eyes danced. "Zat eez my daughter!"

"Get out of town! Forgive me, sir, but you don't look nearly old enough to have a grown daughter."

He shrugged. "*Oui?* Zen again, perhaps eet eez she zat does not look young enough."

"Uh—right."

"Do you recognize hair?"

"Excuse me?"

"My daughter. Do you recognize hair?"

"Actually, I do recognize her. I mean, she looks very familiar—but I can't quite place her."

"She works for zee robbers."

"Come again?"

"Rob-Bob and Bob-Rob," he said with a flourish of R's. "She eez zer assistant."

"No kidding! Funny, they've never mentioned that. You can bet that as soon as I see them—oh my gosh, look at the time! I'm supposed to have met them inside ten minutes ago."

Monsieur Dupree glanced at his watch. "*Oui,* zee time, she flies. But first we must to talk about zee birdcage, *n'est-ce pas?*"

"Yes, the birdcage. Monsieur Dupree, do you mind sharing why it is you have such a strong interest in this particular cage? Or is it, perhaps, the bird?"

"*Mai non,* eet eez not zee baird. But zee cage— she eez a work of art, no?"

"Indeed it is."

"Eef she wear mine, I would poot hair on zee stage weef zee musicians. Zen peoples would say zees eez zee most beautiful restaurant een Charleston."

"That's it? That's why you bid so high against me?"

"Eez zat not enough, Madame Washburn?"

"I suppose it is," I said, half believing him. For the moment I had no more questions.

My timing stank. I had no trouble finding the Rob-Bobs, supine upon their Pier One pillows, but an extraordinarily large belly dancer all but blocked the entrance to their velvet hideaway. She had good peripheral vision, and before could I sneak past her, she turned to face me.

"Excuse me," I said. "I just want to get by."

"Oh no you don't, sister. These two are mine."

"Yours?"

"Are you hard of hearing?" she shouted above the deafening music. Meanwhile she shimmied and shook, although not in sync with the music.

"My hearing is just fine," I shouted back. "Now, if you'd be so kind as to get out of my way—"

"I said they're mine. I got first dibs."

"You can have them. I just want to join them for lunch."

"Get lost, you hussy." She advanced, and her belly, which had been shaking like a paint mixer, began a series of slow downward rolls, known in her business as belly rolls. Unfortunately, the dancer had, during the course of her lifetime, consumed

74

more than a few jelly rolls. The spectacle was both gross and engrossing.

"Look lady, I'm a happily married woman," I told her. "And besides, they're my cousins. I just want to eat couscous with my cousins."

"Yeah, right. Yesterday this woman claims to be this guy's wife, and she's his mistress."

"And you know that how?" I tried to look away from her stomach, but the rolling had been replaced by a move called the flutter. Frankly, it was rather alluring.

"Intuition, honey. It ain't just something you use for college. Now beat it, sister."

I stood my ground, all the while trying hard not to look at her titillating tummy. "Not that it's any of my business, but do you think this is the best place to look for a single man?"

"Honey, do you know how hard it is for a woman with four children to find herself a husband?"

"No, but I wouldn't go trolling for one in a family restaurant."

"A gal's gotta do what a gal's gotta do. Honey, I don't want no trouble, and you look like the troublemaking kind, so I tell you what. You let me have the big handsome hunk—the one with the hair—and you can have that skinny bald guy with the glasses."

"I don't want the skinny bald guy!" I shouted at the top of my lungs.

Alas, the music had stopped abruptly, a signal that the belly dancers were to scurry back into the kitchen. But there was no scurrying just then, only stares. I could feel the eyes of everyone in the tent trained on me.

"Not that there's anything wrong with skinny bald guys," I said, my words echoing as if I were in a tomb the size of the Taj Mahal, and not a tent. "As a matter of fact, I prefer my men scrawny and hairless. And as for the glasses, the bigger the better I always say."

"Abby," Rob whispered, "what the heck is going on?"

"Nothing," I whispered back. I turned to the tart with the twitching tummy. "You can have the hunk—after you get off work, of course."

"Promise you won't touch him until then."

"Girl Scout's honor."

Satisfied, she shimmied her way back to the kitchen, leaving behind a trail of cheap perfume.

I dove into a pile of cushions. "Pull the drapes please," I choked.

"What just went down?" Rob asked, after sealing us in a cloth cocoon.

"You've got a date tonight."

"A *what?*" Bob brayed.

"Don't worry, dear, it's with a woman. That dancer has the hots for Rob."

"What about me?"

"She has the hots for you, too, but I thought it was only fair that she share, so you're mine."

"Ah, so that's why you shouted out a description of me. Let's see, how did it go? Scrawny, hairless—"

"But I forgot the good cook part. Did I say good? I mean excellent."

Bob beamed. "Abby, you're not going to believe what I'm making for dinner tonight."

"I'm sure I won't."

"Well, we're having some discerning friends over for dinner—not that you're not discerning, dear—so I'll be serving squab giblet pâté on toast points as the appetizer, marinated turkey wattles on a bed of endive for the salad, and then for the main course, it's alligator balls in alfredo sauce over homemade pasta, and topped with a special parmesan cheese that has been aged for three years in caves above a monastery on an island in the Aegean, where the only woman allowed to set foot is the Virgin Mary—although I'm told she seldom visits."

"Whoa, back up a bit. I didn't know alligators have—"

"Like meatballs," Rob said, "but made from ground alligator meat. Just be happy you're not invited, Abby. And speaking of invitations, you promised to give us the scoop on the other bidders if we met you here for lunch. So spill it, girlfriend."

"Ah, the other bidders. As it turns out, y'all have a connection."

"We do?"

"Your shop assistant, Simone Dupree, is the daughter of Blackmond Dupree, owner of this fine establishment."

"Well, I'll be damned. And here I thought she was a struggling grad student at the College of Charleston."

"She may be that. Restaurants often operate in the red for the first couple of years. Or she may have a bad relationship with her father. All I know is that they are father and daughter."

"How did you find out?"

"I was just interviewing him in his office. I saw a photo of her and asked."

Bob caught on first. "So you're saying that the swashbuckling Blackmond Dupree was one of the five top bidders on your birdcage?"

"I'd hardly call him swashbuckling," Rob said, clearly annoyed.

I winked at Bob. "A little jealousy is a good thing. Yes, he's one of the five. Believe it or not, he wants to put the Taj—it's far more than just a birdcage—up on the stage with the musicians. Sort of a centerpiece."

"But this is a Moroccan restaurant, not Indian."

"It's an eclectic restaurant. The last time I was here they had paella on the menu. So tell me, guys, why would someone be willing to pay ten thousand dollars for a stage decoration?"

Bob shrugged.

"Why did you?" Rob asked.

"I bought it because it was beautiful, because it spoke to me—thanks, Rob, I think I just answered my own question."

"Think nothing of it. And anyway, it's not the

most outrageous thing I've heard of. I was once asked to design a room around a piece of chewing gum that had supposedly seen the inside of Elvis Presley's mouth. The gum was on a gold dish, under a glass dome, on a pedestal in the center of the room. The owner was so proud of that thing—claimed it held Elvis's DNA—that she couldn't help bragging about what she'd paid for it." Rob took a chug of his sweet tea, just to taunt us.

"How much *did* she pay?" I finally demanded.

"Fifty thousand smackeroos. Can you believe that?"

"Holy Toledo!" Bob barked. That's his favorite expression, which isn't surprising, given that he's originally from Toledo.

Rob grinned, happy to be the center of attention. "The story doesn't end there. One of my client's friends stole the gum, hoping to clone Elvis and have his baby. But when the thief took the gum to a lab for analysis, she learned that the gum had only been chewed by a woman. Anyway, the thief sued my client for causing her "undue stress," and won a judgment of a hundred thousand dollars."

"It sounds like my partner's been spending too much time in the supermarket checkout line," Bob said.

"I swear it's true!"

I tapped my water glass with a spoon. "Okay, guys, I've got this one figured out. There is no limit to how much an object is worth—as long as there is a buyer who meets the asking price. But given the fact that most restaurants struggle the first few years, and that Simone Dupree is working for minimum wage, it's unlikely he would be willing to spend ten grand just to pretty this place up some more. The Taj Mahal birdcage means more to Blackmond than he's letting on. Therefore, I am putting him at the top of my list of suspects."

"We most certainly do not pay Simone minimum wage," Rob hissed.

"Plus, I bring in leftovers just about every day," Bob growled.

It was starting to sound like a menagerie in our private booth. "Sorry guys, I didn't mean to ruffle any feathers."

"Besides," Rob said, "people spend money all the time on things they can't afford. Granted, those things usually involve mortgages or horse-power, but the operating principle is the same. When we humans desperately want something, we're willing to throw caution to the wind. Before you circle his name in ink, tell us the other four names on the list."

"I only know two of the others; Wynnell is tracking down the other two. But the names you want are Catherine Deephouse and Martin Gibble."

"*Our* Martin Gibble?"

"Is there any other?"

"The one who hates your guts?"

"He doesn't—okay, maybe he does, but that's not why he made the list. First of all, he wanted the Taj so bad he could taste it, and second, he was unduly concerned about Monet pooping in it, and third, when I told him the mynah was missing, he jumped to the conclusion that Monet had been stolen. How suspicious is that?"

My friends exchanged smiles. "Not very," Rob said. "The Taj, as you call it, is uncommonly beautiful, so who wouldn't lust over it? And nobody in their right mind—sorry, Abby—would allow a starling, no matter how exotic, to foul a work of art. And frankly, what other explanation would there be for a missing bird, especially one that has been replaced by a stuffed look-alike?"

"I didn't tell him about the stuffed look-alike."

"Even so, it's a logical conclusion for him to make."

Bob, who is more sensitive than his partner, picked up on my vibes. "Hey, we love you. You know that, right?"

"But you think I'm nuttier than a Payday."

"No, make that a small Snickers. And Abby, I mean it when I say that in the past you've done some dynamite sleuthing."

"But now I'm so far off base even the Jolly Green Giant couldn't tag me?"

"So tell us about your visit to Catherine Deephouse," Rob said.

The diversion worked. "She claims she was

bidding on the Taj for a secret client. Believe it or not, she offered fifteen grand for it."

Bob whistled. "A fifty percent markup! Not bad."

He was just trying to humor me. It was a good offer, but not outstanding. In this biz we try to resale for three times what we've paid for an item. This allows us to mark down merchandise that's been taking up valuable space too long, as well as give our customers discounts upon request.

"Yeah, well I might have taken the fifteen grand, but I want to see if she'll go any higher. She's being cagey, so I know she's hiding something."

"Good one, Abby."

"What?"

Before Bob could point out the clever thing I'd said, albeit inadvertently, the drapes that formed our cubicle were drawn back to reveal a trio of waiters bearing silver-plated salvers. The men were dressed in white tunics and leggings, and red slippers with curled-up toes, and each sported a red, ill-fitting fez. All three had handlebar mustaches, none of which were real.

"We took the liberty of ordering for you," Rob said.

"I hope you like sheep's head," Bob said. "In a nice cumin and yogurt sauce. Yummy."

"I think I'm going to be sick," I said, and struggled to my feet.

"But Abby, we're only kidding. It's shish kebab, rice pilaf, and salad."

I bolted anyway. When I was out of sight of the Rob-Bobs' cubicle, I ducked into the ladies' room. Just as I'd hoped, one of the waiters was right on my heels.

CHAPTER 8

"Wynnell! What on earth are you doing in that costume?"

"You told me this was where you were having lunch. Abby, couldn't you at least have kept the drapes open? Yours was the third table I had to serve."

"The costume, Wynnell!"

"Oh that. My neighbor, José Garcia, works here. He also owes me a few favors. How did you recognize me, Abby? I've got my hair tucked up under this fez and I'm not wearing any makeup."

My friend would have been hurt if I told her it was her unibrow that gave her away. Especially since I'd helped her wax only a week before.

"Your boobs," I said kindly.

"Funny, because José is a bit on the pudgy side. I've always thought he was bigger than I."

Suddenly we both heard loud female voices. Just in time I ripped the mustache off Wynnell and snatched away her crimson fez. The poor woman screeched in pain. At least I wouldn't have to wax her upper lip for a few days.

The women were so involved in their conversation they didn't hear Wynnell's screech or notice her curled shoes. They kept a steady stream of gossip going throughout their business, and then left without washing their hands.

"Gross," Wynnell said.

"Wynnell, out with it! Why the charade?"

"Abby, I went out to see John at the auction house, like you told me."

"And? Did he give you the names and addresses of the folks who bid against me?"

"You bet he did. The African American man who bid against you is Bubba Johnson. He owns a string of dry-cleaning shops. Hi-N-Dry is the name of the business. John said that Bubba Johnson is very successful. In fact, he owns a mansion on Battery Street."

"I use Hi-N-Dry! In my opinion they're the only establishment that can do a decent job of pressing silk. Most cleaners leave shiny areas— never mind. Who was my European-American blonde competition?"

"Abby, you shouldn't be making fun like that."

"I'm not. I'm trying to prove a point. If we qualify every American except for white ones, aren't we then saying that white is the norm? There may be more of us, but that doesn't make us the gold standard. An American is an American. Adjectives divide."

"Well, I don't agree. But anyway, the gorgeous blonde is George Murphy."

"Excuse me?"

"That's what he said. Here's her phone number, and Mr. Johnson's."

More voices alerted us to the fact that the door was about to swing open. On impulse I dragged Wynnell into a stall. To avoid the problem of two pairs of feet being visible, I hopped up onto the toilet seat.

"The trouble is she knows she's cute," Voice One said. "Thinks she can get away with anything. You should see how messy their house is."

"She's just so tiny!" Voice Two said.

"Abigail this, Abigail that, that's all Harry seems to say anymore," Voice One said. "He's absolutely smitten."

"Linda admits she's jealous," Voice Two said.

"Why that little bitch Abigail!" Voice One said. They both laughed.

"Why I never!" I said, but Wynnell has lightning-quick responses and covered my mouth almost immediately.

"What was that?" Voice One said.

"I think someone's in there," Voice Two said. "Anyway, I warned them. I told them getting a Chihuahua puppy was like giving your heart away."

The second they closed the restroom door behind them, Wynnell and I came tumbling out of the stall like a pair of acrobats. She was the first to recover.

"We're taking this back to the alley," she said, grabbing my arm.

"Why don't we just join the Rob-Bobs?"

For the record, Wynnell is eight inches taller than I and probably outweighs me by a good sixty pounds. I barely got a glimpse of the Chez Fez kitchen on my way to the rear entrance. But the glimpse I did get included about a dozen belly dancers standing around, spooning couscous into their mouths.

"Does this mean I get the bald one, too?" one of them yelled.

In the alley, Wynnell propped me up against a brick wall. "Abby, I know that Rob Goldburg and Bob Steuben are close friends of yours. I'm fond of them as well. But they're human like the rest of us."

"I can't argue with you there. What's going on, Wynnell?"

"I'm not suggesting they kidnapped Mozella. She could identify them and then they'd have to—" She let go of me with one hand and made a slashing motion across her throat. "Of course if it came to that, I'm sure they'd hire an expert to do the job for them, and your mama wouldn't feel a thing. Come to think of it, there's any number of Yankees who would be only too glad to do that kind of work for free. After all, Mozella was—I mean, is—the quintessential example of the Deep South; gracious to a fault, and as eccentric as they come."

I squirmed out of her reach. "What on earth are you talking about, Wynnell? Are you on some new medication? Has C.J. been giving you samples of her granny's home remedies again?"

Wynnell's unibrow formed a hairy V. "I wish I didn't have to tell you this, Abby. Bear in mind that I'm only the messenger."

"The message, please!"

"Not only did John Norman identify Bubba Johnson and George Murphy as your top contenders, but there was a telephone bidder as well."

I'd forgotten that Auction Barn allows telephone bids, provided the caller is preregistered and agrees to pay a one-hundred-dollar non-refundable deposit. This ensures serious buyers, who may preview the items to be auctioned. However, most folks enjoy the excitement and atmosphere of an in-person auction, so phone bidders are rare.

My knees felt weak. "Are you saying the phone bidder was one of the Rob-Bobs?"

"Bingo."

"Was it Rob—never mind, I don't want to know. They're like the Bobbsey Twins, or the Robbsey Twins, take your pick. I'm sure they're in it together. But why didn't they tell me? They know I'm tracking down the finalists who bid against me. This is bizarre, Wynnell."

"That's why I couldn't tell you in front of them. Abby, I think you should stay away from them until we find your mama."

"To heck with that. I'm marching right back in there to confront them."

"No, you're not."

"You just try and stop me."

She tried, but to no avail. For the record, after kicking her in the shins I immediately apologized.

Alas, the Rob-Bobs' curtained cubicle was empty, except for a busboy who was flirting with the belly dancer, who was back on duty.

"You chased them off," she growled, "and we had ourselves a deal."

"I did no such thing."

"Everything was going just fine until you showed up, claiming to be their friend."

"Which I am." I started for the front door, but she grabbed my arm and spun me around.

"You think you're special with them expensive clothes and that la-dee-da accent. Well, welcome to the real world, sister. In the real world we fight for what's ours. Ain't nothing handed to us on a silver spoon."

"You mean tray, don't you? A spoon doesn't hold that much."

"Bitch!"

"Ladies," the lad said, "I'm all for a catfight, but can we do it after my shift? Say four o'clock this afternoon at my place?"

"Where do you live?" the belly dancer asked.

"He's jailbait," I said helpfully.

"I'm old enough to drive," he whined.

I dashed out front. The Rob-Bobs were nowhere to be seen. Wynnell, however, was limping around the corner, having come directly from the alley.

"I'm sorry, again," I said.

"Abby, I was only trying to look out for you."

"I know, and I appreciate it. Say, do you want to come with me to interview Bubba Johnson?"

"At his mansion?"

"I don't know, I haven't called him yet. I assume he has an office somewhere."

"Hmm. If it turns out that he's at home, I'll come. I've always wanted a peek inside one of those mansions."

"What about your clothes? Don't you need to go back for them?

"Nah. I was wearing a dress that I'd outgrown anyway. I kinda like the Casbah look. And these curly-toe shoes are much more comfortable than you'd think."

I rang the number Wynnell gave me. It was Bubba Johnson's office, but when I identified myself as the owner of the Taj Mahal birdcage, I was told Mr. Johnson was at home and that he'd been hoping I'd call. I called him there and was told to come by the servants' entrance off the alley.

"The servants' entrance!" I said with righteous indignation. "Can you believe that?"

"Welcome to the real world, Abby."

I drove, taking Society St. over to East Bay. A cruise ship towered over the Customs House, and I felt a longing in my belly. Ever since moving to Charleston I've wanted to take a cruise—to anywhere—just as long as it started and ended in my hometown. What a luxury it would be to not have to worry about missing connecting flights, or airline strikes, and how wonderful it would be to know for a fact that I would be sleeping in the world's most comfortable bed the night I disembarked.

"Dang, I wish I were on a cruise right now," I said aloud. "No worries, unlimited gorging—I could live my life on a cruise ship. Did you know, Wynnell, that people actually do that? You can buy an apartment aboard a cruise ship, and never have to get off."

Wynnell pursed her lips. "You know Ed and I have never been able to afford one. I don't think I'd like to do it if I could. Our neighbors went on one. Maynard, that's the husband, died halfway back from Hawaii. The power to the morgue went out, and they had to store him with the blocks of ice they use for those fancy ice carvings at the gala dinner. Everybody complained about the lack of sculptures. It was just awful for Lydia."

We rode in silence until we came to Market Street. That double intersection was clogged with tourists who believe that since they are on vacation they are immortal. While Wynnell prayed audibly, I cursed softly. I am pleased to say that we made it across without the loss of life.

I never get tired of looking at Rainbow Row, made famous by the musical *Porgy and Bess*, and that day I got plenty of time to enjoy the brightly painted houses, stuck as we were behind a horse-drawn carriage. Just when I was about to blow a gasket (as was my car), Wynnell reminded me how fortunate I was to live in the world's finest city.

"If you had all the money in the world—and sometimes it seems like you do—would you want to live anywhere else?"

"No. The sea air, the lush semitropical gardens, all this history—there's no place else in the world like it."

Immediately the horse pulled over to let us pass. Soon after that we were fortunate enough to find a parking space near the corner of Stolls Alley and East Battery, directly across from the Charleston Yacht Club. Do you see the benefits of extolling the glories of the Holy City?

But even benefits from above are dispensed sparingly to the very stupid, like myself. Bubba Johnson had described his house as "the big brick one with white pillars and lots of fancy trim." Since he made it sound so obvious, and didn't offer more specific information, I didn't think to ask for his house number. Trying to match his house to his description was like trying to identify a bowling ball by its three holes. Finally Wynnell and I resorted to climbing on the seawall for an overview. One of the mansions did seem to be marginally more impressive than the others. The smallest one, by the way, probably exceeded ten thousand square feet.

"I'll be danged if I'm going around to the service entrance," Wynnell declared with surprising vehemence. "I want all these tourists to think I'm company."

"You're dressed like a Gypsy who's lost his guitar. Give it up, Wynnell."

She would not. To the contrary, she opened the splendid wrought-iron gates and sauntered up the walk like she was the Queen of Sheba. I trotted after her at a respectful distance. But as we mounted the steps I edged past her.

"Let me do the talking," I said.

"Could I stop you?"

"I mean it. This is serious business."

"Yes, your majesty," she said without a trace of irony.

There wasn't any bell—at least not that I could see—so I rapped with a bronze ring hanging from the jaws of a life-size bronze lion head. I could feel the thuds reverberating under my feet. After eons of time had passed, and every tourist in Charleston had a chance to see us being shut out of this grand house, the brass-plated massive oak door creaked open, perhaps less than an eighth of an inch. It was impossible to see in.

"Go to the service door," a voice rasped.

"She has an appointment," Wynnell said.

"Go around back to the alley." The monstrous door closed with a thud that was felt all the way up to Columbia.

"Well, that bites," Wynnell said bitterly.

"We're disgraced in front of dozens of people we don't care about. We'll never be able to show our heads in Charleston Society again."

"Unlike you, I haven't had the opportunity. But if I did, I wouldn't blow it by going in drag to the most coveted event of the year."

"Don't even *start* blaming me for Mama's disappearance. I'm blaming myself too much as it is."

"Sorry, Abby. I'm not blaming you. To be honest, I'm just jealous that you ladies didn't invite me to go with you. How come C.J. was invited and I wasn't? You're my best friend, for crying out loud."

It is always awkward when someone considers you to be their best friend but they're number two or three on your list. To be honest, Greg and Mama notwithstanding, I'd have to say Rob Goldburg is my very best friend, my confidant. Then maybe Wynnell—or maybe Bob. It isn't cut-and-dried.

"It wasn't like we meant to exclude you," I wailed. "It just sort of happened. Besides, C.J. wasn't invited at all. She crashed Mama's little party, and much to our surprise she has deep Charleston connections that go back centuries. Prick C.J.'s finger and you'll get royal blue."

"You're talking about *our* C.J.? Calamity Jane from Shelby with the whiskered granny and the Ledbetter cousins that belong in Ripley's Believe It or Not?"

By then we were back on the sidewalk. "That's her. She presents herself as such a yokel, and so over the top with her Shelby stories. If she were a fictional character, I'd find her unbelievable."

"You know what they say—the truth is stranger than fiction."

We arrived at a service entrance that was another brass-plated door. It would have looked nice on your run-of-the-mill mansion in, say, the South Park area of Charlotte, North Carolina. This one had a bell, which I let Wynnell buzz. That the dear woman took a bit of her frustration out on that bell was clear when the door was yanked open.

"We have ears, you know," a uniformed maid snapped.

"And we have feelings. Why the back door?"

"Are they white?" It was the same raspy voice we'd heard in front.

"Yes," the maid said.

A man appeared, as she disappeared. He was dark skinned, with a short natural Afro that was streaked with white. Although he was dressed in a polo shirt, slacks, and a pair of comfortable-looking moccasins, he had the air of a wealthy man about him. I knew at once he was Bubba Johnson.

"My mother was a maid in this very house," he said. "She spent her entire life going through back doors. I made a vow when I was a kid—maybe just ten years old—that someday I would own this place, and all the white folks would have to go through the back door."

"But that's discrimination," Wynnell said. "I've

never made anyone go through my back door, and Abby here has an African-American cousin."

He looked at me with bemusement. "Is that so?"

"Actually, she's a second cousin. But definitely a blood relative."

"I'm sure I have one of those, too," he said with just the hint of a smile. "Come in."

We stepped into a mud room, and then into a large breakfast room, beyond which I could see the makings of an industrial-size kitchen. French doors and floor-to-ceiling glass windows in the breakfast room offered a view of a spectacular garden. A brick walk, flanked by tightly clipped boxwood, led to a large fountain set against a brick wall traced with creeping fig. On either side of the walk in lush profusion grew camellia bushes, cycads, and a species of dwarf palm with strikingly blue fronds. But it was definitely the fountain that was the eye-catcher.

"That's Leda and the swan," I said aloud.

"Very good," Bubba Johnson said.

We shook hands.

"What's that girl doing with the swan?" Wynnell asked. "Swans can be dangerous."

"The swan is raping her," I said. "It's from the poem by William Butler Yeats. After being raped, Leda produces an egg that contains three babies, two boys and a girl. The girl is Helen of Troy."

"I thought that was a movie with Brad Pitt."

"Same Helen," Bubba Johnson said. "Would you ladies care for something to drink? A little sweet tea, maybe, or something stronger if you like."

"Something stronger," Wynnell said without a second's hesitation. My friend is strict Southern Baptist, but only at home.

"Name your poison. I have just about everything."

Before Wynnell could open her mouth we heard a thundering crash in another room, and seconds later the door to the kitchen was flung open by the maid. Along with her came the stench of ammonia so intense it stung my eyes. Adding to the assault on my senses was a shrill, high-pitched noise at mind-boggling decibels. It was like listening to the Vienna Boys Choir while on speed—not that I've done a whole lot of that, mind you.

"Number fifty-two toppled," the maid said between gasps.

"What the flock!" Bubba Johnson ran to the door, the maid at his heels.

Not wanting to appear standoffish, Wynnell and I ran after them. What we witnessed that morning was so astonishing, it almost defies description. Lying on the floor of what should have been a dining room were dozens of overturned birdcages. Inside the cages were dozens, maybe hundreds, of chirping birds. A quick glance around the room informed me that the toppled cages had just seconds before been stacked from the floor to the twelve-foot ceiling. Other stacks of cages covered the walls like three-dimensional wallpaper. And there were stacks of cages in the middle of the room as well, although a number of them had been knocked to the floor.

It is hard to say how many birds had been

liberated by this unfortunate event, or how many were flying free to begin with, but the air was filled with them. It was also filled with floating feathers and falling excrement. Wynnell and I were content to stand in the doorway and stare.

Bubba Johnson turned and saw us. "Get the hell out of my house!" he roared.

CHAPTER 9

"What was that all about?" Wynnell asked, badly shaken.

I was balancing on the seawall again, this time trying to look into Bubba Johnson's front windows. No luck. The heavy drapes may as well have been walls.

"I don't think he was lashing out at us," I said. "He was just upset about the cages falling over."

"No, I meant what's with all the birds? That's more than just a hobby. That's even more than a business. Do you think it's some kind of fetish?"

"A fetid fetish? I think you mean obsession. It's definitely that. It's a danger all collectors face. I knew a woman who collected Raggedy Anne dolls and memorabilia. She finally had to declare bankruptcy. At that time, she had over five thousand dolls and was thirty thousand dollars in debt."

"Dolls, I can see. Birds, I can't."

"People collect matchbooks, sheet music, orchids, palm trees, cars—anything you can think of. Even husbands. There's that unbeatable excitement of the next acquisition."

"It sounds like you know from experience, Abby."

"Merely observation. Well, at least we know why Mr. Johnson was interested in the birdcage. It was unique, and it was bird-related. That was enough."

"Where to next, Abby? The beautiful blonde named George Murphy?"

"Sounds like a plan," I said, and jumped from the seawall to the sidewalk.

Unfortunately, my body objected to the rude jolt, forcing me to limp back to the car.

George Murphy was a licensed physical therapist who worked at the Lowcountry Arm and Shoulder Therapy on Ben Sawyer Boulevard in Mount Pleasant. To get there we had to cross the Cooper River. This is, by the way, one of the most important rivers in the world. At the southern end of the Charleston peninsula, the Cooper joins with the Ashley River, where together they form the Atlantic Ocean. That this important piece of geography is not taught in classrooms is yet another sign of the great power the Northern States continue to wield. While it's not on the tip of my tongue at the moment, I do remember reading about the two rivers that come together to form the Pacific Ocean. Do you see what I mean?

At any rate, Mount Pleasant, which lacks a mountain, was until just two decades ago a sleepy, moss-festooned fishing village. Today it is home to thousands of retirees, many of whom were fortunate enough to cash in on their nest eggs while still in their fifties, and before the dot-com crash. With money to burn, and in relatively good health, this new generation of retirees eschews rocking chairs for golf, jogging, tennis, and that most revered physical activity, "the workout." But where there are workouts, there are injuries, and thus in Mount Pleasant there exists a plethora of physical therapists.

I'd confirmed over the phone that George Murphy was indeed a woman. My purpose for calling, I told her, was that I was having second thoughts about the birdcage. She got off at four and agreed to meet Wynnell and me at the Starbucks in the Barnes & Noble in Towne Center. She described herself as blond and ordinary looking, but the blonde at Starbucks at the appointed hour was a woman who looked like a young Dolly Parton. I, who have never had a hankering for other women, found that it was almost impossible to look her in the eyes.

"Mrs. Washburn?" she asked.

"George?"

She had an easy, pleasant laugh. "It was my mother's maiden name. She loved her daddy very much and wouldn't even consider Georgia, or anything like that. I've kind of gotten used to it."

I introduced Wynnell, who was similarly

transfixed by the woman's attributes. In fact, my dear friend couldn't look at George at all, so although her head was turned in the young therapist's direction, Wynnell's eyes were doing something her mother had no doubt warned her against as a child.

"She suffers from a rare disease known as putyoureyesbackinyourheaditis," I explained to George.

"I do not!" Wynnell said.

"Forgive her," I said. "It's the medication. Would you care for some coffee or a snack, Miss Murphy? My treat, of course."

She allowed as how she did, so we all got lattes and scones before cornering the most secluded table. While I did the hostess thing and removed a pile of magazines from the table, Wynnell slid in next to George Murphy. I was thereby forced to confront the Himalayas head on, or settle for a side view, which was even more unsettling. I chose the tips of twin peaks.

"George," I said, "you're probably wondering why we asked you to meet us here."

"No, ma'am. You said it was about the birdcage. That you'd changed your mind."

"I said I was having second thoughts. I didn't say I'd changed my mind."

"Oh, that's okay." She took a long sip of her latte and smiled. I couldn't for the life of me figure out what was going on. To have made it to the final five contending for the Taj took fast and furious bidding. It showed she was serious about owning that splendid work of art. But now suddenly she didn't care about it? What was up with that?

"George, don't you want the Taj Mahal?"

"The what?"

"The fancy birdcage."

"Yeah, well I did want it. But that was then, this is now. Hey, have you guys seen that new movie everyone's talking about?"

"*Scary Movie Six?*"

"No, I think it's called *Blonde, Blonder, and Blondest*. Hey, would you guys like to go?"

"Excuse me?" Wynnell said.

"We can see another one if you want. The Palmetto Grande theater is just around the corner."

"I know where it is," Wynnell said. "I just can't figure out—"

"How we could possibly fit it into our schedule for today," I said.

"Tomorrow, then?"

"If we have an opening, I'll give you a call," I said. I made a show of looking at my watch. "Goodness me, look what time it is already. If we don't hurry, Wynnell, we're going to be stuck in rush hour traffic."

"But Abby, most of the rush hour traffic at this time of the day is coming *into* Mount Pleasant, not—"

George gasped. "Ouch!"

Silly me. I'd tried to kick Wynnell, but in

103

sliding down into my chair in order to reach, I'd inadvertently changed course by a few inches. It was George's knee my tootsie jabbed.

They say the best defense is a good offense, but I'd like to suggest flight as a solution. Unfortunately Wynnell had yet to start on her scone, so I had to grab her by the arm and pull her from Barnes & Noble.

"What the heck is going on, Abby?" she demanded as I virtually stuffed her into my car.

"That buxom blonde is trying to stall, that's what."

"You're not making any sense, Abby. Did you slip a little something special into your latte?"

"I did not! Think about it, Wynnell. Why would a complete stranger invite us to the movies with her?"

"Because she likes us?"

"Think again. She's trying to keep us away from the Den of Antiquity as long as possible."

"Now you're being paranoid, Abby."

"C.J.!" I dialed the shop number, and when I got the answering machine, I left a cryptic message, commanding my assistant to lock the doors and stay put. Then I tried to dial her cell phone.

"No answer either place?" Wynnell asked, her unibrow bunched together again.

"She could be using the restroom," I said, trying to keep hope afloat. I couldn't press the pedal to the metal in traffic that heavy, but I did try to drive nine miles above what the law allows. In my experience, it's that tenth mile that will get you the ticket. But both lanes on Route 17 southbound were bumper-to-bumper and, for some inexplicable reason, moving along at well below the speed limit. I was about to bust a gut with frustration.

"It's a Yankee plot," Wynnell said, shaking her head.

"What is?"

"This traffic jam—all these retirees. Sure, they sent down a few carpetbaggers after they won the War of Northern Aggression, but that was just the tip of the iceberg. They were really just biding their time until air-conditioning was invented. Now they send us their old folk by the thousands, maybe even millions, and there is nothing we can do to stop them. If we were still the Confederate States of America, we could refuse them visas."

"Now who's being paranoid?"

"Oh, Abby, I was just kidding. You know that."

"As much kidding as you think you can get away with, given that one of your granddaddies hailed from north of the Line."

My buddy snorted and crossed her arms. It bothers her something fierce that she's not one hundred percent Dixie. But all was forgiven, if not forgotten, when we pulled into my private parking space behind the Den of Antiquity.

"C.J.," I cried, letting myself in the back entrance,

"are you all right?" Wynnell was right on my heels, sometimes literally.

We were still in the storeroom when we heard the loud, off-key sounds that signify the big galoot is attempting to sing. Although I've never heard one, this noise brings to mind a donkey in heat. At any rate, I was right: C.J. was in the john.

I pounded on the door. "Are you okay?"

The door opened unexpectedly, and I staggered backward, knocking over a stack of dining room chairs. If Wynnell hadn't been so quick to react, I could have spent the rest of the summer in traction.

C.J. grinned with delight at seeing us. "Hey guys, what's up?"

"You," I said between pants. "Why didn't you answer the phone?"

"Don't be silly, Abby. You know the cord doesn't reach that far. You should buy a cordless phone, like I keep telling you."

"What about your cell phone? I tried to call that, too."

She shook her giant head. "Everybody knows that talking on cell phones in bathrooms is dangerous. Abby, I'm surprised you'd even suggest such a thing."

"It's not dangerous. Tell her, Wynnell."

"I'm having too much fun watching," Wynnell said.

"You see, she knows. But I guess I can't blame

you, Abby, because I didn't know either until Cousin Olea Ledbetter slipped away."

I refused to respond.

"She'd taken her cell phone into the bathroom with her, you see, and was standing on the seat, because she could get better reception that way. Suddenly she slipped and slid right down that hole. Her husband had to break down the door, and all he found was the cell phone floating in the bowl."

"Are you sure that wasn't Cousin Olive Oyl Ledbetter?" I asked.

"You don't need to be mean, Abby. You know Cousin Olive Oyl died by choking on a pit."

The outside front buzzer rang, and I had never been so happy to answer it in my life. I literally left Wynnell and C.J. behind in the dust (my storeroom needs a thorough cleaning). But my steps slowed when I saw the navy blue uniforms of Charleston's finest through the beveled glass. Good news, I've learned, most often comes by phone. Bad news begs to be delivered in person. One major exception, I am told, is Publisher's Clearing House. I'll have to take someone's word for that.

I turned the dead bolt slowly. My stomach turned as well.

"Yes, Officer Tweedledum?" I used his real name, of course.

"Police business," he said.

"Duh!" I said cheerfully. With enough forced

cheer, one can get away with saying just about anything. It's much like saying "bless your heart," but with fewer words.

For a moment they were so relieved to be in from the blistering heat that they acted almost human. "I'm glad to see you've taken precautions," Officer Tweedledee said.

"Say, you wouldn't happen to have any cold sodas on hand, would you?" Officer Tweedledum asked. I believe that's the longest string of nonhostile words the man has ever spoken to me.

"Sorry, I don't. But I can send my assistant out for some."

"Yes, please," they said in unison.

"Would you like her to bring back a couple of Krispy Kremes as well?"

"Is that supposed to be a joke, ma'am?"

What a relief. It was business as usual. No more worrying about the Stepford police.

"C.J.," I called. "Come here, please."

"In a minute, Abby."

"Come now, please."

"No can do, Abby. Wynnell and I are arm wrestling."

I shrugged. "Good help is hard to find these days," I said, stalling the inevitable.

"Mrs. Washburn, I think you should sit down," Officer Tweedledee said in a rare moment of kindness.

My knees were suddenly incapable of holding up a mynah bird, much less ninety-eight pounds.

I stumbled backward until my bottom connected with a Shaker chair. It took every ounce of strength for me to hoist my patootie, petite as it may be, up to the seat.

"It's about Mama, isn't it?"

"I'm afraid it is."

CHAPTER 10

I closed my eyes and balled my fists. "Let me have it. Straight up."

"We found her rented wheelchair."

"And?"

"That's all. We thought you might like to know."

My eyes flew open. "What do you mean 'that's all'? What about Mama's body?"

"There was no body, Mrs. Washburn. Just the wheelchair. By the way, the rental company says you owe them $79.82 in late fees."

I felt the resurgence of energy. It was just enough to enable me to leap at them and knock their heads together, or to continue my investigation once they left. For Mama's sake, I chose to be a lady.

"Where did you find the chair?"

"I'm afraid that's on a need-to-know basis," Officer Tweedledum said.

"Give her a break," Officer Tweedledee whispered, earning her my temporary gratitude.

"St. Philip's cemetery," Officer Tweedledum

growled. "A parishioner discovered it yesterday, but didn't report it until this afternoon."

"He confessed to taking it home for his wife to use," Officer Tweedledee said, "but she couldn't fit. Then his conscience started bothering him, so he turned it over to the department. You'd be surprised how many times that sort of thing happens."

"Makes you proud to be an American," Officer Tweedledum said. "Yes, ma'am, right proud."

"Wait a minute," I said, as a thought came to me, "lots of people use wheelchairs. How do you know it's the right one? Did you check for prints?"

"We're not stupid," Officer Tweedledum said. "We just look that way. Of course we checked it for prints."

"And?"

"There weren't any."

"But we called the rental company," Officer Tweedledee said. "On the backs of the chairs they advertise a book they publish—*Geriatric Sex for Dummies*—along with their phone number. Anyway, your mother's was their only rental last weekend."

"May I assume you turned the chair back in so that the rental fee won't accrue?"

"Look, Mrs. Washburn," Officer Tweedledum said, "we don't all have your kind of money. My wife's been needing a bigger chair for a long time now and—"

Officer Tweedledee poked her partner in the ribs.

"Sorry you folks have to run," I said, and at the earliest opportunity locked the door behind them.

C.J. finally answered my call. By then her hair was mussed and her red face was bulging with so many veins it looked like she'd dipped it in a bowl of spaghetti.

"Where's Wynnell?"

"She went out the front way. She said to tell you she was going home to make supper for Ed. Personally, Abby, I think she's no longer interested in sleuthing."

"It has been an extraordinarily long day. How was business?"

"Pretty good. But just about everyone asked where the bird is."

"What did you tell them?"

"I said we sent it over to Berlitz so it could learn to speak a lot of languages."

"Good one." It was an inside joke; C.J. speaks seventeen languages fluently. At least she claims she does. Who is to know if the Sino-Tibetan dialect she rattles off is really gibberish?

"Abby, I don't care if a million customers stop by, it gets lonely here without my little friend."

"I'm sure we'll get Monet back, dear. It's just a question of time."

"I meant you."

Does it get any sweeter than that? "C.J., what are your plans for this evening?"

"I was going to go home and wait for your brother to call. Abby, do you know what it's like to be in love with the handsomest, sexiest man in the world, and not be able to hold him in your arms every night? I long to feel Toy's lithe body— if I overlook the love handles—pressed hard against mine, his full, but somewhat rubbery lips—"

"Ew! That's my brother!"

"But it will all be worth it someday. I'll be Mrs. Toy Wiggins, and you'll be my sister-in-law. How cool is that, sis?"

"Cooler than an unheated igloo in January. C.J.—sis—he can call you at my house just as well."

She hesitated just long enough to make me repeat my invitation, and then we were off. When we got home I was doubly glad to have the big gal for company. Greg had left a message saying his boat was having engine troubles and that he'd be spending the night with a buddy, Mark Gallentree, up in McClellanville. Of course I trusted my husband, but I will admit that it helped that I knew Caroline Gallentree, Mark's wife. The fact they were neither politicians nor preachers added to my comfort level.

Dmitri adores C.J., and while I kicked my shoes off and dug through the freezer for a couple of Lean Cuisine dinners, he kneaded her lap and purred. "I had a cat once," C.J. said loud enough so I could hear from the kitchen.

"What was his name?" I called.

"Liger."

I brought her a tall glass of sweet tea. "That's a cute name. Short for Little Tiger, right?"

"Oh, no, Abby. We called him Liger because that's what he was—half lion and half tiger."

"C.J., please. I'm too tired for Shelby stories tonight."

"But it's true, Abby. Granny Ledbetter bought him from a traveling menagerie. Of course he was just a cub when we got him, but then he got so big that granny put a saddle on him and let me ride him. Ligers, you know, are the biggest cats in the world."

"Stop it. Lions and tigers are different species and they come from different places. Lions are from Africa and tigers from Asia. They can't interbreed. There is no such animal as a liger."

"Are you calling me a liar, Abby?"

"No, just highly imaginative."

"You *are* calling me a liar." She pushed Dmitri off her lap and stood.

I wasn't in the mood to play games. Neither did I wish to be mean. But if we constantly let C.J. get away with her preposterous tales, we weren't doing her any favors.

"I'm sorry you can't stay longer," I said.

C.J. put her hands on her hips and gave me the evil eye. Her bottom lip was trembling, but she didn't say a word. Then, still without saying a thing, she grabbed her purse and stomped out the door.

I must say that her silence unnerved me. I would have much preferred a stiff rebuttal, even one laced with Shelby stories. Just to make one hundred percent sure that I wasn't in the wrong, I ran to the computer and typed "liger" in the search blank supplied by Google. The results came up immediately.

"Holy guacamole," I said aloud, "there is such a thing."

The big gal was right as rain. Due to a phenomenon biologists refer to as hybrid vigor, ligers—the offspring of a male lion and a female tiger—can weigh as much as a thousand pounds and, when standing on their hind legs, reach twelve feet in height.

I dialed C.J.'s cell phone. She couldn't have been gone more than two minutes, so she was definitely not indisposed. I hung up and tried again. Not having any luck, I did the only thing I could do, which was leave her a message, telling my dear friend how sorry I was for not believing her. I even went so far as to promise to believe all her future Shelby stories. Frankly, I hadn't made such an insincere vow since I was confirmed at age fourteen.

Depression either steals my appetite or makes me ravenous. That evening it made me hungry enough to devour both Lean Cuisines, a Hungry Man, and half a pint of Cherry Garcia ice cream. I tried to distract myself by reading, gave up to watch *Last Comic Standing,* and then, after an hour of not chuckling once, I turned out the light and fell asleep almost immediately.

I dreamed a thousand pound liger, with C.J. astride, was roaming the streets of Charleston South of Broad. But I was the only one who could see the giant cat. My calls to police were cruelly mocked, then ignored altogether. Even my honeybuns, Greg, who had returned from McClellanville married to Caroline Gallentree, refused to take me seriously. The only person in the entire world to believe me, other than C.J., was Bob Steuben, who said he had an old family recipe for liger burgers and would be right over to help me catch the behemoth. Before Bob could get there, the ferocious beast leaped through my bedroom window—Greg and the new Mrs. Washburn were in the kitchen yucking it up—knocked me to the bed, and started clawing at my eyes.

It was one of those dreams more real than reality, in part because I dreamed it mere minutes before waking, and when I did finally awaken, Dmitri was lying on my sternum, batting at my fluttering eyelids. It was a sport he'd engaged in on numerous other occasions. Still, it took me a couple of seconds to realize what was happening. Just before it clicked, I let loose with a bloodcurdling scream. Dmitri leaped into the air, landed on my chest, then tore from the room in a streak of orange. There are not many places in our house where a ten-pound cat can hide and not be found, but there must be at least one. Even a freshly opened can failed to do the trick.

While my poor pussy pouted, I got on the phone to McClellanville. First I called Greg's cell phone, but couldn't get through. When I called the Gallentree's landline, Caroline Gallentree picked up on the first ring.

"Hey Caroline. Is Greg there?" Only Yankees (and recently arrived Southerners) identify themselves to folks they've met more than once.

"Abby! I was just about to call *you*. I take it you haven't seen Mark, then?"

"Not since we rode to Clemson together last fall for the homecoming game."

"I was afraid of that."

My phone hand trembled. "Greg left a message late yesterday afternoon. Said he had engine trouble."

"Funny, because that's what Mark said. And that he was closer to Charleston than to McClellanville, so he was spending the night with y'all."

"Well, he didn't. Have you tried calling Mark on his cell?"

"Only a million times. Always get the same answer: the party I'm trying to reach is out of his calling area. How about you?"

"Same here. Caroline, what are the odds they both had engine trouble?"

"What are the odds we'll see a hundred pounds again—sorry, Abby. Damn them, Abby. Damn them all to hell." She started crying.

"Caroline, do you want me to come up there?" I crossed my fingers and prayed that she didn't.

"No, I'll be okay. I just need to focus on what I do next. Should we call the Coast Guard, Abby? Mark's boat isn't in his slip."

"Doesn't he have a partner?"

"He has two employees, Jesus and Chico. They're from Mexico. I called them both. Jesus said they never went out yesterday. Abby, have you checked with Greg's partners?"

"I just woke up. Give me five minutes and I'll call you right back."

Skeeter and Bo Evans are Greg's partners. They're also his cousins. Bo fancies himself a lady-killer. Unfortunately, not many women fancy him. Nonetheless, when Bo's done trawling for shrimp, he trawls the bars for women. Skeeter, on the other hand, is a family man with four children, three of them in braces and one bound for college. I chose to call him.

He read his caller ID. "Abby?"

"Skeeter, have you seen Greg?"

"Not since Friday. Why?"

"He didn't go out in the boat yesterday?"

"I don't think so. He said he needed off—to be with you. So Bo and I decided to take the day off as well. I want to spend as much time

118

as I can with my oldest before she goes away to school. Say, any word about your mother, Abby?"

"No, not really. Thanks, Skeeter."

"Any time."

I called Caroline back. "His partner said he didn't think Greg took the boat out. I'm going to drive over to Mount Pleasant and see for myself. Do you have *my* cell phone number?"

"Yeah. Call me—promise?"

"As soon as I find out anything."

When I hung up, I tried calling C.J. again. Still no answer. It was getting to the point where it was almost funny. First Mama, then C.J., then Dmitri, then Greg. Who was going to go missing next? Of course it wasn't funny. Except for my first wedding day—and the seven or eight times since when I've almost gotten myself killed—this was shaping up to be the most stressful day of my life.

Who should a stressed-out woman turn to? Yes, God is a good answer, but being only a lapsed Episcopalian, I ran straight into the arms of a good-looking unmarried man.

Rob Goldburg gave me a long, hard hug, and then passed me over to Bob.

"You look like hell, Abby," Rob said. "What happened?"

"Greg didn't come home last night, and he wasn't where he said he would be. C.J. is missing

119

as well—at least she won't answer her phone. Oh, and Dmitri is hiding somewhere in the house sulking. Can it get any worse?"

They led me into their kitchen. "Tell us everything," Bob said. "Don't leave out a single word, but tell us between bites. I made a pigeon egg soufflé. It's hot from the oven. I haven't even taken it from its bath yet."

"A what and a what?"

Rob laughed. "That's what I said."

Bob was not amused. "For your information, fresh pigeon eggs are hard to get in Charleston. I had to put my order in weeks ago."

"He serious?" I asked.

Rob rolled his eyes. "I'm afraid so. Do you know how many pigeon eggs it takes to make a soufflé? I don't, either, but I can tell you it takes forty-eight bucks worth."

"That's because I had to have them air-freighted from San Antonio. Orange juice or grapefruit, Abby? I've even got kumquat, if you like."

"Coffee, please."

"You take it like you like your men, right? Weak and white."

"I'll take it strong and white this morning. Why on earth would anyone eat pigeon eggs?"

"They have a rich, almost buttery taste, that's why."

"They smell like a paper processing plant," Rob said.

"Look guys, I'd love to stay and give you my

opinion, but I'm headed over to Shem Creek in Mount Pleasant. I want to see if Greg's car is parked anywhere nearby. But first I need to rake one, or both, of you over the coals."

"Uh-oh," Rob said, "we've been outed."

"I outed myself years ago," Bob said, "so she must mean you, Rob."

"Ha ha, very funny," I said. "And yes, you are outed. Why didn't either of you tell me that y'all made a phone bid on the Taj Mahal?"

My buddies exchanged worried glances. For all their sophistication, suddenly they were now just boys caught with their hands inside a cookie jar.

I tapped my sandal against their hardwood kitchen floor. "I want the truth, and I want it now."

"Careful, Abby, you'll leave a mark," Bob said. "Your floor has a better finish than that."

"He's just worried you'll make his soufflé fall," Rob said with a smile.

"Then maybe I should slam a few doors," I said, but without a smile.

"Uncle!" Bob boomed. "We were bidding on it because we wanted it for you."

"For me?"

"As a birthday present," Rob said. "You've got one coming next month, in case you haven't remembered."

"I try not to. But why the Taj?"

"Well, when we went to the presale viewing the

night before, that's all you could talk about. Most beautiful thing you'd ever seen, you said—like a million times. We got the hint. To make it more of a surprise, we stayed away from the auction and bid over the phone. But some jerk kept bidding against us."

"That would be me. So why did you stop?"

"We love you, Abby, but not ten thousand dollars worth." Fortunately, that line was delivered with a grin.

"Well, thanks for the thought. And remember, whatever figure you stopped your bidding at, that's how much I expect you to pay for my birthday present—when you do get around to buying it."

The look of terror in Rob's eyes may have been staged, but it was priceless. "Yeah, sure thing, Abby."

"Okay guys, it's been lovely, but like I said, I need to bop on over to the pleasant side of the Cooper to look for Greg's car."

"We'd love to go with you," Bob said, "but there's the soufflé to consider. You understand, don't you, Abby?"

"Of course."

"Nonsense," Rob said, "we're going with you." He grabbed a set of keys hanging from the tooth of a scowling wall gnome.

"No fair," Bob moaned. "The soufflé is going to fall without anyone even tasting it."

"That doesn't have to be the case," Rob said.

"Bob, why don't you stay and give it a test taste? I'm sure Abby won't mind."

I didn't, but I knew Bob cared. As much as he knows better, my homely friend lives in constant fear that his very handsome partner will suddenly become a raging heterosexual—in other words, Anita Bryant's poster boy.

"Let's all three taste it, and then go," I said.

Rob glared at me while I smiled sweetly.

"So," Bob said, "who wants to go first?"

I needed to get the show on the road, so I took the plunge. Actually, it was a series of stabs. The soufflé had a surprisingly thick crust on it, which has yet to be explained. It was, however, quite tasty.

"Pretty good," I said. "Does it have blue cheese in it?"

Bob beamed. "I always knew you had sophisticated taste buds, Abby."

Rob barely licked what was on his spoon. "Funny, because I would have guessed dirty socks."

"You're right as well! You see, this particular blue cheese is made in a very poor monastery in the Carpathian Mountains. The monks use old socks—clean ones, of course—to separate the curds from the whey."

"You're kidding," I said.

Rob stared at his partner. "I'm afraid he's not. Bob always blinks when he's not telling the truth."

The phone rang, and Bob, who was the closest, glanced at the caller ID. "It's blocked."

"Pick it up anyway," Rob said. "I've got this feeling it might be important."

"Hello?" Bob said into the phone. Then his eyes widened as he turned to me. "It's for you, Abby."

CHAPTER 11

I took the phone hesitantly. "Who is it?" I asked, one hand over the mouthpiece.

Bob shrugged.

"Hello?"

I was greeted by silence.

"Hello? Is anyone there? There's nobody on the line!"

"Sorry, Abby," Bob said.

"Was it a man or a woman?"

"That's the thing, I couldn't tell. The voice was all over the place."

"Maybe an adolescent boy," Rob said, and put his arm around my shoulders.

"Could it have been a bird, Bob?"

"A bird? I guess so. You mean like Monet, right?"

"Right."

"Shoot, Abby, I should have said something to keep him—uh, or her—on the line."

"You didn't know. But *they* know—they know where to call me. Guys, I'm being followed."

Rob squeezed my shoulder. "Sort of looks like it, doesn't it? But don't worry, darlin', we're not

125

going to let anything happen to you. From now on Bob and I are sticking to you like glue."

"But not Goofy Glue," Bob said. "That stuff can't hold two pieces of paper together, much less suspend a truck from an I-beam like in those commercials."

"They'll follow us to Mount Pleasant," I said. "How am I going to look for Greg's car?"

"How do you feel about suitcases?" Rob asked.

"Excuse me?"

"I'll be right back," he said.

"He better make this quick," I said to Bob. "I'm being followed by some maniacal kidnapper, and he wants to show off his new suitcase?"

Rob kept his word, and was back in less time than it takes a Yankee to say the pledge of allegiance. He was pulling a very large suitcase in a floral tapestry design. He opened it immediately.

"Hop in," he said.

"I beg your pardon?"

"Don't worry, it has air holes all over the place. The center of each rose in fact."

"What the heck is going on?"

"It's the perfect way to sneak you out of here. I'll open the garage door first and make a big show of loading the car, and then Bob and I will take off, presumably on a trip of some kind. They'll sit and wait here, watching for your car to leave, but of course it won't."

"I see—no, I don't. What are you doing with a suitcase full of holes?"

126

Rob blushed.

"It was a fraternity," Bob said. "You don't want to know. Trust me."

I am not a claustrophobic person. I'm sure that is in large part because I'm such a small person. What is a tight squeeze for most adults is plenty big for me. But just the thought of being locked up in a suitcase, no matter how roomy it might be, gave me the willies.

"I think I've seen too many horror movies, guys. This isn't going to work."

The Rob-Bobs sighed in unison. "Somehow I'm not surprised," Rob said. "Back in college when I had to—never mind. We could just stick you in the trunk when the garage door is closed. The trunk has a safety pull, so you don't need to worry about—"

"I'll do it."

"Excuse me?"

"But you have to put this suitcase on the back-seat, not the trunk. Fill the trunk with other suitcases. That will make it look like you're going on a long trip, and I get to see out."

"Not much, you won't," Bob said. "Whenever I—"

"Never mind," Rob said. "We'll let you out as soon as we get over the bridge and into Mount Pleasant. You'll be out of here in fifteen minutes, twenty tops."

I must admit that once I got in and found a comfortable position, it started to be fun. It was very much like playing hide-and-seek, or reading under the covers with a flashlight. Confining spaces can actually be comforting, seeing as how they remind us of the womb. The trick to enjoying them is that one must be sure that an exit is in the offing. Therefore I chose to think of the Rob-Bobs—more specifically, my trust in them—as my birth canal.

"Do you want to listen to some music?" Rob asked once we were buckled in and on the move.

"Sure," I said, speaking through a peephole. "Just as long as it isn't rap."

"Rap isn't music," Bob said. "Music has to have a tune."

"There are millions of people who disagree," I said.

We didn't listen to any music. Instead, the Rob-Bobs kept a running commentary on the cars they could see through the rearview mirrors. As I might have expected, Bob thought every other car was following us, whereas Rob didn't see anything suspicious. Bob was right about one thing: there wasn't much I could see, besides the back of their heads.

Because I was literally in the dark, I didn't react at first when I heard the siren. Fire, ambulance, or police, they seldom have much to do with me. It was only when I heard Rob swear like an Air Force plebe—which he was at one time—that I realized that the three of us were in potentially deep doo-doo.

"Sir, do you realize you were going fifty-five miles an hour on that bridge?"

"No, sir."

"The speed limit is forty-five."

"I am very sorry, sir. I did not realize it."

So far, so good. Rob was polite, without being servile. He was acknowledging his error, but not excusing it. There is a fine line one must walk at moments like that, and yet so much depends on whether the officer is having a good day, or his boxers are riding up and driving him crazy.

"Mr. Goldburg, the fine for exceeding the limit by ten miles is—What's in that suitcase?"

"Uh—the suitcase?"

"I just saw an eye."

"An eye, sir?"

"There are holes in that suitcase, Mr. Goldburg, and I asked you a simple question."

I closed my offending eyes. So much for wanting to see, as well as hear, what was going on.

"Yes, it is a simple question, one easily answered, I am sure—"

"If one had a brain in one's head," Bob boomed, almost making me jump, which would indeed have given the officer an eyeful. "I keep telling my friend that the dog is a basenji, but I might as well be talking to the walls."

"A basenji?" the officer said. "My sister has one of those."

"You're kidding! A red and white, a black and white, or a tricolor?"

"The kind with all three colors. What kind is yours?"

"Red and white?"

"Can I see it?"

"Man, I sure wish you could," Bob said, "but the little bitch has taken to biting lately. That's where we're headed right now, to obedience school."

"Yeah? They say biting is a hard habit to break." I could hear the policeman rip a page from his book. "Mr. Goldburg, I'm going to give you a warning ticket this time, on account of you had a legitimate reason to be distracted."

"Thank you, sir," Rob said, with just the right amount of sarcasm.

"Don't thank me. Thank your little four-legged friend in the backseat. Lucky for you I have a soft spot for dogs."

"Yes, sir."

I heard the window close, then open again. "Hey," the cop said, "just one more thing. How come you got the bitch in a suitcase and not in a crate?"

Bob spoke up. "Like I said, sir, the bitch bites a lot. Chewed up the crate so bad you can't close the door. This is just an old suitcase I wasn't using anymore. I plan to swing by Pet Smart in North Charleston after her training session and get a new crate."

"Good move. Those basenjis are something else, aren't they? The little rascals come from Africa, where they use them as hunting dogs. Even use them to hunt lions and elephants, my sister says, because they aren't afraid of anything. Interesting reason why they can't bark—"

"They can't bark?" Rob asked.

There was a long period of silence.

"Mr. Goldburg, you led me to believe the dog was yours."

"It is! I thought the rascal was silent all the time because she didn't like me." He turned and stuck his finger through a hole not far from my face. "Does daddy's little girl like him after all? Does her? Does her? Oh, there's a good widdle girl."

I despise baby talk when not issued from the mouths of babes. Plus which, the finger came dangerously close to jabbing me in the eye. Can this little bitch then be blamed for what she did next?

"Damn!" Rob jerked his finger from the hole. "She bit me!"

"Serves you right," Bob said.

I could hear the officer chuckling as the window went back up.

"What the heck, Abby," Rob said, "was that all about?"

"This widdle bitch bites a lot, didn't you hear?"

"Bob said that, not me."

"Bitch," Bob said, "is the preferred term for a female dog. Ask any breeder. Go to any dog show."

"What's a male dog called?"

"A dog."

I made Rob pull into the nearest parking lot and release me from the valise. If the maniacal kidnappers saw me, so be it. I was through with suitcases and canine identities.

The Mount Pleasant shrimp industry is based on Shem Creek, a tidal creek that bisects the old part of town like a jagged sword. Years ago the docks were jammed with shrimp boats. Today restaurants almost outnumber the boats, and the seafood they serve is not always local. The shrimpers—many of them Vietnamese—struggle to stay in business. I don't know how Skeeter and Bo manage to survive financially. If Greg and I didn't own the Den of Antiquity (and its sister store in Charlotte), we could never afford to live like we do. At any rate, Greg's boat, the *Brown Pelican,* was deserted except for an ornery, territorial bird of the same name. But it was *there.* How could Greg have lied to me like that? How could he say he had the boat up in McClellanville, and that it was giving him engine trouble, when it was tied up at its home berth? Greg didn't even have it in him to tell a white lie, for Pete's sake. I learned early on in our relationship never to ask him if I look fat or if my hair looks nice.

We checked all the parking areas within half a mile of the creek. I even thought to push the horn button on my set of keys. I got no response—well, I got one. A Hummer took to bleating like an oversized lamb and unfortunately there was no way to make it stop.

"Let's get out of here, guys!"

Rob was still smarting from his warning ticket, plus he can be stubborn upon occasion. I can run faster than he drove away from the Hummer.

"This reeks," I said, on the edge of despair. "First the stupid bird, then Mama, and now Greg. What's next? Will my shop burn down?"

"You forgot Dmitri," Rob said.

"Thanks a lot. But at least he disappeared at home. He's probably leaving me a little present of apology right now—in my shoes."

"This girl needs something to eat," Bob said.

My heart pounded. I knew that the Rob-Bobs had put at least four suitcases in the trunk of their car before stashing me in the backseat. I had assumed those suitcases were empty, but like they say, when you assume, you make an "ass" out of "u" and "me." Perhaps Bob had packed a picnic lunch, in which case the already horrible day was going to get even uglier. I had no stomach for sweet and sour llama brains, or whatever Bob had dreamed up.

"I want to go to IHOP," I practically shouted.

My buds were stunned. Their philosophy of restaurants can be covered in one sentence: *if it's part of a chain, it's cool to disdain.* But I had a hankering for flapjacks, and what better place to get them than at the International House of Pancakes?

Rob found his voice first. "You're kidding, Abby, aren't you?"

"No, I'm not. And there is an IHOP on Route 17, just before you get to Towne Center."

Rob drove even slower, if that was possible. I had to remind him that one can be ticketed for driving too slowly. I had to say it about a dozen times. When we got to the restaurant, I was in such a hurry to get inside that I stubbed my toe on the curb. As a consequence, I hopped into the IHOP hopping mad. Fortunately, a plate of pancakes was all it took to placate me. As the sugar surged through my body, my brain became functional again. Although it may be fleeting, there is nothing as immediately satisfying as a high-carb high.

"Sorry if I was bitchy, guys."

"No prob," Rob said. "How else should a widdle bitch be expected to act?"

"Very funny. Guys, I want to get serious for a minute. Greg never, ever lies to me. He said he was spending the night with a buddy up in McClellanville, that he had the boat up there when it had engine trouble. But he never even showed up. That is so not like him. And why would his buddy, Mark, say he was going to be staying with us? Nobody told *me*."

The Rob-Bobs exchanged looks. They both cleared their throats, but Bob spoke first, all the while smearing leftover syrup around his plate with a fork.

"Abby, has it ever occurred to you that Greg might be one of the boys?"

"He's in his late forties, for crying out loud, and he's happily married. I'm not saying I'm against a boys' night out from time to time. But *all* night? Give me a break!"

Bob smiled. "I meant gay. Do you think Greg might be gay?"

"Save it, Bob, this is no time to joke."

"I'm afraid he's not," Rob said.

"We had a friend in Atlanta," Bob said, "who told his wife he was going to church. Well, he did go to church. That's where he picked up the pastor, who had his bags waiting there, and the two of them took off across the country."

"That's cowardly."

"Agreed, that's why I said 'had.' I was just trying to illustrate that these things happen."

I started to laugh. I couldn't help myself. The thought of my Greg being gay was absurd. They may as well have been trying to convince me that Greg was really a chimpanzee that was into heavy-duty body waxing.

"You think it's absurd, don't you?" Bob asked.

"Yes, of course!"

"But it's not. We could tell you so many stories—"

"I'm sure you could. I know a few myself. But guys, you're forgetting that I don't have a homophobic bone in my body, and neither does Greg. If he and Mark Gallentree were having an affair, there would be no reason not to tell me."

"Would he tell you if he was having an affair with a woman?"

The three pancakes I'd eaten, plus the bacon and eggs they came with, felt like a bowling ball in my stomach. I couldn't breathe, thanks to the pressure on my lungs.

"You're turning gray, Abby," Rob said. He reached across the table and grabbed my hand. "Do you need to lie down?"

"I'm fine guys, really."

"Take a deep breath, Abby. In through your nose, out through your mouth. Keep breathing like that until you stop feeling light-headed. I know this is a lot for you to deal with—"

"I'm not feeling light-headed."

"Denial is also a part of the process," Bob said.

"Denial is in Egypt," I snapped, "and Greg is not gay."

"Abby, we're your friends. We only want to help you."

The bowling ball left as fast as it had arrived, and I could breathe again. "If you two are though yapping, you might want to turn around and see who is seated two booths behind you."

CHAPTER 12

"**B**ut don't let her see you," I whispered. Bob is as subtle as a marching band. His glasses nearly flew off he whipped his head around so fast.

"That's Catherine Deephouse."

"Indeed. Look who's with her."

"I don't know him, Abby, do you?"

"He's definitely a hunk," Rob said. "Uh—if you don't mind robbing the cradle, which I don't— do, that is. I definitely do mind."

"Good save," Bob growled. He was only half kidding.

"So, Abby, who is he?" Rob demanded.

"I don't know. But don't you think it odd that in all the restaurants in the Charleston area, Catherine Deephouse would show up at the same one that I choose? And with a muscle-bound hunk in tow?"

"She's got to eat breakfast someplace."

"Yes, but Catherine lives on Wadmalaw Island," I said, referring to a community that is so posh, dirt roads are considered chic. "That's all the way over on the other side of Charleston.

Frankly, I'm surprised she has the energy to keep her shop downtown. That commute would kill me."

Rob shook his head as he geared up to poke holes in my theory. "Catherine is an interior decorator. She has clients all over the tristate. As long as they have the bucks, she's happy to oblige."

"That could be her son," Bob said. "I see a family resemblance."

"Otis and Catherine Deephouse don't have children," I said. "I'm telling you, this guy's some kind of bodyguard—no, make that a thug."

"He's married," Rob said. "Not that I pay attention to ring fingers. I just happened to notice."

Bob glared at him. "Abby, coincidences do happen. I bet she doesn't even know you're here."

"We'll just see about that." I put my napkin down beside me on the banquette and slid across the faux leather.

"Stop," Rob hissed. "Come back."

I don't take orders. Looking straight ahead, I walked to her booth, stopping when I was halfway past her. Feigning responses, especially surprise, has always come easily to me.

"Catherine! I almost didn't see you there."

She did a pretty good job of faking as well. "Abby, how nice to see you."

"Do you come here, to the Pleasant side, very often?"

"You know how this business is, Abby. You go

where it takes you." She must have caught a glimpse of the Rob-Bobs. "Heavens, there's a crowd of you here."

"Yeah, well—"

"Why on earth would the three of you drive all the way over here to eat breakfast?"

"But I was just—"

"What gives, Abby? Some big auction I don't know about? Some collector die and leave his estate to the wolves?"

"I'm not a wolf, thank you. But the answer is yes. There's a fabulous yard sale going on down on Pitt Street in the Old Village. You wouldn't believe the quality of the merchandise, or the ridiculously low prices. Supposedly the couple is going through a nasty divorce and the husband, who collects, is overseas. I just bought an eighteenth-century writing desk for two hundred dollars!"

Catherine Deephouse and her male companion, whomever he was, slid out of their booth like butter from a hot pan. They must have already been given their check, because they made only a brief stop at the register before bolting out the door.

I returned to my seat feeling as stupid as the woman who claimed to have given birth to a circumcised child she'd stolen from a hospital.

"What's with them?" Bob asked.

I shrugged. "Beats me."

Rob sighed. "Abby, Abby, Abby, what are we going to do with you? Catherine said something that pissed you off, so you fired back with a volley of your own. It was obviously a good shot, little Miss Big Shot, but the question remains: did you find out what you need to know? Namely, what she's doing all the way over here, and just who the heck the hunk is?"

"Hey!" Bob said. "He wasn't that cute."

I hung my head. "Okay, I screwed up. I blew it. But they obviously aren't following me. Let's leave it at that, can we?"

We finished our second carafe of coffee in silence.

"I've been thinking," Bob said.

"Uh-oh," Rob and I said in unison, and then slapped palms. I might have gotten a little syrup on him.

"This is serious. I want us to review what we know so far. First, there is this furious auction over a birdcage. Then the bird gets stolen, then Mozella disappears, and then Abby starts getting phone calls from the bird, then C.J. disappears, then Greg, but do you know what's *not* missing from this picture?"

"What?" I said.

"The birdcage," Bob said.

"Duh," I said, and slapped my forehead. There was indeed syrup on my hand.

"Abby," Rob said, "I hate to say this, but he is so right. On the way over here you said that there are five people who wanted that darn thing so bad they could taste it. Enough even to make them seem suspicious. But the cage has just been sitting there in your shop. It wasn't taken when Monet was filched. It wasn't taken last night, or the night before. It probably doesn't have anything to do with this case, so you've been barking up the wrong tree."

"Make that a forest," I said.

"Nonetheless, if you don't mind my suggestion, I think you should put it someplace safe until we solve this mystery."

"Let us keep it for you," Bob said.

"Thanks, guys. I'll take you up on that. But Rob, you're wrong about one thing: one of those trees could stand a little more barking. I told you that Bubba Johnson owns a string of dry cleaning stores, but I didn't tell you that he is obsessed with birds."

Rob smirked. "How obsessed? Two parrots and a canary? Or one of those terrariumlike deals that you rent from some service that comes in the house and cleans it for you?"

"I'm talking hundreds of cages, maybe thousands of birds. You've got to see his house to believe it."

"Where does he live? Out in the country someplace?"

"Downtown, South of Broad."

The Rob-Bobs whistled, but not together, and not in the same key. It sounded a lot like a wolf whistle, and heads turned. I pointed at myself and smiled.

Bob, as usual, sounded the first sour note. "Whoever took Monet didn't do it to add a new species to his, or her, collection. They did it as a means to get something else. After all, they could have gotten a mynah from any pet shop—even off the Internet. They would have us think that the bird Monet leads to the real Monet—possibly one of his paintings. But we all know that Monet's paintings were huge. It's not like one could be hidden somewhere inside the cage itself. Just the same, Abby, how well have you searched the cage?"

"Excuse me?"

"Could there be a false bottom?"

"There is a tray that slides out, of course. That's how you get rid of his droppings."

"Have you ever held the tray up at eye level?"

That was a silly, if thought-provoking, question. Who, in their right mind, holds a birdcage tray at eye level? Perhaps the same folks who behold their toilet rims at eye level. I haven't done that since college.

"No, I did not."

"Perhaps we should go do that."

I felt like a fool, but a hopeful fool. Perhaps Bob was on to something. I would find what it was my mamanapper was looking for and get her back, Greg would return to me straight away, and even the prodigal C.J. would come home. Then, if I could get my daughter Susan married off to a doctor, and my son Charlie married to the second or third woman president, I could begin to live happily ever after.

"Lunch is on me," I said generously.

But the Rob-Bobs were already headed for the door, while our check remained on the table. Oh well, IHOP had been worth those few extra bucks.

All the way to my shop I worried that the Taj Mahal would be missing. I couldn't even enjoy the spectacle of a massive container ship passing directly below us as we crossed on the new Thomas Ravenel Bridge, the longest single-span suspension bridge in North America. I couldn't enjoy the pair of dolphins that arched and looped near the shore between Drum Island and the peninsula. Worst of all, I couldn't enjoy the residual bits of bacon caught in my teeth, or the aftertaste of sweet maple syrup.

At my direction, Rob parked in my reserved spot behind the shop. My heart was beating so hard I couldn't concentrate to put the key in the lock. I certainly did not pay much attention to the package by the door. I get deliveries, or returns of small purchases, on a daily basis. When at last I got the door open, I kicked the package inside, and then ran through the storeroom and out into the selling area. The miniature replica of the most beautiful building in the world was right where I'd left it! I collapsed into a Biedermeier armchair while I caught my breath. This particular chair is a favorite of mine because, like me, it is functional without being frilly.

"Hot damn," Bob said, "it's still there."

"In all its avian glory," I gasped.

"Mind if we check it out?" Rob asked.

"Knock yourselves out."

There, before my eyes, two of Charleston's most elegant men turned into the Hardy Boys. They were all over that birdcage, like butter on grits. Bob pulled out the tray and held it to eye level. Finding nothing unusual, he had Rob hold the cage aloft while he got on his knees and peered upward. The four outside minarets were of such intricate and delicate design that I insisted the Taj not be laid on its side.

"Hurry up," Rob said. "This thing is heavy."

"I'm hurrying as fast as I can."

Rob switched arms. "What's this thing made out of, Abby? Gold?"

The Taj was painted white. I had assumed it was made from wire scrollwork. But what if it wasn't? What if that was gold under the paint? What if Monet the bird and Monet the artist weren't even part of the equation? That much gold would be worth a mint, particularly if it was of high purity. But gold, being a "noble metal," remains unaffected by most elements. Getting paint to adhere firmly to gold is like getting it to stick to glass. But what if one first coated the Taj with an epoxy of some sort, or a resin?

I leaped to my feet. I am no expert on precious

metals, but ever since the third grade I've been an expert on scratching things. One spring day when Jimmy Campbell was out on the playground trouncing the other kids at dodgeball, a shy but precocious Abby Wiggins removed a barrette from her stick-straight hair and scratched A. W. + J. C. on the front of her hero's lunch box. Then, carried away by my newfound skill at engraving, I gave Lassie horns and a billy goat beard. When Jimmy saw what I had done, he burst into tears and ran from the room. A part of me blames myself for Jimmy's metamorphosis into playground bully and later into a petty criminal, one who spends more time in the slammer than out. At any rate, the time to scratch painted metal again had arrived.

"Y'all have any barrettes on you?"

"What the heck is that supposed to mean?" Bob said.

"I need something sharp."

"There's a tweezers somewhere in my left pocket," Rob said.

"Be a gentleman, will you, and fish it out?" A lesser woman might have paused to wonder what he was doing with tweezers in his pants.

Rob fumbled a bit with his left hand before retrieving the smallest tweezers I'd ever seen. "It came off a Swiss army knife," he said. "Sometimes when I'm out driving in the sunlight and look in the rearview mirror, I spot a stray hair. You know, in my nose or ears."

"TMI!" I grabbed the tweezers and gave one of the cage bars a good scrape.

"Hey," Bob cried in dismay, "you're going to ruin this thing. I'll admit I wasn't so wild about this birdcage in the beginning, but it kinda grows on one. It's really quite camp, Abby."

I examined my handiwork closely. There were, in fact, many layers of paint, but at the bottom of the gouge I spotted the telltale glint of gray.

"Oh phooey, it's just base metal."

Rob laughed. "You didn't really expect to find gold, did you, Abby?"

"Don't be silly, Rob. But if it was made in India— well, they're famous for their silver filigree."

"This isn't a ring, Abby. This is an animal house the size of Grand Central Station. Say Bob, you making any progress on discovering your false bottom? My arms are about to fall off."

"*My* false bottom?" Bob boomed.

My desk phone rang before I could think of a clever quip. I ran to answer it, but thanks to my less-than-perfect floor plan, the machine picked up before I got there. And just a second after that the front buzzer sounded.

"It's our assistant," Rob shouted. I heard the jangle of bells as the door opened, and then Rob's voice again. "A small crisis across the way, Abby. We'll be back in two minutes." The door slammed.

By then my caller had had ample time to leave a message. The caller ID read "blocked" again, a good indication that a telemarketer had been itching to waste my time—either that or it was the kidnapper. But there was no way I could resist listening to the message. For the first time I found myself hoping against hope that the caller was trying to convince me to refinance.

"Damn," the voice said, "I was hoping to get you. Listen hon, I just want you to know that I'm with Mark, and that I'm okay. Love you, babe. Catch you later."

I was still holding the receiver to my ear when the Rob-Bobs returned. I must have listened to that message a hundred times. When I became aware of their presence, I set the phone gently back in its cradle, as gently I would lay an infant in its crib.

"You were right," I said.

"Of course," Rob said. "I'm always right."

"Not you—Bob."

"Uh-oh," Rob said, and moved in to hug me, but I backed away.

Bob cleared his throat. "What was I right about?"

"Greg. He's run off with his buddy from McClellanville."

"*What?*"

"She's kidding," Rob said. "Good one, Abby."

My legs felt rubbery so I backed up until I was leaning against a file cabinet. "I'm not kidding. If you don't believe me, pick up the phone and dial Star 98."

147

Rob's jaw tensed as he listened to the message. He listened to it twice. When he was done, he set the receiver down slowly as a grin spread across his face.

CHAPTER 13

"That doesn't sound like a man in love, Abby. That sounds like a drunk trying to talk despite his hangover."

I grabbed the phone and retrieved the message. I listened to it three more times Greg's phrasing, the slight slur of certain words, it was all reminiscent of a call I received the morning after a bachelor party from which eight men—all of them detectives—disappeared. They were later found in the basement of the best man, most of them so drunk they couldn't stand up.

"Holy smokes," I shouted, "you were right, Rob!"

"Of course I was. Aren't I always?"

Rob wasn't being arrogant, just cocky. There is a boyish quality about him that makes his self-confidence endearing. Poor Bob, on the other hand, revisits every decision, and agonizes over his mistakes. As Rob strutted with his chest out, Bob studied the moons on his fingernails.

"I'm really sorry, Abby. I guess I succumbed to Gay Fantasy Number One."

"Which is?"

149

"That inside every good-looking straight man there is a gay man waiting to come out."

"Forget about it. I'm just as guilty for jumping to conclusions. Okay, guys, what do we do next?"

"Well, for starters," Rob said, "we're not leaving your side for a minute—well, maybe for the occasional minute, but we'll be right outside the door. And of course you're spending the night at our house. As will the birdcage."

"Thanks, guys."

"We'll have a good time," Bob said. "I'll make us a nice squab salad—got them from the pigeon egg dealer—followed by hare simmered in white wine and served with a cream sauce, and top it off with a bleached loganberry torte. After dinner we'll watch the *Amazing Race* on TV. And just so we get really into the international spirit, we'll munch on freshly popped millet drenched in melted yak butter."

"Sounds good."

"Abby," Bob said, "you still seem distracted. I apologize again for misleading you."

"It's not that. I've been thinking: I've been spending too much time investigating everyone who really wanted to acquire this stupid cage—"

"Tut-tut-tut," Rob said. "It's not a stupid cage; it's the Taj."

"Whatever. But what I haven't done is trace its origins."

"You mean you've been chasing after the who, and not the why."

"Exactly."

"In that case, it's back to my car, and out to the Auction Barn."

"Makes perfect sense to me," Bob said. He was obviously relieved that I seemed to be recovering.

"Last one to the car is a rotten pigeon egg," I said.

Of course I was the rotten egg. After all, my legs are about as long as Rob's thighs. Besides, the Rob-Bobs didn't hesitate, however briefly, to glance at the package, which still lay where I'd tossed it, just inside the door.

The Lowcountry Auction Barn is located right across the highway from the Binh Minh Vietnamese restaurant, which, incidentally, serves the best Vietnamese food east, or west, of Ho Chi Minh City. If you're ever up that way try the beef satay, as well as the salty lemongrass chicken. You won't regret it.

At any rate, the Lowcountry Auction Barn parking lot was deserted except for John Norman's car. The auctions are only on Saturday mornings and Tuesday and Thursday evenings, but there is more than enough paperwork to keep John busy the rest of the week. We found him in his window-less office, practically hidden by stacks of invoices, receipts, and photographs of various pieces too large, or redundant, to make their presence feasible. John is a quiet, unassuming man who expresses himself with his neckties, which he insists on wearing even on the hottest days. This afternoon his choice of tie depicted a portion of a Salvador Dali painting. The melting timepieces reflected the way I felt walking from the car.

John Norman seemed pleased by our interruption. "I'd offer y'all cold drinks," he said, "but the soda machine needs servicing. The best I can do is lukewarm. What's it like outside? Still hot?"

That silly question is one I hear thousands of times during the dog days of summer. *Yes,* it was still hot. The air was so thick that one could practically slice it with a knife. Having done that, one could conceivably ship the slice to one of the poles and exponentially hasten global warming. The melted polar ice would increase rainfall and winter snow. The increased snow amounts would create new glaciers and subsequently usher in a new ice age, thus eventually cooling the Carolinas. In the meantime, I'd have to put up with that rhetorical question about the stupid weather.

"We're fixin' to have a bodacious thunderstorm," Bob said without cracking a smile. Every now and then the transplanted Yankee trots out what he considers to be a southernism. One must at least appreciate his attempt to assimilate.

John winked at me. "You mean a frog-strangler?"

"Well—"

"Or do you mean a gully-washer? Or a trash-toter? Or a fence-lifter? Or a chunk-mover? Or a clod-buster? Or a goose-drowneder? Possibly even a turd-floater?"

Bob knew his chain was being yanked, and good

sport that he can be, grinned. "It's going to rain hard."

"We sure could use it," John said. He scrounged up three cracked plastic chairs.

"John," I said, now that the ice had been broken—so to speak, "I need to ask you some questions about that birdcage shaped like the Taj Mahal."

"Funny, because you're not the first one this week."

The hair along the nape of my neck saluted. "Oh?"

"Yeah. Yesterday this woman with one eyebrow comes in—"

"Those are two eyebrows, just very closely spaced. And her name is Wynnell Crawford. She's a dealer from West of the Ashley."

"Right. Anyway, she wanted to know who the five people were who bid against you at crunch time. Said you sent her."

"I did indeed."

"Good, because I had a busy day staring me in the face and didn't have time to check her story. Just gave her the info she wanted and sent her along. It's not like it's a secret or anything."

"Then you won't mind giving me even more information?"

"It'd be my pleasure, Abby. Assuming I can."

"Anything would help. But for starters, where did you get the birdcage?"

"Well, as you know, that particular day I was

selling the Cornmesser-Thornbright estate, along with some odds and ends on consignment. That piece, however, was one of my own."

"Your *own*?"

"Yeah, that's what I call a 'pity buy.' This sailor comes by one day—takes a cab over from the docks—had that birdcage tied on the roof. Says his captain won't let him keep it any longer, but that he didn't want to sell it, either. Said he wasn't sure what he was going to do, but in the meantime could I keep it as collateral and loan him some money. I asked him what he thought a fair price would be, and he says a hundred bucks. I figure I can't go wrong. A lot of work went into that thing. I'm no expert on the Taj Mahal, but that looks pretty darn close if you ask me. And all those stones got to be worth something. A shame to use it as a birdcage. I can picture something like that in a folk art museum, or as a foyer showpiece in a large home."

My head swam. "Uh—did you say *one* hundred dollars?"

"Yeah, I'm afraid so. To be flat-out honest with you, I've been feeling kinda bad about that ever since. I should have given him at least two hundred. In fact, I would have tracked him down and given him the extra money, but I didn't have anything to go on. Then about two weeks later I read in the paper about this guy who gets killed on one of the loading docks when a crane operator sets a container down right on top of him. Well, that's what the police think at first. But the autopsy showed that the man had been dead for a couple of hours before being squished like a pancake."

"Ew," I said, the taste of IHOP still in my mouth.

John Norman is a kind man, quick to show concern. "Is something wrong, Abby?"

"Our Abby is a recovering pancaholic," Rob said.

"I cannot deny that," I said. "John, can you describe this man? Could he have been Indian? From India, I mean."

"Perhaps. Or maybe southern Mediterranean. Heck, he could have been any number of things, but he was a good-looking guy, I can tell you that."

"What kind of accent did he have?"

John shrugged. "Well, he wasn't from around here. But he didn't sound like Peter Sellers, either, if that's what you mean. He didn't even speak English that well."

"What can you tell us about the bird?"

"Clever, isn't he? Speaking of the weather, I was getting dressed one morning, and I thought I heard the weatherman from Channel 4 telling us a tornado watch was in effect. I looked at the window, and there wasn't a cloud in the sky. It was that darn bird."

"So he came with the cage, right?"

"You better believe it. I told the sailor I didn't know the first thing about caring for a bird, but he just kind of shrugged. Like I said, his English wasn't the best."

"But he did tell you the bird's name was Monet, right?"

"Something like that. I wrote that on a note that went with the cage. But it was more of a guess."

I felt lower than the belly of a mole. Monet the mynah and Monet the painter might not even be connected. My disappointment must have shown on my face.

Bob cleared his throat, which is usually the preamble to speech or a morality lecture. I cringed.

"John," he said, "you made it sound like there was a connection between the loading dock incident and the guy who sold you the cage. Was there?"

"Yeah. Thanks, Robert. When you get to be my age, your thoughts tend to wander a bit, and you don't always get back to where you started. Anyway, that container really did a job on that guy—sorry, Abby. As a result, the police were unable to even get a good set of prints, much less a positive ID on the victim. The coroner wasn't much help, either, other than determining the time of death based on body temperature. The deceased may have died of a heart attack and gone unnoticed, or he could have been the victim of foul play. The best the police could do was to check the crew manifests and the lists of people cleared to work on that dock, but no one showed up missing. But when I read that article I just somehow knew that the sailor who brought me the birdcage and the dead guy on the dock were the same person. And I knew in my gut that he was indeed the victim of foul play."

I hate sounding like a moralistic prig, but John is a mature adult, and by now should be used to people like me. "So," I said, unable to help myself, "you decided to keep mum about the Taj."

"Wouldn't you?"

"I would," Rob said.

"Well, I wouldn't," Bob said.

I gave him the thumbs-up. "Thank you. No offense, John, but you might have been able to help the police. You might still be able. Yes, they might hold the Taj Mahal as disputed property—until you can prove rightful ownership, or no one else claims it after ninety days—but it would be worth it if it helped put a killer away, right?"

"You tell me."

"I beg your pardon?"

"The Taj isn't mine to hand over now, is it?"

Stupid, stupid me. I'd been so sure about walking the high ground that I walked right into quicksand. "Well, uh—it's different now. I paid ten thousand for the Taj, you only shelled out a hundred."

"I see. So we get to lower our moral standards if enough money is at stake?"

"He's got you, Abby."

I glared at Bob. "Well, it really is different now. I didn't know anything about the sailor when I bought it, and I haven't had that so-called gut feeling John had. In fact, I don't remember reading anything about this in the paper." I turned to John. "How long ago was it, anyway?"

"A year."

"A *year*?"

"I guess I'm not as morally bankrupt as you thought."

"Hmm. You could have told me you waited a year. A year ago—wait, how close to a year is it?"

"A year and two days from when he brought it in until the day I put it up for auction. The two days were insurance for my ailing conscience."

"Touché. Well, this explains why I never read about him in the papers. At the time he was found, Greg, Mama, and I were whale-watching in Nova Scotia." I turned to Rob. "I suppose you guys read about him, too."

"Abby, you know Bob and I only read the *Times*."

"New York or London?" John asked with a straight face.

"Touché," Rob said, and we all laughed.

The tension I'd caused appeared to have been eased.

The intersection of Ashley Phosphate and I-26 is an accident waiting to happen. Even on good days traffic backs up, due to the proximity of Northwoods Mall. On bad days it's possible to observe the growth in one's fingernails between approaching this intersection and leaving it. The best way to handle this kind of stress, I've discovered, is a candy bar, a bottle of water, and a good radio station. Or, one can play word games with the Rob-Bobs.

"I have a five letter word for the world's largest cat," I said smugly.

"Tiger," Bob said without a second's hesitation.

"That's not it."

"Well, it isn't lion, because they're smaller than tigers, and besides, you said five letters."

"That's correct. Do you give up?"

"No."

"I do," Rob said, "because you're yanking our chains. This is a trick question and you know it."

"This isn't a trick question. Let's make a bet. If neither of you can supply the right word by the time we get back on I-26, you will be at my mercy for the entire evening."

"Kinky," Rob said. "I love it already."

Bob, the mild-mannered man from Toledo, blew a Bronx cheer at the car in front of us, which had applied the brakes for no apparent reason. "What happens if we guess the word in time?"

"Then I'll be yours for the evening."

"In how many ways?" Rob asked.

"As many as you want, darling."

"Deal," Rob said.

"Then you better guess," Bob growled, "because we're moving again."

But neither of my buddies came up with liger, the correct answer. What's more, they didn't believe me—especially when I told them I'd gotten the word from C.J. To make matters worse, the word liger did not appear in the *Merriam Webster's Collegiate Dictionary* Bob keeps under the passenger seat for just this sort of situation. However, he did find "tiglon." When we got to the Den of Antiquity he looked up liger on the Internet, and then shook his head in disappointment.

"That C.J.," he said, "she tells the truth just enough times to keep one off balance."

"She probably believes most, if not everything, she tell us," I said. "I don't think she's capable of lying."

"Everyone's capable of lying," Rob said. He started to unbutton his shirt.

"Rob, what *are* you doing?"

"Aren't you going to have your way with us?"

"Yes, but I want you fully clothed."

"Like I said, you're kinky."

"Yes, kinky enough to treat the two of you to dinner tonight at Chez Fez."

The men exchanged looks of genuine horror. "You're not serious, Abby," Rob said. "Are you?"

"As serious as the plague."

"But the belly dancer hit on me."

"And the chef uses canned cumin," Bob moaned.

"A deal's a deal. I'm not taking no for an answer."

"But what will I do with my llama lasagna?"

"Send it to some hungry llamas."

They tried to bribe me. Bob was willing to freeze the lasagna and treat me to dinner at a restaurant of my choice—anything but Chez Fez. Rob said he would give me unlimited back rubs for a month. When I refused their offers, they pouted like little boys.

"If that belly dancer has her way with me," Rob

whined, "I'll have to go to therapy." His eyes, however, were twinkling. If I was a wishy-washy Washburn, we wouldn't be such good friends.

"Now remember, guys, you're mine for the rest of the day."

"Must you rub it in?"

"Which means we're off to Hocus Pocus Costumes on Savannah Highway."

"Abby, need I remind you that Halloween is still three months away?"

"And please," Bob said, "try something a little more convincing this year. Last year's Condoleezza Rice was a bit of a stretch, even for you, seeing as how you're, uh—a bit more petite than she."

I hustled them back into Rob's car, refusing to say more about my harebrained scheme until we got to the costume store. Meanwhile, the package just inside the back door to the Den of Antiquity was ignored yet again.

CHAPTER 14

It was hard to focus at Hocus Pocus because they carry so many interesting costumes. But I was a woman on a mission, which meant I had to keep my nose to the rhinestone. The store didn't carry adult belly dancer outfits in my size, so I had to settle for a child's. The two looked essentially the same, but nonetheless, it was a blow to my ego.

The Rob-Bobs, on the other hand, seemed bent on proving they had no egos. Bob was the first to emerge from a dressing room, but I wouldn't have known it was him. He'd have made a convincing Tweety Bird, if not for his voice. The quite masculine Rob made a stunning Achilles, down to the arrow shaft emerging from his heel. Who knew he had such good-looking thighs! But so far so good. Then Achilles decided to chase Tweety Bird around the room with a plastic sword. Tweety Bird flapped his little yellow wings and flitted about the shop, all the while bellowing in his basso profundo.

Both customers and clerks got a kick out of

my friends' antics, but I was embarrassed to the core.

"Can't take them anywhere," I said to the cashier who was waiting on me.

She barely glanced at the price tag she was scanning. "Oh my gosh, that guy's so real-looking, isn't he? Looks just like Brad Pitt—oh my gosh, you don't think it's really *him*, do you?"

"Sort of looks like him. But this guy's quite a bit older."

She looked at me for the first time. "It *is* him, isn't it?"

"No."

"You're just saying that because you don't want me to know. Oh my gosh, oh my gosh, this is too cool!"

I sighed. "Then you've probably guessed I'm Jennifer Anniston."

"No way. You're like, an old lady, or something. You're probably his mother, right?"

"Or something," I growled. Rob is four years and six days older than I. And he doesn't cover the gray at his temples, for heaven's sake.

Daddy taught me to whistle with my fingers when I was ten. It is a skill I'd almost forgotten, but never will again, given the amount of practice I had that day. The Rob-Bobs finally stopped horsing around and changed back into their street looks. When Rob emerged from the dressing room in chinos and polo shirt, the young clerk nearly burst into tears.

"You tried to trick me," she said.

"What?"

"You tried to make me think that was Brad Pitt by using adverse psychology."

"That's reverse, darling—"

It was obvious that Rob had seen me. Alas, given my mode of dress, I couldn't very well run outside and take refuge in another shop.

"Abby, is *that* what you came for?"

"Yes, do you like it?"

"Before I say yes, does this have anything to do with Chez Fez?"

"And what if it does?"

"Bob and I are not going to be a part of this, Abby."

"Don't presume to speak for me," Bob boomed as he materialized, looking entirely presentable again, if perhaps a mite sweaty.

"But she's going to make a fool of herself. We can't let her—"

"I'm a grown woman, Rob. Why, I'm practically old enough to be your mother." I paused to give the clerk a well-deserved glare. "Besides, this is my evening, remember?"

"Abby, be reasonable. They're not going to let you wear that costume out of the shop."

"I've already paid for it," I chirped, and sashayed out into the bright Charleston sunshine.

The astonishing thing is, no one gave me a second look.

★   ★   ★

164

"I don't plan to do any dancing," I said, much to Rob's relief. "But I do need to do a little snooping— incognito."

"Why do Rob and I have to be there?"

"To make sure I'm safe. You wouldn't want me to be kidnapped by a white slaver and shipped off to Lapland, would you?"

"Why Lapland?"

"To do lap dances, of course."

If they hadn't groaned I would have disowned them. But I could have done without Rob's ensuing safety lecture and Bob's last lament over his languishing llama lasagna. They dropped me off in the alley behind the restaurant, and gave me kisses and hugs as if I was their child going off to trick-or-treat on my own.

Frankly, I was nervous about crashing the belly dancing scene, but the second I stepped foot in the kitchen, I felt a surge of confidence. There were eight or nine dancers hanging out, so they were obviously between sets. Away from the main floor, and not twitching their tummies, they looked just like regular women having a coffee break—well, except for their clothes. And much to my relief, the dancer whose pheromones had tried futilely to snare Rob was not in evidence.

"Hi there," a stout woman with a Yankee accent said. "You new?"

"Well, uh—"

"Name's Brenda. You'll get used to the ropes in no time. I'm sure Mr. Dupree gave you the rundown, but it doesn't hurt to hear it again, does it? Repetition is the cardinal law of learning, isn't that what they say? Anyway, we're only supposed to dance twenty minutes at a time, and then we get a ten-minute break. This is so the customers aren't distracted all the time and can look at their menus. But when the music starts, we have to be out there at our stations in thirty seconds. Which station are you, by the way?"

"Uh—"

"Oh, I know. You must be subbing for Geraldine. She had an appendectomy last week. Was supposed to come back today, but I guess the doctor's making her stay out longer. She's station ten. Say, you must be pretty good."

"I must?"

"He puts only the most experienced dancers at station ten because that's where he seats the VIPs."

I gulped. "How many minutes are left on this break?"

Brenda pointed to a grease-splattered clock above one of the massive stoves. "Six. You need to use the john, you have to use the employee one over there." She pointed to a door, above which hung a crooked cardboard sign that read: KEEP OUT! "That's the chef's idea of humor."

"No, I'm good." I shivered as I watched the second hand tick off until I was expected to shake my stuff at station ten.

"Hey," my new acquaintance said, "you never told me your name."

"Fatima." Thank goodness I'd given that some thought on the ride down from the costume shop.

"That's a beautiful name. Where are you from? Someplace really exotic, I bet. You have such a lovely accent."

"I do?"

She glanced around the crowded kitchen. No one seemed to be monitoring our conversation.

"Some of these Southern accents grate on my nerves. Of course I'm sure all we Americans sound strange to you. Now come on, Fatima, tell me where you're from."

I am, of course, a South Carolina girl, born and bred. I have also spent a great deal of time in Charlotte, North Carolina. My accent is as Southern as grits and magnolias. But that's not what Brenda wanted to hear.

"I'mjustafakeistan," I said.

Brenda beamed. "And here I thought I was far from home. You must find living here quite an adjustment, Fatima. When Henry and I first moved here from Pittsburgh, I was so homesick I thought I would die. I couldn't find pierogies, and all the sunshine they have down here—I just found it unnatural."

I looked at the clock again. Just five minutes until I made a fool out of myself doing the shimmy—unless I got the skinny on Blackmond Dupree.

"Brenda, how long have you worked here?"

"Since it opened—eight months or thereabouts. Henry was opposed to it at first—thought the

167

customers might hit on me—but after he lost his job, he was really glad I had this one."

"What do you think of Mr. Dupree?"

She recoiled in apparent shock. "Mr. Dupree?"

"Our boss."

She moved closer and lowered her voice. "Funny you should ask. I didn't know what to think at first, him being a foreigner and all like yourself—no offense intended—then I decided that I really liked him. But lately he's been acting kind of strange."

"Strange, how?"

"It's hard to put my finger on it. He's still nice and everything, but he's just not as friendly as he used to be."

"Would you say he's distracted?"

"That's it. He used to spend a lot of time back here in the kitchen flirting with us—you know, the harmless kind—but now it's like we hardly exist. Oh well, there's not one of us worth looking at anyway. We're all just middle-age housewives trying to fill the voids in our lives. Aren't we?"

I would have protested, but the sound of sultry music seeped into the room and insinuated itself into the assembled women. Bodies began to sway as one by one the women fell under the spell of the three musicians.

"Break's over early," Brenda gasped, and the next thing I knew, her eyes had glazed over and she was undulating like a cobra in a snake charmer's basket.

"What do I do now?" I wailed.

"Dance."

That was the last thing she said before joining the line of women snaking its way out of the hot kitchen and into the cool, dimly lit dining area. The customers began to applaud and whistle. Some even stamped their feet. I could imagine the Rob-Bobs doing the same.

"Wait up!" I called, and chased after Brenda.

Belly dancing is an art, and an ancient one at that. It takes years of practice to become skilled, and there are different levels of competence. Wearing a costume rented from Hocus Pocus does not make one a belly dancer, any more than wearing a stethoscope makes one a doctor. It can't be faked.

Of course that didn't stop me from giving it my best shot. Unfortunately, station ten was at the far end of the tent. It was also on a dais, surrounded by heavy velvet drapes pulled back slightly by thick gold cords. There was no way I could dance my way over to it, so I abandoned any pretense. Fluttering my veils, I simply ran to the dais and hopped up the steps. Once in place, in front of the narrow opening, I twirled and I twitched, I shimmied and I shook. I must not have looked too ridiculous, because nobody laughed or booed. After a while I began to enjoy what I was doing and relaxed somewhat. It was then that I remembered station ten was reserved for VIPs.

Sure enough, sprawled across a divan, his miniature fez at a rakish angle, was none other than Blackmond Dupree. Sprawled across an adjoining divan was a beautiful young woman whom I recognized at once as Simone Dupree. Seated across from them, his back turned to me, was a heavyset man with a shaved head. A green and red dragon tail wound its way to the base of his bulging neck. He was wearing a black T-shirt and black denim pants. I took him to be the bouncer, although I'd seen no need of one at lunch.

"She's still very much alive and kicking," he said. His voice was almost as deep as Bob's, and I had to dance as close as possible to hear him. He smelled of Irish Spring, possibly both the deodorant and the soap.

"Where is she now?" Blackmond Dupree asked.

"Her summer house in Portland, Maine. That thing must have fifty rooms. Tell me, boss, why does one woman need all that space?"

"She sober?"

"Nah, she's still hitting the sauce just as hard as she ever was. Neighbors claim she tried to make love to a moose that wandered into her backyard."

"Did you give her my ultimatum?"

Wait just one cotton-picking minute. Exotic Blackmond Dupree, he of French-Moroccan descent, the restaurateur who spoke like Pepe Le Pew with a mouthful of marbles, didn't have a foreign accent at all. He spoke perfectly good Charlestonese.

The bouncer—or was he a hit man?—snorted. "Hell yeah, boss. I leaned on her hard, but she didn't budge. That's one tough old lady, drunk or not. Said she'd go to the authorities if you didn't leave her alone. Said she didn't care what happened to her, as long as you got what was coming to you."

A vein along Blackmond Dupree's right temple began to twitch. Then again, it may have been an illusion, given all the twitching I was doing. I switched to a slow undulation on the half beat, to better see and hear what was going on.

"I'm going to make her worst nightmare come true, that's what I'm going to do to her."

"Easy, babe," Simone Dupree said.

Easy, babe? What kind of daughter calls her father "babe"?

"She's going to wish she'd never set eyes on me."

"Hey boss," the bouncer said, "I ain't gonna do anything that's gonna land me in jail. I've served all the time I'm gonna."

"Don't worry. I'll come up with something slow and torturous, and it will be entirely legal."

"I love it when you talk that way," Simone said. Then she lunged at Blackmond Dupree and kissed him hard on the mouth.

I was so shocked that I stopped dancing altogether. I stood stone still, staring at the bizarre scene in front of me. What I saw did not compute with what I had been led to believe. Perhaps my eyes were deceiving me, or perhaps I was having an early stroke. I opened and shut my eyes several times to see if the picture changed. It did not. Only gradually did I become aware that three pairs of eyes were staring back at me.

The bouncer clambered to his feet. "What the hell you staring at?"

"Uh—uh—"

Blackmond Dupree had freed himself from his lip-lock and was standing also. "Hey, don't I know you?"

What's good for the gander is good for the goose. "I dun't sink so."

"Now I know who you are. You're Felicia's daughter, aren't you? Look, I told your mama that I can't have you dancing here, no matter how talented you are. Sorry kid. Come back when you're sixteen and we'll talk. But keep up the dancing. Your mama's right: you're a natural."

Moi? A natural-born dancer? Well, slap me up the side of the head and call me Betty. I couldn't recall ever having gotten such a nice compliment.

"Beat it, kid," the bouncer growled.

"Yeah, scram," Simone said, and reached out to tickle the back of Blackmond Dupree's knee.

I'd seen all I needed to see. Gathering my veils, and clutching my pantaloons tightly, I leaped from the dais and fled across the room, swerving only to miss the stage upon which the musicians sat. I don't know what made me think the Rob-Bobs would be in the same pavilion as per our previous visit, but unfortunately they weren't. Feeling every bit the fool, I dashed from table to table, my panic mounting.

"Abby," I thought I heard Rob call when I was halfway back to station ten.

The next thing I knew I was flying through the air like a ninety-eight-pound bag of potatoes.

CHAPTER 15

I hit the floor every bit as hard as a sack of spuds. Thank heavens the Chez Fez has plush carpeting; otherwise, potato chips would have flown everywhere. Even so, I was left breathless and gasping like a fish out of water. A grounded guppy, as it were.

"Well, if it isn't little Miss Greedy," a familiar voice said. "Coming back for seconds, are you?"

I looked up to see the belly-dancing mother of four, the housewife from North Charleston who'd had the hots for Rob the last time we were here.

"I'm—not—af—ter—him. You—can—have—"

"Okay, I believe you," she said, and grabbed one of my arms and yanked me to my feet. "Your cousin isn't into women. Found that out the hard way."

Upright, the air rushed into my lungs. "My cousin?"

"Cousin!" Rob cried, appearing magically on the scene.

"Relax, honey, I'm over you," the woman said. She turned to address me. "Gotta watch them plug outlets in the floor. At least once a night some poor waiter goes flying—just like you did. A body could

174

sue Mr. Dupree, if they had a mind to." She seemed to notice my costume for the first time. "Hey, when did you start working here?"

"Tonight."

"What station are you?"

"Station ten."

She stared at me openmouthed. Even though the room was dimly lit, I could see the glint of a gold tooth where a back molar should have been. By the time she found her voice, I knew as much about her bite as her dentist did.

"Why that no-good, lying, son of a—"

Mercifully, Rob pulled me into his pavilion and jerked the drapes closed. "Abby, are you all right?"

"Of course she isn't all right," Bob said. "That man-eating Amazonian stuck her foot out and tripped her. That plug stuff is all nonsense."

I waved my arms like a maniac. "Guys, we gotta get out of here."

"Hold on, Abby," Rob said. "We ordered our mutton well-done. Our waitperson said it was going to be a while."

"*You* ordered the mutton well-done," Bob boomed. "Honestly, Abby, this man is a Philistine."

"I thought he was Jewish," I said. "But never mind that. Guys, this isn't the time to bicker. We need to get out of here pronto. Look, I'll treat you to dinner at anyplace you want."

"*Anyplace?*" they chorused.

"You got it. Now let's am-scray."

★   ★   ★

Charleston Grill is arguably *the* best place to dine in the Holy City. That's fitting considering its location; *the* best hotel in town. Occupying an entire city block, Charleston Place Hotel is downtown, smack dab in the heart of the shopping district. The bottom floor of the building is an arcade of exclusive stores that cater to brand-name wallets. During the Christmas season a large model train display is erected in the space between the two sets of sweeping stairs that connect the lobby to the second floor. Anyone who is anyone stays at the Charleston Place Hotel when in town. A few high-ranking politicians stay there as well.

I had only eaten at Charleston Grill three times prior to this, but I had fantasized about it many times. Forget the word grill if it conjures up images of backyard barbecues or greasy diners. This is a white tablecloth establishment with haute cuisine. Lay your napkin down to use the ladies' room, and upon return you will find it replaced by a fresh one, along with clean cutlery. Between courses, complimentary minicourses are served, so that one is not left staring at a vacant place setting. Servers hover about like guardian angels, but are never intrusive. Wish for something and it will appear—well, almost. You get the picture.

We were lucky to get a table, for which I thanked my lucky stars (and you can be sure I changed my clothes first). Bob is one of the dearest, kindest men in the universe, but he takes complaining to a new level.

"Can we order any wine we want?" he asked, the second we were seated.

"Absolutely. The more expensive, and the more obscure, the better."

"Abby, are you making fun of me?"

"Absolutely."

He gave me a hurt look, but when the wine steward came along, Bob ordered a bottle of Chateau de Moron Neuf de Boston Pops 1949, or something like that. Anyway, it cost $189, and that was just to smell the cork. The wine itself was fifty dollars extra.

"Listen guys," I whispered, after we placed our food orders, "you're not going to believe what I overheard at the Chez Fez tonight."

"Spill it," Rob said.

"Please don't say that word while a drop of this wine remains." I took a sip. It was as astringent as mouthwash, and far less tasty. "Hmm-hmm," I said, trying to clear my throat.

"You like?" Bob asked.

"It's really special," I said, which is Southern for "it sucks."

"Don't feel bad, Abby," Rob said. "I can't stand it, either. Drink enough of this and you won't need to be embalmed."

Bob started turning red, so I got right down to brass tacks. "Blackmond Dupree is a fake, and he's hired a hit man to knock off some poor old lady in Maine."

The Rob-Bobs exchanged glances.

"And that's not all, guys. Simone Dupree, y'all's assistant, is not his daughter."

"Abby," Rob said, "you've had a long hard day—heck, a long hard last couple of days. Maybe we should pass on dinner and get you home early."

"The guest room is all made up," Bob said. "One-thousand-thread-count sheets, just as you like them." It's not a secret that when Rob's mother comes to visit, the sheets are 180 count. Mrs. Goldburg never stays long.

"Don't patronize me! I was dancing at station ten—that's the VIP table. I heard, very clearly, what was going on. In real life Blackmond Dupree is Charleston County born and bred. Not South of Broad, to be sure, and not aristocracy, but he's pure Lowcountry. As for that so-called daughter of his, well, she certainly isn't that. The two of them were exchanging tonsil juice like there was no tomorrow. And the hit man—he's one ruthless dude. Looks the part, too, what with that dragon tattooed across his head and down his neck."

Rob came around first. "You're serious?"

"I swear on Dmitri's life."

"You shouldn't say something you'd regret," Bob said, before taking another sip of liquid snobbery.

"I can't regret something that won't happen, because every word I said is true."

"You really *are* serious."

"As serious as the plague. What do you think we should do? Call 911?"

Rob laid a hand gently on my arm. "Did you get the name of the intended victim?"

"No, but Blackmond Dupree—if that's even his real name—said it would be slow and torturous."

"Abby, did you hear the words 'shoot' or 'stab' or 'kill'? Or maybe 'poison'?"

"No."

"Did you hear a time or place?"

"Portland, Maine!"

"A street address?" Bob asked.

"Not really."

"Portland, Maine, probably has more than one resident," Rob said, but his eyes twinkled.

"She owns a bookstore! There can't be that many."

"Now we're cooking," Bob said. "Do you have your cell phone, Abby?"

"Hold it," Rob said. "We're not calling anybody just yet. No offense, Abby, but what you just told us could be interpreted a number of ways."

"Oh really? How? He said slow and torturous."

"Sounds like a visit from Rob's mom," Bob said, and then hid behind his wineglass.

"I'll choose to ignore that," Rob said. "But Abby, you of all people should know that the police need something concrete to go on. What would be the motive for this—long and torturous whatever?"

"It sounded like blackmail. He said something about payments—Rob, did you not hear me when I said Simone and Blackmond Dupree are having an affair?"

"I heard. But Abby, we seem to be forgetting

why it is you went undercover to begin with. Weren't you trying to see if Blackmond Dupree had anything to do with Mozella's disappearance, not to mention that stupid bird?"

"Yes."

"And you were hoping to maybe learn of some connection between him and the exotic stranger who brought the Taj Mahal to Charleston in the first place, right?"

"Yes," I hissed softly.

"Instead you jumped to conclusions, blew your cover, and now instead of gathering facts, you're sitting in Charleston's finest restaurant."

"*Arguably* the finest. Besides, it was your choice."

"My point is that you could be back at Chez Fez rifling through Blackmond Dupree's desk if you hadn't lost your head."

"Well, I'm about to lose my temper. Y'all are supposed to be my friends. But oh, no—" My cell phone rang. There are few folks ruder than those who carry on phone conversations in restaurants, especially in loud voices. The one exception I'm willing to make is myself. Besides, I had mitigating circumstances.

"Hello?"

"Hi, Mrs. Washburn."

"You must have a wrong number," I said crisply.

"This is George. We had lattes together at Barnes & Noble, remember?"

"Yes. George, if you don't mind, I'm really terribly busy at the moment—"

180

"Mrs. Washburn, I was hoping you'd agree to have breakfast with me tomorrow morning."

Then it struck me. "George, how did you get my cell phone number?"

"The same way you found out where I worked."

"John Norman!"

"He's such a nice man, isn't he? Mrs. Washburn, I called your shop, and your machine said you didn't open until ten, and I don't have to be at work until eleven, so I thought we might meet downtown for breakfast. I was thinking of the Bookstore Café. And how does eight sound?"

I might well have jammed the phone back into my overstuffed purse had it not been for Rob's stinging accusation that I'd lost my head. I'd show him.

"Breakfast tomorrow would be lovely. 'Bye."

I smiled at the Rob-Bobs. "Just keeping my head. That was one of my suspects."

Rob waggled his neatly trimmed eyebrows. "Do tell, Abby, is George cute?"

"Very." My stupid phone rang again. "What?" I barked into it.

"Abby, hon, didn't you get my message?"

"Greg?"

"I called you twice. The first time I was a little out of it, but the second time I gave you a number to call and asked you to call back. Left the message on both our home phone and your cell."

"When was that?"

"About an hour ago."

An hour ago I was shakin' my bacon for a fake foreigner. That would explain why he hadn't reached me on my cell phone, a fact I was not about to try and explain to Greg.

"Silly me, I must have had the ringer turned off. So what was your message? And where the heck are you, Timbuktu?"

"Norfolk."

"What in tarnation are you doing there?"

"Where is he?" the Rob-Bobs chorused.

Timbuktu, I mouthed. "Explain, dear."

"Well, like I said in my message, I was drunk. *Really* drunk."

"Go on, I'm listening."

"Well, Mark—you know, my buddy up from McClellanville—"

"Yes, I know Mark. The one whose wife, Caroline, is at her wits' end because he's missing as well. What's the deal, Greg, are the two of you having an affair?"

Two pairs of ears rotated forward, as if set on hinges.

"An affair?" Greg had the effrontery to laugh. "Come on, Abby, give me a break. He's hardly my type. Heck no, we aren't having an affair. I was about to tell you that the shrimping business hasn't been panning out for Mark, something Caroline doesn't seem to understand. She's gotten addicted to online shopping, and that's all she does now. Abby, you should see their house. It's wall-to-wall stuff; a lot of it she doesn't even bother to unwrap. Anyway, he's had to sell his boat. The best offer was from a fellow who lives up in Norfolk, Virginia. Mark asked if I would drive up there, while he took the boat, then I would drive him back. So that's what I did, except that we went on a bender afterward because Mark was really taking it hard. Tried to call you earlier—I think I did, actually. Just can't remember what I said. Anyway, I'm sober now and we're headed home. We're in Fayetteville, by the way. I'm coming straight home after I drop Mark off in McClellanville."

"Okay darling, I understand. Take as much time as you need."

"Love you, hon. You're the best. 'Bye."

I hung up, trying to look as sad as a puppy dog in a cattery.

"Oh gawd, Abby, he didn't!" Rob leaned forward and tried to put an arm around my shoulders.

I shrugged him away. "I'm afraid he did. They ran off to Virginia together."

"This is unbelievable," Bob said, although he sounded like he not only believed it, but was hoping for details.

I threw my shoulders back bravely. "Well you know what they say: Virginia is for lovers."

"But Abby," Rob protested, "Greg seemed so, uh—well, so hetero. I was only joking before."

"I blame it all on metrosexuals," I wailed. "They seduced him with their fragrances, girlie foods, manicures, and sensitivity. It was only a short leap from good hygiene and manners to another man's arms. And to think he used to be a stinky meat and potatoes eater."

"I'm sure he still stinks," Bob said, doing his best to comfort me.

"You really think so?"

They both nodded.

Our meals arrived just in time. So as not to ruin what is invariably a delightful dining experience, I put on a stiff upper lip—although I let it quiver a bit. Yes, it made eating a trifle more difficult, but I'm sure it endeared me further to my friends. Every now and then one or the other of them would glance up from their food and bestow upon me a loving, supportive look. And yes, I knew I would have to pay the piper dearly when I came clean, but in the meantime it was worth it.

Of course I couldn't keep the charade going all night, not with my darling, handsome husband expected home in three hours. I waited until the last spoonful of crème brûlée was safely down my gullet before coughing up the truth. Strangely enough, the Rob-Bobs were not amused.

"B-b-but Abby," Bob bleated, "how could you!" He folded his arms across his chest and waited for an explanation.

"Well, it was Rob's fault. He jumped to conclusions. I just played along."

"For shame, for shame, for shame," Rob said, but try as he might, he is just too suave and good-looking to do a decent Gomer Pyle imitation. "I suppose this means you won't be spending the night with us. We were going to put you in the Queen Anne suite and serve you breakfast in bed."

When the Rob-Bobs talk about their Queen Anne bed, they are not referring to a period or style of furniture, but to a bed in which the old gal herself counted sheep. Frankly, it's not all that comfortable, which is probably why she enumerated ewes. As for breakfast in bed, I was all too glad to escape another of Bob's creative repasts.

"Thanks guys, for everything. I really mean it. I love you two like the brother I wish I had."

"We love you, too, Abby," Rob said.

Bob immediately concurred. We might have progressed to a group hug had it not been for the fact that we were still sitting, and the table had very sharp corners. Since it would have been wasteful to let those good vibes dissipate unused, I asked my dear friends for a favor. They hemmed and hawed, but I put on the sugar. In the end they relented, but only after I promised to be in touch by cell phone the entire time. They also insisted on following me home—not because of any criminal threat to my person, but because a humdinger of a thunderstorm was brewing. Still, I felt like I was under house arrest.

I wasn't being stupid when I asked the Rob-Bobs to drop me off at the shop so I could pick up my car; I was merely being deceitful. If my car wasn't home, safely ensconced in the garage, when Greg returned he would suspect that I'd been playing detective and that something had gone wrong. I would then be forced to listen to a safety lecture from a man who had just returned from a drunken spree in an unfamiliar city.

I'm pretty sure I would have kept my promise to drive straight home and lock the door behind me had it not been for the impending thunderstorm. High winds often accompany these fast-moving fronts, and while I was positive that the Den of Antiquity was locked up as tightly as a mass murderer on death row, I was not as sure about the small ventilation window in the storeroom toilet. This opening is too small and too high up to be of interest to a cat burglar, but in heavy downpours, overflow from the rain gutters sometimes finds its way inside. I once had a seventeenth-century gate-leg table ruined by water seeping out from beneath the bathroom door.

Rain damage is a perfectly good excuse, and no doubt about it, I would have been more responsible and informed the Rob-Bobs of my change of plans had not a second reason to return to my shop wedged its way into my already overloaded head. What if the package I'd been bent on ignoring had something to do with Mama and her disappearance?

I drove out of the alley first, the Rob-Bobs following, until I hit Queen Street. Normally I would take a right at this point, but when I glanced into the rearview mirror and saw that my buddies had somehow managed to disappear, I knew luck was with me. The instant the light turned green, I leapt across the intersection, slid over to the left lane, and turned on Broad to circle back to the store. Just as I was about to turn off my engine, Rob's voice came over my headset like the voice of Big Brother. That's not the sort of filial relationship I had in mind.

"Abby, where are you?" he demanded.

"The question is, where are *you*?"

"Bob saw something in a store window that he just had to see. We stopped just for a second, but you'd disappeared."

"Well, don't worry. I'm almost home."

"Are you telling the truth, Abby?"

"No. I'm already there." I unhooked my phone, grabbed my purse, and slammed the car door. "You hear that? Now listen while I unlock the door."

"I'm listening. Abby, this better be on the up-and-up. I'll tell Greg all about your belly dancing escapade if you're lying."

I jangled the keys into the phone, opened the back door to my shop, and punched in the security code. "You hear that?" I asked.

"Abby, if you're not telling the truth, so help me I'm going to tie you up and force-feed you Bob's llama lasagna."

"Hey," I heard Bob say in the background, "you're going to regret that, buster."

I picked up the package, which was really just

an overstuffed envelope. It was as light as I remembered; practically weightless. I pulled the tearaway tag on the back. As the contents pushed their way out I let loose with a bloodcurdling scream.

CHAPTER 16

Mama's crinolines weigh only a few ounces each, but I dropped this one as if it were made out of lead. There was no mistaking this was hers. Puffy slips are out these days, unless one is a member of a wedding party, or a square dancer. But Mama doesn't buy her undergarments from bridal shops or Western stores. She makes her own, and into the waistband of each she proudly sews her initials: MW. She is also amused by her own cleverness. "If I'm drunk at a party," she's fond of saying, "I'll be able to find my own crinoline, even if I'm holding it upside down." Never mind that Mama never gets drunk and seldom goes to parties.

"Abby, Abby!" I heard the sound of a distant voice.

Slowly I became aware that I was still holding the phone, clutching it tightly even, as if it was a proffered hand and I was dangling over a precipice. It seemed to take all my strength to get it to my mouth.

"It's Mama," I croaked.

"Mozella? Abby, where are you? What's happened?"

189

"I—I'm at my shop. There was this package—Rob, please, you've got to come right away."

"We're on it. Abby, are you inside?"

"Yes, just barely. I'm in the storeroom—" The outside door, which I'd left open, closed with a bang, and I found myself enveloped in darkness. I screamed again and fumbled for the light switch. I found it after several long seconds, but when I flipped it, nothing happened.

"Oh shoot," I said into the phone. Actually I used a stronger word, one which no lady should employ.

"Abby, I'm calling the police."

"No!"

"Too bad, Abby, I'm doing it." He hung up.

I groped for the door, found the release bar, and threw my weight into it. The door wouldn't budge. My fingers felt for the latch, which turned, but still the door would not open. Senselessly, I began pounding on the heavy metal. My fists might as well have been biscuits for all the sound they made. The panic I felt at being trapped, even in a place as familiar as my storeroom, caused my chest to tighten, and I felt like I could barely breathe.

"Stay calm," I said aloud to myself. "Help is on its way."

Immediately I heard a crash at the other end of the storeroom and a high-pitched scream. I gave the door one final, futile push, and then dropped to my knees. There is an Indonesian armoire to the left of the rear door, one that I have been planning to restore but had somehow never gotten around to. I scuttled in its general direction now, like a crab trying to escape a hungry gull. Crawling seemed a safer way to travel in utter darkness, but even then I slammed into a copper bin and banged my nose on the rung of a Shaker chair.

When I finally reached the armoire, my heart was pounding so hard that I was convinced the intruder could hear it. It was certainly louder then the squeak made by the hand-hewn door. Thank heavens the Indonesians are master carvers. The lotus pattern cut all the way through the panel, so I was able to pull it closed after me by wedging my fingers between the wood blossoms. No doubt it was an irrational feeling, but I felt safer surrounded by the faint smell of sandalwood incense and extraordinary beauty.

But a second crash, followed by another scream, made short shrift of my ill-perceived security. I curled in a fetal position on the floor of the armoire and, even though a lapsed Episcopalian, prayed for divine protection. Normally I listen in disbelief to those folks on television who credit God for saving them from the ravages of weather, or perhaps a plane crash, while ignoring the fate of others who perished in the same event. Did God not have enough free passes for everyone? But let me tell you, just as there are no atheists in foxholes, there are none inside Indonesian armoires.

It is difficult to measure time by heartbeats, especially if they are accelerated. But perhaps a million and a half heartbeats after taking refuge inside a piece of furniture, I heard a familiar voice.

"Abby! Abby! Where the heck are you?"

"Rob!" I shrieked, and flung open the door to the armoire so hard it slammed against the opposite side and bounced back, smacking my rather petite proboscis. The poor thing was taking a beating.

I saw the beam of a flashlight sweep across the top of a breakfront. What he thought I'd be doing on top of a seven-foot bookcase was beyond me.

"I'm over here—to the left of the back door."

The light bobbed around the room like a giant firefly.

"The heavily carved Indonesian armoire!" I screamed.

"Why didn't you say so?" He scooped me up in his arms a second later. "Are you all right?"

"Yes—oh, Rob! The package—it's Mama!"

His arms shook. "What do you mean, 'it's Mama'?"

I wiggled free of his embrace. "Not *her*, but her slip. Her crinoline—well, one of them. And the door's locked, and"—I started to whisper—"I heard two crashes and two screams."

"That would be the pair of cats that streaked out the front door when I let myself in."

"B-but the crashes. There was someone in here, Rob."

"Yes, the aforementioned felines. Apparently they knocked over a lamp and a large urn. Were either of them particularly valuable, Abby? I can't remember."

I was rapidly losing patience. "We're in the dark, for crying out loud. Someone cut the power to my shop."

"It was the storm, Abby."

"The storm?"

"Blew through here a million miles an hour. They said a tornado might have touched down briefly West of the Ashley. Thousands of people are without power, not just you."

"Oh. But what about—"

"The piece of pipe scaffolding jammed between the concrete tire stops and your alley door? It's from that remodeling job going on behind you. Bob and I tried to yank it loose, but it's going to take some power tools. Don't worry about your car—it's fine."

"Where's Bob?" I was only a teensy bit suspicious; Rob's answers were too convenient. But mostly I found it hard to take that I'd been cowering in an armoire all because of two amorous pussies.

"He's outside still trying to get through to 911. The lines are jammed."

"Tell him to stop!"

"Don't be foolish, Abby. What about Mozella's crinoline?"

"Mama's kidnapper said not to involve the police."

193

"They all say that, Abby. You know that, you've seen the movies. You also know you can't solve this alone."

"I don't have to—I've got you. And Bob. And Greg, when he gets home. Besides, the police aren't taking this seriously. Officially, she's only just now gone missing."

"Let me see the crinoline, Abby," Rob said gently.

I showed him the package and its contents. He examined them both closely with his flashlight. There was no note of any kind, no blood or anything else gruesome on the half-slip, and of course no return address on the envelope.

"You see," I said. "This isn't going to prove anything to the police. It's bizarre, granted, but hardly criminal evidence. They might take it with them, file it away in some storage facility, but it won't be of any help in finding Mama."

"Abby, how did you get to be so cynical?"

"By living four-plus decades. And watching presidential campaigns on TV. When I last checked, you were a couple of years older than I. Why is it you're *not* cynical?"

"Because if I allowed myself to go down that path, even just a little way, I might never get back to where I want to be."

"And where's that?"

"Believing that most of the time the majority of the people are honest and competent. It's in my best interest to think the best of everyone until

194

proven wrong. If I didn't do that, Abby, I couldn't get out of bed in the morning."

I hugged my friend. "Now let's go tell Bob to put away his cell phone."

It took only a cursory glance up and down King Street to make me realize just how lucky I was. The Den of Antiquity had essentially been spared, as had The Finer Things, but some of the neighboring stores had not. The Shabby Sheik, an importer of Persian carpets so old that Aladdin had ridden one, lost its plate-glass window. Pandora's Box, a jewelry boutique, was missing part of its roof.

When Bob saw that I was all right, he threw his spindly arms around me. "Thank God you're okay, Abby."

"Right back at you. Now please, put your phone away."

"But—"

"No buts. I insist."

Bob sighed. "You know we have your best interest at heart, Abby."

"Right back at you again."

No sooner did Bob put his cell back in his shirt pocket than my phone rang. My heart skipped a beat, thinking as I did that the call might have something to do with Mama.

"Hello?"

"Hon, are you all right?"

"Greg! Yes, darling, I'm fine. Why do you ask?"

"I heard it on the radio. About the storm."

"Yup, it was a doozy."

"Your shop okay?"

"Essentially. There's something jamming the back door."

"Look, hon, Mark wants me to be there when he tells Caroline. Do you mind terribly if I stay as long as he needs me?"

Of course I minded. Gregory Morris Washburn owed me big-time for going off on a drunken binge with a buddy and not telling me. Yes, he was looking out for his friend, but that was no excuse for letting me worry. But now that I knew where he was, and that he was safe and sound, I would just as soon he stayed away longer. It is hard to do a little personal detecting when your husband, a former professional detective, is monitoring your every move.

I sighed for dramatic effect. "You have to do what needs to be done, right? Give Mark and Caroline both my love."

"Hon, you're the best, you know that? Did I luck out marrying you, or what?"

"Back at you, darling." That seemed to be my new mantra.

"Well, hon, I better go. The signal's getting weak."

"One last thing, darling. There was a package—"

"Sorry, hon, you're breaking up."

"I said there's a package—" There was no point in talking further; our connection was essentially terminated. "Well, at least I tried," I said, turning my attention to the Rob-Bobs.

"Lost your signal?" Rob asked, a smile tugging at the corners of his mouth.

"Yes. Oh, and he's not coming home tonight after all."

"Hip hip hooray!" Bob brayed. "Now we get to tuck you into the Queen Anne and serve you breakfast in bed."

"The bed part sounds nice, but I have a breakfast date with George."

"Abby," Rob said, "who is this George? We demand to know."

"I told you before, she's one of my suspects."

"He's a she?"

"*She's* a she, and a lot of it too. She was one of the top five bidders for the Taj Mahal. Do y'all want to join us?"

"No, thanks," Rob said, his interest in George greatly diminished. "At least we still get to tuck you into bed."

"There is one caveat," I said.

"Uh-oh. I don't like the sound of that."

"It's Dmitri. I've left him alone too much lately. Right now he's hiding somewhere in the house, pouting. You know what this means, don't you?"

"Scratch marks on the Queen Anne?"

"Throw up on my throw rugs?" Bob moaned. "The silk one in the guest room was handmade by a reclusive order of blind Tibetan nuns. It took them ten years to weave it, and it cost us a fortune. It's irreplaceable."

"We could roll it up and put it away," Rob said, "or we could simply replace it with a machine-made carpet that's attractive."

"*Machine*-made carpet?" Bob had grown pale and beads of sweat were gathering on his forehead in front of our very eyes.

"Sorry I can't eat breakfast in bed, but I'll eat your lunch," I said. "And I won't crack a single joke."

"You'll eat *anything* I make?"

"Anything."

"Deal," Rob said. "I gotta see this."

"Deal," Bob said. "Have you ever eaten poached eels?"

"I can't say that I have."

He grinned happily.

As for Dmitri, we found him in my laundry basket, doing what cats his age do best: sleeping.

The power was restored sometime after midnight, allowing me to keep my breakfast date with the buxom George Murphy at the Bookstore Café. She was already seated, facing the door, and she waved me over with a big smile on her face. You would have thought we were best friends.

"Abby! I'm so glad you could make it."

I allowed her to lean over the table and do the kissy-cheek thing. "Good morning, George. Did y'all lose power over in Mount Pleasant last night?"

She shrugged. "I don't live there; I live here—on Tradd Street."

Thanks to the magic of computer imaging, Tradd Street, which is not waterfront property, was transformed into just that in the movie *The Patriot*. Nevertheless, homes on this historic street sell for a premium. Normally, a physical therapist, even one employed in prestigious Mount Pleasant, would be hard-pressed to purchase a home on Tradd Street by herself.

"Do you rent?" I wasn't being rude, merely curious.

"No, I own. Where do you live, Abby?"

"Squiggle Lane."

"Oh, I just love that little street. Which house is yours?"

"It's the one—that's hard to find," I said, changing horses in midstream. If she was the one who had stolen Monet and mamanapped my minimadre, then she already knew where I lived. Darned if I was going to let her have fun at my expense. And even if she wasn't involved in these crimes, she no had business asking such a personal question.

If she found my answer peculiar, she didn't let on. "Abby, where are you going to put the birdcage?"

"I don't know. Any suggestions?"

"Well, if it was me, I'd put it in a sunporch. Do you have a sunporch?"

"George, if you don't mind, could we skip the small talk and get right down to business."

"Business?"

The server came by to ask if we wanted coffee. "We'd like to order our meals as well," I said.

George tossed her blond locks and bobbled her bosoms. The server, a young man, quite possibly a student at the College of Charleston, was reduced to a bundle of salivating hormones.

"I'm not ready to order yet," George declared.

"She's not ready to order yet," the server drooled.

"I can hear," I said pleasantly. "Very well, I'll start with a large orange juice and coffee. Lots of half and half."

"I don't consume dairy," George said. "I'll have a small orange juice and black coffee. No half and half."

"No half and half," the server intoned, as if chanting a liturgical response.

"She does eat dairy," I wailed. "I saw her drink a latte yesterday."

"And no carbs, either," George said, jiggling her D-cups for emphasis.

"But I do eat carbs," I said, waving my Moo-Roo pocketbook, which, alas, held no more than a B-cup. "Besides, doesn't orange juice contain carbs?"

"No carbs," the server chanted.

"Listen young man," I said, still waving my handbag, "there are tips, and then there are *tips*."

"What would you suggest I order?" George purred, her finger digging seductively into her lower lip.

In all fairness, even I, who had heretofore never even considered batting for the other team, found myself breathing a mite harder than normal. The poor college boy never stood a chance. His tongue hung out like that of a dog in an August heat wave, rendering him incapable of even the most rudimentary speech.

"Do you think I'd like your low-carb-forget-about-calories-and-exercise-eat-too-much-gain-weight-anyway special number one?" she asked, crossing and uncrossing her legs. "Or should I go with the high-carb-pump-you-full-of-energy-watch-you-crash-an-hour-later special number two?" Of course those weren't her actual words, but she may as well have been saying them for all the difference it made.

"Ma'am?" the server said, when it finally dawned on him that he'd been asked a question.

I got up, took his order pad, and wrote: *Two juices, one small, one large; two coffees, LOTS of half and half; and two Breakfast Special #2.* "That will be all, darling," I said, and gave him a gentle push.

The young man bounced back like a weighted punching bag.

"The sooner you bring our orders, the sooner you can stand there and ogle," I said, losing patience.

It wasn't until George dismissed the libidinous malingerer with another toss of her mane that our server remembered he had feet.

"Don't you just hate that?" George said the second the coast was clear.

"I absolutely despise it," I said. I'd seldom meant anything as fervently.

"So what should we do today, Abby? Since we're already here, I thought we could do some shopping. I haven't popped into Saks Fifth Avenue for ages. Afterward we could have lunch at Cypress, or wherever you'd like. Then we could hit a matinee, unless you'd rather go to the beach."

I couldn't believe my ears. I'd only met the girl yesterday, and now she was laying out a day trip that would be the envy of many a mother and daughter team.

"Don't you have to work today?"

"Not unless I want to, and today I don't want to."

The mother part of me kicked in. "What about your boss?"

"She'll get over it."

"Excuse me?"

"She always does, you know. Maybe it's because I don't ask for a raise, like the other girls. Besides, I already left a message on her machine."

It was starting to make sense. "George, this is none of my business, but you don't need the money, do you?"

She shook her head, sending her golden curls swirling in all directions. It was like waving a red flag in front of a herd of bulls. Every male in the restaurant began pawing the floor.

"No, not really. I was raised by my grandfather— my parents were killed in a car wreck when I was a little girl. I was with them, but I don't remember a thing. The car flipped over in the rain on I-26 between here and Orangeburg. It landed on its roof in a wooded area and wasn't discovered for three days. They say I survived on rainwater and mints from my mama's purse. Anyway, Grandpa wanted me to have a profession, in case I ever ran out of money, but just between you and me, I don't think that's going to happen. There was a lot of insurance money, and Grandpa was a shrewd investor."

I kept my voice down so the pawing males wouldn't charge. "With all that money, George, why do you work?"

"Why do you work, Abby?"

"Touché. I love my work. Sometimes I think I'm the luckiest woman in the world."

"Physical therapy is okay—but I thought I'd like it more. If it wasn't for the physical therapists that worked with me after the accident, I probably wouldn't be able to walk now."

"You still haven't answered my question."

She looked down at her lap. "I—I . . . well, I get lonely sometimes. It isn't easy making friends when you look like I do."

"More of us should have your problem. I'm sorry, I shouldn't have said that. It just seems—on the surface at least—that someone with your attributes would be swamped with friends."

"Well, I'm not. The men all want just one thing, and the women—and I know this sounds in-credibly vain—the women all hate me. That's why I go to auctions and concerts, and even the movies. When I'm surrounded by a crowd, I can pretend that I'm with somebody. Like my friend has gone to the bathroom and I'm saving her seat, or my date's gone off to buy popcorn. I even go to two churches, and everybody's nice enough, but after they say 'Hey' at coffee hour, they go home to Sunday dinner, and I go home to my TV dinner. But then along comes you."

"Excuse me?"

"I said 'then along comes you.'"

"I know what you said, but I'm not sure what you mean."

"When I saw you bidding at the auction, you smiled at me. I thought, now there's a woman I could be friends with. So I kept bidding just so you would notice me. I was going to outbid you, so that afterward I could offer to sell you the birdcage myself, but I could see how much you wanted it. I thought you might get mad if the bidding went too high, so I stopped. Then when you called and asked me to have coffee with you—well, I was really happy, Abby. I knew you were just being nice for business reasons, but like I said, women aren't usually nice to me. I know it was silly of me, but I was hoping we could be friends."

Lordy, but didn't I feel like something the cat dragged in and the dog wouldn't eat. The poor child only wanted to make a friend, while I had turned her into a murder suspect. How would I feel if that happened to my daughter, Susan? The least I could do was to be as upfront with George as possible.

"I called you because I'm interested in why you, and the others, bid against me for the birdcage. I know this must sound strange, but I'm not at liberty to tell you why I'm interested—"

"That's okay, Abby, I don't need to know. Clay Aiken is coming to the North Charleston Coliseum on the thirtieth. Do you want to come?"

"I think I'm busy that night." So much for being upfront.

"They're third row seats, dead center."

"Oh, what the heck, it's only a Pilates class."

George beamed, which made her all the prettier. "Abby, I'm so glad I met you."

Mercifully, my cell phone rang. Ironically, it was a Georgia number, but one I didn't recognize. I answered anyway.

CHAPTER 17

"Agnes, darling, what a surprise to hear from you."

"Ooh, Abby," a very familiar voice said, "you always were a little bit strange. Not strange like Cousin Urethra, of course, but still very strange."

"C.J.! Where on earth are you?"

"I'm in Sewannee, at the Episcopal Seminary."

"What in heaven's name are you doing there?"

"I'm with your brother, Abby. Or have you forgotten that Toy and I are engaged?"

"I most certainly haven't forgotten. What I meant is, why aren't you here? Where you're supposed to be—minding the store?"

"Because you think I'm a liar, Abby."

"I do not!"

"Yes, you do. You think I make up things."

"Well . . ."

"Well what, Abby?"

"I think you have an active imagination, that's all. There's nothing wrong with that, C.J. That's what makes you so special."

"Ooh, Abby, do you really think I'm special?"

"Definitely one of a kind. And I'm really sorry that I hurt your feelings."

"I forgive you, Abby."

"Thanks. But C.J., you don't really have a cousin named Urethra, do you? I mean, you were just kidding about that, weren't you?"

"Oh no, Abby. Aunt Clemantine Ledbetter, up in Moon Pie Hollow, led a very sheltered life. When she was pregnant for the first time she visited a doctor in the big city—that would be Shelby—and there was this chart on the wall. Aunt Clemantine saw the word urethra and thought it was the most beautiful name for a baby in the entire world. Now there are six Urethras living up in Moon Pie Hollow, but you just don't hear that name very much anywhere else."

"What a pity. C.J., does that mean you'll come back to Charleston and help me out at the Den of Antiquity?"

"Do you need me?"

"More than ever."

"Did you find your mama yet, Abby?"

"No. What have you told Toy?"

"I told him that she went missing at the St. Ophelia Society dance, but he said not to worry. Abby, did you know Mozella went missing for five days once, and finally showed up at a Shriners' convention driving one of them little bitty cars?"

"No! That can't be true—I mean, I don't remember that."

"He said it happened when you were just a little

girl, before your daddy got dive-bombed by that seagull with a brain tumor the size of a walnut."

"I don't remember Mama running away," I said, "except to the convent, and she kept in constant touch."

"Abby, the main thing is that you shouldn't worry. I got up with the birds this morning, so I'm already in Augusta, Georgia. I'll be there before you know it."

"What about Toy?"

"Ooh, Abby, I shouldn't be telling you this, but your brother will be just fine for a while—if you know what I mean."

"I do, and TMI! But C.J., you're the best, you know that? You're a really good friend."

Out of the corner of my eye I saw poor George's hangdog expression. "Gotta go, C.J."

"See you soon, Abby."

"Family," I said to George, shaking my head, "can't live with them, can't live without them."

"I have no family," she reminded me softly.

Even a size four foot can be too much to fit into a minimouth like mine. I was struggling to find the right words when our waiter returned with part of our drink orders. His tongue was still hanging out, and his eyes were never going to fit back into their sockets without the help of a shoehorn. Poor George cringed.

"Will that be all, ma'am?" he asked as he poured the coffee. It seemed like he hadn't even bothered to glance at our cups. I suppose as long as no one screamed, he figured there was no harm done.

"There is the small matter of our orange juice, not to mention our meals."

"Yeah, right." He stopped pouring, all the better to stare.

"You were saying," I said loudly to George, "that you're an undercover cop. Are you're here to make a drug bust?"

"Uh—be right back with your orders." Our waiter lit out of there like he was carrying a shovelful of fire.

It was the manager who finally brought us breakfast, and it was delicious as always. I stayed just as long as I had to, and then after thanking George profusely again for the Clay Aiken tickets, I too beat a hasty retreat.

Charleston is a fast healer. The enormous damage visited upon the city by Hurricane Hugo in 1989 can now only be appreciated by viewing photographs and film.

The Finer Things deserves its name. It was my idea to move to Charleston from Charlotte, and to open an antiques shop on King Street. I was pleased, but not surprised, when the Rob-Bobs did the same. I was less pleased, and even less surprised, when their new store not only outclassed, but eclipsed, mine.

Of course there already were upscale antiques stores on King Street, but none quite as elegant as the Rob-Bobs' new venture. To begin with, one has to buzz to gain admittance. This feature automatically eliminates the faint of heart, who also tend to be timid with their greenbacks. Once inside, the shoppers are greeted warmly (usually by the Rob-Bobs) and offered a glass of champagne. I know for a fact that the bubbly served is disgustingly sweet, as well as cheap. This is the second stage of the winnowing-out process. If the shopper grimaces at the first sip and sets the glass down, the odds are he or she has discerning taste. On the other hand, if the shopper makes a face but continues to hold the glass, he or she not only has good taste, but good manners as well. But if, after tasting the vile brew, the customer smacks his or her lips, smiles, or clutches the glass tightly, he or she would be happier shopping at a collectibles store in a strip mall.

Although a frequent visitor, I must be buzzed in like everyone else. Needless to say, I was quite surprised that morning when Simone Dupree did the honor.

"Where are the guys?"

"They're taking the day off, Mrs. Washburn. I got the impression they were with you."

"Sort of—I had a breakfast date. Simone, darling, we need to talk."

Up until last night I'd thought of Simone Dupree as a beautiful but enigmatic young woman. After seeing her paw the man who was supposed to be her father, I found myself looking at an entirely different person. Was that a look of alarm on her face, or merely innocent surprise? Did her dark eyes hide unspeakable secrets, or could it be that this was nothing more than a simple case of mistaken identity?

I'd heard nothing of a Mrs. Dupree, but there probably was one. My nervousness at performing, combined with the seductive lighting at Chez Fez, might well have been responsible for me shaving twenty years off a woman's age. If that combo could be bottled and sold, I'd soon be a billionaire. At any rate, many daughters look like younger versions of their mothers, and it was quite possible that the real Simone Dupree hadn't gone anywhere near Chez Fez the night before.

The woman in question stepped aside to let me enter the cool sanctuary of the serious collector. "Would you care for some champagne, Mrs. Washburn?"

"No thanks, I just ate."

Her long dark lashes fluttered. "Sorry, it's a habit. What did you want to see me about?"

"May we sit somewhere? I know the Rob-Bobs have some cushy chairs in their office."

"Certainly, but I may have to answer the door."

"By all means."

While the Rob-Bobs are big on French furniture, the office resembles the drawing room of a nineteenth-century Italian nobleman. Perhaps that's because it *is* the drawing room of a nineteenth-century Italian nobleman. I'm not up on Italian aristocracy, but I do know that the previous owner was a count, and Bologne was part of his name. Trust me, I'm not the only antiques dealer on King Street who refers to this pretentious place of business as the "baloney room."

A frequent visitor, I knew exactly where I wanted to sit—or should I say recline? The emerald-green silk damask daybed of yesteryear is a perfect fit for my diminutive frame. Once supine, I got right down to brass tacks.

"I'm not going to beat around the bush, Simone. I know you're having a sordid affair with Blackmond Dupree and that the two of you want to murder some poor old lady in Portland, Maine. Normally, this would be none of my business, but my mama is a poor old woman as well, and she just happens to be missing. Not to mention the fact that a stupid bird calls me demanding something I don't have, and that your beloved was one of the people who wanted to get his hands on that bird—or its cage—and was willing to spend almost ten thousand dollars to do so. Although I believe in his case it was a mere $9,560. Oh, and just so you don't go getting any funny ideas, not only am I wired, but this room is wired as well."

The fact that Simone stayed around to listen to my spiel was surprising enough. That she crumpled like one of Bob's soufflés when the oven door is slammed was downright shocking. If I hadn't already been reclining, I might well have tasted the authentic Italian marble on the floor.

"Mrs. Washburn, I had no idea you were an IGS agent."

I had no idea what IGS meant, but I had a cousin who once worked for IGA. The truth, once stretched, soon becomes rather flexible.

"I'm chock-full of surprises, Simone."

"You need to know this wasn't my idea. Charlie told me he was single. How was I supposed to know about the old biddy up in Maine?"

Charlie? Aha, so I was right. Blackmond Dupree was not his real name. But that not-so-insignificant detail was going to have to wait.

"How can you be so callous, Simone? Don't you have any regard for human life?"

"What?"

"The plan to make the old biddy pay. What was it Charlie said? Ah yes, he'd make her 'worst nightmare come true.'"

Simone's soufflé crumpled even further. "You mean Vladimir is an agent, too?"

Vladimir? Wasn't the cold war over? Perhaps I'd gotten in over my head. Oh well, it was too late now. It was either sink or swim; it had certainly gotten too deep for me to wade back through.

"Vladimir is definitely involved," I said. "Now, this is how it's going to work. If you tell me everything you know about Charlie—and Vladimir—I'll tell the higher-ups to go easy on you. Of course I can't promise anything, you understand."

"I understand."

"Good. Now if you please, sing like a canary."

I settled back on the daybed and folded my hands.

"Well, I met Charlie at a party in Myrtle Beach last summer. We kinda hooked up right away, and when he said he was moving to Charleston to open a restaurant, I just sort of tagged along. I was really surprised because I found a job almost immediately. Working here. I couldn't believe my luck at first. New boyfriend, new job—it was like my life was finally working out. I didn't have such a good time growing up, you see."

"Not many of us do."

"What?"

"Never mind, darling. Please, continue with your story."

"Anyway, we hadn't been here but a few days and Charlie tells me to start calling him Blackmond. I say okay, because what's in a name, right? I think Madonna said that. But I swear I didn't know he was doing anything illegal—not then, at any rate. Then Charlie starts pretending he's a foreigner, because his restaurant has a theme and all, and he asks me to play along with that, too. Mrs. Washburn, there isn't anything illegal about pretending to be a foreigner, is there?"

"I don't know. But I would think it would be rather stupid, considering the threat of terrorism."

"That's what I told Charlie, but he said, 'I'm not pretending to be a Moroccan, but a Frenchman from Morocco.' He also said that a theme restaurant would go over really big in Charleston, especially with the tourists and cruise passengers, who have come here to be entertained anyway."

My attempt at a warm smile may have come across as tepid. "Can you speed your story up, darling? Can you get to the part about the old lady and Vladimir?"

"Right. Well, I move in with Charlie, see, and I think it's like we're almost married, but he wants me to pretend that I'm his daughter. Says it might be bad for business if folks thought we were just hooking up—Charleston being such a conservative city and all. But I tell him that is so nineties, and if it made that much difference, why didn't we just get married? Then he says it's because he already has a wife. Can you believe that, Mrs. Washburn? Do all men lie like that?"

"Not *all* men. Not all women, either." I gave her my hand signal for "hurry up," which is a little bit like Queen Elizabeth waving in fast motion.

"So anyway, I make Charlie tell me everything. He says his wife is this rich Russian woman—her first husband was some kind of communist big shot—and that she offered him a whole lot of money to marry her, so that she could get a green card. That's how Charlie got his money for the restaurant, see. Only now she won't divorce him. She says that if Charlie sues for divorce, then she'll expose his scam, even though that would mean she'd be in big trouble, too."

"He could call her bluff."

"He has. Last time he sent an actor pretending

215

to be a lawyer. She just laughed. So this time he sent Vladimir."

"Do you know *why* this woman won't give Mr. Dupree a divorce?"

"Sex."

"You're joking!"

"Mrs. Washburn, Charlie is—well, let's just say I couldn't be happier in that department. But you see, all the other old bags he's brought over were just as happy *not* to be bothered with that. Then along comes Tatiana, who falls head over heels in love with Charlie. Who would have thought? I mean, how could she think that a good-looking guy like him would really fall in love with her? Like, who is she kidding? Besides, he told her from the get-go that it was strictly business."

Simone looked to be about my daughter Susan's age. I found myself wanting to mother her, to dispense advice on men. Instead I had to grill her like a weenie on the Fourth of July before the Rob-Bobs showed up.

"What exactly does Blackmond—I mean, Charlie Dupree—want Vladimir to do to his wife?"

"Kill her orchids."

"I beg your pardon?"

"Well, threaten to kill them. If that doesn't work, he really might kill them."

"You're talking about flowers, right?"

"Yeah. You see, Tatiana—when she's not drunk, which is most of the time—is really into orchids. Did you know there are clubs for that kind of thing?"

"There's a club for everything. So you're saying that Vladimir is not planning to kill Charlie's wife, but is planning to kill her flowers?"

"Yeah. Sounds pretty silly when you put it like that, doesn't it?"

"I take it that they've been married long enough to get divorced and not cause suspicion?"

Her entire body went on red alert. Her eyes darted about like those of an impala that has caught the scent of a lion hiding in the tall grass.

"Uh—yeah. I'm sure of that. Mrs. Washburn, I can't get into any trouble, can I? I'm only sleeping with Charlie; it's not like I'm doing anything wrong."

It is neither my inclination nor my right to tell others how to live their lives. But like I said, I have a daughter Simone's age.

"Here's some unsolicited advice, darling. If he'll cheat with you, he'll cheat on you. Yes, I know, this is a sham marriage, and he wasn't emotionally committed to Tatiana and all that, but just think about this: the guy tells lies for a living. You're too intelligent and too beautiful to waste your life on someone like that."

"He's the only man I'll ever love, Mrs. Washburn."

My daughter Susan says the same thing—over and over again. The only man she'll ever love is invariably replaced by the new only man she'll ever love. Susan never listens, and if I lecture her too much, I run the risk of straining our relationship. But I had nothing to lose by preaching to Simone.

"How old are you, Simone?"

"Twenty-three."

"How old is Charlie—a.k.a. Blackmond—Dupree?"

"I don't know. Forty-six, I think. Something like that. We don't talk about age."

"Do you think he's cute?"

"Yeah."

"Just think, when you're his age, he'll be pushing seventy. All his muscles will have turned to flab. And he probably won't have any hair—not that there's anything wrong with that. But will *you* still find him cute?"

"Ew!" She remembered we were on opposing sides. "So what? I like bald men. And anyway, if he works out in a gym, he won't be flabby."

I hopped off the daybed. Perhaps the seed had been planted. If it had fallen on stony ground—well, I wasn't going to be around come harvest time. Besides, I'd gotten all the information I needed.

"Toodle-ooh," I said.

I'd gotten only halfway to the front door when I heard the Rob-Bobs coming through the back. I raced back to find Simone, dug a couple of twenties out of my purse, and practically threw them at her.

"Let's keep this conversation between you and me," I said.

She looked astonished, as well she should. "The IGS pays to do interviews?"

"Only for the best." I plastered a smile on my face as the Rob-Bobs came through the back door of the display area. Simone, by the way, faded into the background like a receding shadow. "Hey, I just dropped by to see if you were here. My breakfast meeting is over."

"Guess what we had for breakfast." Rob said, rolling his eyes. "No, don't waste your time guessing. It was yesterday's pigeon soufflé."

"How was it?"

He rolled his eyes again.

"No fair," Bob said. "A soufflé is meant to be served the minute it emerges from the oven, not as leftovers. But you have to admit, the scallion sauce I whipped up just on that account was pretty darn tasty."

"I'm sure it had a lot of taste, darling," I said.

"Moving right along," Rob said, "Abby, I forgot, Bob and I need to do a little paperwork this morning. Would you mind terribly if we—"

"Go right ahead. I really don't need a baby-sitter."

"Tough," Rob said. "You've got one anyway—at least until Greg gets home. We expect you to meet us here at twelve sharp, and we'll take you to lunch. This time it's our treat."

Bob squirmed like a six-year-old who'd been told to be quiet in church.

"Or we could eat lunch at your house," I said generously.

"No, we can't," Rob said.

That settled, I bid my friends adieu and stepped

out into the full blast of a Charleston summer. Even the palmettos along the street appeared to be wilting, like broccoli tops that had lost their turgidity. It was, of course, only an optical illusion. But what I saw transpire *beneath* the shimmering palms was very real.

CHAPTER 18

Stretch limos are not an uncommon sight in Charleston. Movie stars can be tourists as well. And lots of movies are filmed in the Holy City. But this was the first time I saw someone I actually knew emerge from one of these ostentatiously elongated automobiles. The woman who disembarked glanced up and down the street, and presumably not seeing me, leaned back into the rear of the car and gave someone a sloppy kiss. The smooch I couldn't see, but I'm no stranger to the sound. At any rate, after laying lips on the limo passenger, the woman in question straightened her skirt and started walking away from me at a brisk trot.

No one in Charleston (except for tourists and firemen) walks that fast between Memorial Day and Labor Day. To do so is to risk death by drowning—in one's own sweat. Nosiree bob! When we must be out and about in the summer sun, we locals do the "Charleston walk." That is to say, we stroll languidly down the street, keeping to the shade as much as possible. When we must nego-tiate a sunny patch, we walk even slower. As every native Charlestonian knows, perhaps instinctually, to hurry creates even more heat.

"Well, as I live and breathe," I said, barely able to breathe in the saturated air, "but if that isn't Catherine Deephouse." To be truthful, I was more than a mite hurt that she hadn't noticed me upon disembarking. Oh well, I am used to being overlooked, and I mean that literally.

Catherine continued to walk away from me at this breakneck speed, deftly dodging pedestrians. I had to run if I was going to catch up with her. I was steeling myself to do just that when a door two shops down the street opened and out squeezed a herd of tourists. Once outside, they blew up to twice their size, like giant yeast rolls, forming an impenetrable wall of dough from storefront to curb. A cursory glance across the street informed me that foot traffic was no better there.

I briefly contemplated risking my life by stepping out into the automobile traffic—some of the tourists were larger than cars—but fortunately, a better thought popped into my heat-addled brain. Ducking from doorway to doorway, like a GI in a war movie, I worked my down to Queen Street, turned left on it, and then finally right on Meeting. By now I was out of the shopping district, and my chances of being trampled were considerably less.

When I hit Broad Street, I had only to turn left and walk a few yards before arriving at Catherine's shop, Deephouse Designs. Always painfully aware of how dowdy little me stacks up to the stacked designer, I paused in the shade of an awning and surveyed myself in the window of an attorney's office. I smacked my lips a couple of times to even my thinning war paint, and ran my fingers through my short dark hair. Could be worse, I thought. I gave my reflected image the thumbs-up, only to see it give me two thumbs in return. What the heck?

"Oh shoot," I said aloud, when I realized that the second thumb belonged to a receptionist behind the glass. What must she think about my lip smack? I didn't hang around to find out. Abandoning the Charleston walk, I practically leaped the remaining distance to Deephouse Designs.

Catherine's assistant met me at the door as I expected. What I didn't expect was to see the grande dame herself, sitting behind her Brazilian hickory desk. Except for some beads of perspiration above her Botoxed brow, she appeared as if she might have been sitting there all morning. Ah, the glory of Charleston women: they never sweat—they merely dew.

The dew-dotted Deephouse acknowledged my arrival with a smile that was all business. "Abby, what can I do for you this morning?"

"Hi, Catherine. I was hoping you'd have time for a cup of coffee."

She looked past her bosom, which was spilling out from a tight purple blouse, and pretended to scan some papers on her desk. "Sorry, no can do. I have a fabric shipment coming in at any moment that's going to take the two of us the rest of the morning to check, and this afternoon I've got to start work on the Blazer House over in Ansonborough. Have you ever been in the Blazer House, Abby?"

"No."

"Even back in the not-too-distant past, when Ansonborough was more shabby than chic, the Blazer House was to die for. It's one of the oldest mansions in Charleston, you know. Anyway, all the best parties were held there. Anyone who was anyone was on Howard and Blanche Blazer's guest list. Then they retired to Florida—they didn't have any children, you know—and the St. Ophelia Society bought the place." She sighed deeply, causing the tops of her bosoms to rise and fall like the swells caused by a boat wake. "Well, you should have seen the house once those fossils were through with it. Everything was off-white, and anything the least bit architectural had been stripped from the place. All the friezes, all the crown molding, even a Tiffany stained-glass window."

"Excuse me. Did you say the St. Ophelia Society?"

"I did. Thank heavens the new owners—"

"The same organization that holds its annual ball in the basement of the Daughters of Fine Lineage building?"

"The same. Abby, do you want to hear about the Blazer House or not?"

"Not."

"I beg your pardon?"

"I mean I do want to hear about it—just not

right now. You've got me really interested in the St. Ophelia Society. Are you a member of that illustrious group?"

Of course I knew she wasn't. No member would speak disparagingly of it. At least not to an outsider. But the best way to get Catherine to tell me everything she knew about the geriatric gentry was to provoke her on the subject.

"Illustrious my ass. Do you know how many pints of blood it takes to give one of those old fogies a complete transfusion?"

"No."

"Guess."

"Five?"

"None! They run on antifreeze. Or embalming fluid. Take your pick. My family's been in Charleston as long as any of theirs, but just because mine got off on the other side of the ship, I'm not good enough to join."

"I'm afraid I don't understand. If your ancestors got off on the other side of the ship, wouldn't that put them in the water? Ah, I get it now! They were stowaways."

Stay away from botulinum injections if you intend to scowl. Catherine's attempt was downright pitiful.

"Stowaways? I should say not! My people were honest-to-goodness indentured servants. The salt of the earth."

I nodded vigorously to show my support of the working classes. "I take it then that you're not a member of the St. Necrophilia Society."

"Ha! Good one, Abby. Even if I could, I wouldn't join that bunch—not if you paid me a million dollars. And you know what, they're going to have to start paying folks to join, the way they're going. From what I hear, young people these days are far more egalitarian than their parents. Sure, you've got the straight arrow, Junior League types, but they're not into classism, either. Mark my words, those stuffy old society dames are teetering on their last legs."

"That's not what I heard. They apparently have a waiting list a mile long. It's basically a case of waiting for someone to die. That's why the membership is so old, you see. By the time a vacancy opens, the folks on the waiting list have gotten up in years. In that regards, it's somewhat like the English royal family. Prince Charles will probably be long in tooth by the time he gets his turn to reign."

She snorted, a response that doesn't require any facial muscles. "We obviously have different sources. But you should trust me, Abby. Like I said, my family's been here for generations. I know how things work in this city."

I swallowed back my irritation. It was a lot tastier than Bob's soufflé.

"Catherine, how do you think the membership would respond if someone tried to crash one of their functions—incognito, of course?"

"Why I suppose they would be furious. Inbreeding produces short tempers."

"Would they physically harm the intruder?"

"Hmm—I don't think so. For starters, they wouldn't be capable of such a thing. Besides, that's not their style anyway. Their style would be to socially blackball the offender."

"But what if the offender was 'from off'?"

"Like you?" I swear she said that just to be mean.

"Everyone who is anyone goes to church or synagogue, Abby. Not to mention charity events, concerts, and the like. There are plenty of opportunities to snub someone who has broken the rules."

Despite her dearth of working muscles, it was clear to me that Catherine Deephouse had not been shaken by my line of questioning. But I hadn't come to Deephouse Designs to talk about genealogy, or historical houses—although her comments about the St. Ophelia Society were certainly interesting.

"Catherine, darling," I said, "did you know there is another woman in Charleston who looks just like you?"

I was both pleased and surprised that she was able to blink. "I beg your pardon?"

"Just minutes ago I saw her running down King Street. Of course she had to be a tourist, so she won't be here long. But how cool is that? Can you imagine if the two of you were to meet? I mean, you look exactly like each other. In fact, I thought it was you at first."

"Why, that's just silly," she said, glancing down at the canyon between her bosoms. "I doubt if there's anyone else who looks *just* like me."

"Maybe you're right. The woman I saw was built like a brick outhouse."

"Abby," she gasped, "there is no need to be rude. I have a mighty fine figure, if I do say so myself."

"Oh you do! But this woman was sensational. Very classy as well."

Catherine leaped to her feet. "I'll have you know, Abby, that this classy woman you claim to have seen *is* me."

"No way!"

She glanced at her assistant, who was in the far corner sorting carpet samples. "I had some business on King Street, but I didn't want anyone there to think I had to rely on an antiques dealer for help, so when I was through, I made a dash for it. That's why you thought I was a tourist."

That didn't explain the limo. Or the kiss.

"What sort of help did you need from an antiques dealer, Catherine?"

"That was business—my business. Not yours."

"Yes, but I would have been glad to help. Besides, you do business with our shops on King Street all the time."

The best defense is a good offense, and Catherine Deephouse had no qualms about being offensive. "You seem to be gone from your shop a good deal, Abby. If you were more attractive, one might think you were having an affair."

"What I do with my time is *my* business."

"Touché."

"And at least one man finds me very attractive."

"Yes, you are married."

"Only to the most handsome man in all of Charleston County." I gave her an "I gotcha" face. "Well then, I better be going. Nice visiting, Catherine. Oh, and about the birdcage—is your client still interested?"

You could have knocked Catherine over with one of Monet's feathers. "You've changed your mind?"

"Possibly. I mean, I'm giving it some thought."

"You're still asking fifteen, right?"

"I wasn't asking anything; it was you offering. And I believe the sum was sixteen five."

"Abby, you know that's a small fortune."

"Yes, but the Taj Mahal is undoubtedly the most exquisite birdcage in the entire world. It's a real collector's item."

"Hmm. You'll let me know when you decide for sure, right?"

I promised that I would. Then, just to be polite, I nodded at her assistant before leaving. But I hadn't taken three steps outside before someone grabbed my elbow. Thinking it might be a purse snatcher, I whirled around defiantly. It really wasn't my fault that my head met with Catherine's sternum.

"Oo-gah!" she grunted. "What the heck was that for?"

"I didn't know it was you."

"Abby, we need to talk."

"We just did."

"No, I mean *talk* talk."

The last *talk* talk I had was when Mama, bless her heart, tried to explain the birds and bees to me in the seventh grade. This chat was necessitated by my best friend, Tina, having to leave a sock hop early when a red stain mysteriously appeared on her white pedal pushers. Unable to face facts about the facts of life, Mama whispered behind closed doors that from now on Tina would have a monthly visitor, and that if I was lucky, I would, too. Then she served me sugar cookies and lemonade. That was it; not one bird, nor one bee.

"I've already had the talk," I said to Catherine.

"Abby, I'm serious. This means everything to me."

I sighed. "Okay. You want to make a lunch date?"

"Now, Abby."

I can't explain why I agreed to get into Catherine's car. She said it was the only way we could be sure of privacy. But if that was the reason, we could have had our talk in her Cadillac, in her parking place behind her shop. Instead, she insisted we drive across the Ashley and all the way down to Folly Beach Pier. On the way there we discussed vitally important issues like: do those egg-peeling gizmos advertised on TV really work (they don't for either of us), whom is one really kidding by plastic surgery (Catherine claimed she'd never had any, but her scars were plainly visible), and what were Captain and Tenille thinking when they recorded "Muskrat Love" (they either weren't thinking, or had yet to see one of those hideous water rats).

At any rate, Folly Beach Edwin S. Taylor Fishing Pier, as it is officially called, extends over a thousand feet into the Atlantic. One gets the impression that if the pier was just double in length, it would be possible to walk all the way to Africa. A look back at the shoreline certainly offers one of the most impressive views in the country.

And while it is a great place to fish, it is also a popular spot to people-watch. Although tame by West Coast standards, the waves here are among the highest in the state, and it is a common sight to see surfers trying their luck on colorful boards. Even more common are the tourists, many of un-sinkable proportions, who need only roll out of their hotel beds and onto the beach. One sees them even in the winter, when the locals are huddled around their fireplaces. In the summer, when the water temperature is eighty-five degrees, it gets harder to tell the natives from the visitors.

There are fishing stations at regular intervals along the pier, but Catherine insisted that we plod all the way out to the end and sit under the gazebo. At regular intervals she glanced furtively over her shoulders, as if we might have been followed by the FBI. For the first time, I was grateful for all the tourists. If not for them, I was beginning to fear, Catherine might do me in, and toss my life-less body into the sea. While I have always wanted to go to Africa, floating was never my conveyance of choice.

"Okay, Catherine," I said after we'd taken seats at a picnic table, "we're closer to Casablanca than we are to Charleston. Tell me your big secret."

CHAPTER 19

"I'm in love."

"*What?* You dragged me out to the edge of the earth to tell me that?"

"I'm in love with a man who is not my husband."

"Oh. The limo, yes?"

"I knew you saw me. I thought I could get away with not acknowledging you, but I could see that when you left my shop you thought I was hiding something. Well, Abby, everyone knows that once you sink your teeth into something, you're like a rat terrier that never lets go."

"Please don't use the word 'rat.'"

"You know what I mean. You weren't going to stop until I told you everything. Yes, I wanted to buy that splendid birdcage for Nelson, because he really seemed to like it, and yes, that was him you saw at the IHOP, and of course you saw his limo. But you see, Abby, I still love my husband. I can't explain it—loving two men. They're very different, so I guess they fill different needs. I thought I was being discreet by meeting him for lunch at the pancake house in Mount Pleasant—it never occurred to me that somebody I know would actually eat at one of those places."

"I love pancakes and I love IHOP. What's wrong with that?"

Catherine shuddered. "Well, it's so—gauche. So middle class. People eat in flip-flops and shorts."

"Forgive me, but how many home decorators are upper class?"

"Abby, you're being rude again."

"Sorry. Catherine, were you really willing to pay over sixteen thousand dollars for a birdcage?"

"What does one get for a man who has everything? And it's not like Willard—my husband—would miss the money. This would have come from money my mother left me to do whatever I please with. It's in a money market account with my name only on it. Willard never asks about it."

"Is your lover married?"

"Yes—but his wife is a witch."

"I'm sure they all say that. So tell me, how would he explain such a gargantuan birdcage to his wife?"

"He's getting us an apartment. A love nest where we can be together and not worry about being seen."

"Catherine, tell me, if your paramour is so wealthy, why didn't he buy the birdcage himself?"

"As you recall, Abby, it was a dealers-only auction. I sneaked Nelson in. And although he really liked the piece, it wasn't like he was egging me on to bid. That's why it would make such a good gift. I mean, how many times have you admired an outfit that you wouldn't buy for yourself, but if your husband did, you'd be happy as a bag of peaches?"

"What?"

"Nothing—just something my daddy used to say."

I don't know what possessed me to do so, but I leaned across the table and gently peeled the sunglasses from her face. "Is that really why you want the Taj Mahal?" I asked, staring into her eyes.

"Yes, of course," she said without blinking. "Why would I lie about that? I already told you the secret part."

"Okay, I believe you." I did, in fact.

"You won't say anything to Willard?"

"I don't know Willard that well, and besides, it really isn't any of my business."

"But you will sell me the birdcage—if you decide to sell it, that is?"

"Like I said, it isn't any of my business. In other words, I want nothing to do with your love triangle. That includes helping to feather your nest."

She snatched her glasses out of my hand. "Why I never! This is the last time I'm confiding in you, Abby."

I didn't know what to say. It wasn't like we were even friends, much less bosom buddies who shared confidences. I just happened to be the business acquaintance, who just happened to walk outside some friend's shop at the wrong time. The best thing, I felt, was to say nothing.

Catherine was not okay with that. "You should at least say you're sorry," she told me on the way back from the island.

"Sorry for what?"

"You know."

"No, I don't."

"If you apologize, I'll tell you what you really want to know."

"I'm not interested in the sordid details of your love affair, Catherine."

My tone was gentle, and my spoken words far kinder than the thoughts that were swirling about in my head. Nonetheless, Catherine slammed on the brakes and jerked the car over onto the shoulder of the road, practically landing us in the marsh. The driver of a pickup, which was towing a boat behind us, leaned on the horn while shouting colorful obscenities. I'm sure I said a few impolite things myself.

"Abigail Washburn," Catherine shouted over the din of two pounding hearts, "don't you dare take that high tone with me. I know that you're a divorced woman. I'm sure there are a few skeletons in your closet I could drag out."

"Drag away, darling. Yes, a love affair—make that multiple love affairs—contributed to the breakup of my marriage. The thing is, I wasn't the one cheating."

Unable to glare at me, she snorted a couple of times and pounded the steering wheel. "Fine!" she said. "Condemn me for having an affair. Well, it isn't my fault, Abby. I just fell in love. One can't help that."

Again I chose silence. One doesn't just fall in love, like they fall off the edge of the Grand Canyon because they couldn't see it coming. There are always signals of some kind, and we either choose to back away or continue on a life-altering course. Not that my views on the subject mattered. I hadn't gotten up that morning, leaving behind the comfort of the Rob-Bobs' one-thousand-thread-count sheets, intending to preach to anyone. All I wanted to do was to find Mama.

"Very well," Catherine said, and jerked her car back on the road. "Even if you won't apologize, I'll still tell you what you really want to know."

"I'd appreciate that."

"It's the dry cleaner who stole that bird of yours."

I stomped on an imaginary brake. "Bubba Johnson?"

"I guess that's his name. I've seen his ads on TV, but he just calls himself Bubba. Anyway, he was there that day at the auction, bidding against me. And you, of course. Then a couple of days ago I saw him walking down Broad Street—right in front of my shop—and he was carrying this thing with a towel draped over it. It was kind of breezy that day and he was having trouble keeping the towel on. So then he stopped—right outside my door—and took the towel off, and rearranged it. I could see then that it was a birdcage he was carrying, and that there was a bird inside. Abby,

I swear, it was the same bird that came with the Taj Mahal."

"What makes you think I'm all that interested in this?"

"Isn't that why you came around the other day and started up a conversation about the cage? You were really interested in who stole your bird, weren't you?"

"Jig's up," I said. "You got me."

We made small talk all the way back into town. Against my wishes, and despite my complaints, I learned that Catherine's lover, Nelson, was a real estate developer, which of course explained his great wealth; there is oodles of money to be made by raping the South Carolina coast. It's been several thousand years since God stopped creating new coastline, but there has been no shortage of new humans, many of whom desire to live near the ocean. As a consequence, development, especially along the salt marshes, is spreading like an insidious cancer, eating up the very vistas that made the Lowcountry a popular place to live. And Nelson, apparently, had a gift for getting his projects past the zoning boards.

But raping coastlines is hard work, so much so that poor Nelson hadn't found the time to develop a permanent relationship—not since the collapse of his third marriage, at any rate. That's why Catherine was such a godsend—that, and the fact that she could decorate all his spec houses. So you see, theirs was a pseudomarriage made in heaven.

Just as long as Willard didn't find out—which was all up to me. Go figure.

"You promise you won't tell him," Catherine said for the umpteenth time.

I'd asked her to let me out on the corner of Broad and East Bay. This is the defining line of historic Charleston, and this junction is always overrun by tourists.

"Promises are made to be broken," I said, and ducked into the crowd.

I know it was cruel of me to leave Catherine swinging like that, but she hadn't been paying attention, now had she? Feeling not in the least guilty about my glib answer, I decided to enjoy the walk to my next destination. Along the way I got caught up in a throng of tourists who were far too happy for that hour of the day. It soon became clear that they were from Minnesota, which explained their ebullient mood. With only three frost-free months a year at their disposal, they knew that they needed to make hay while the sun shone.

The good folks from Duluth either didn't care or didn't notice that I was along for the walk. I wisely kept my mouth shut, my vowels safely crammed down my throat. I wouldn't have known what to say anyway. My temporary friends were all doctors, and were discussing a medical case. You would have thought they were speaking Latin.

They were headed for the Battery, which was

perfect for me. I stayed with them until we approached Stolls Alley and the mansion owned by Bubba Johnson, bird collector extraordinaire. My plan was to gradually lag behind them and then stealthily cross the street and then—well, I really didn't have a "then."

Needless to say, I couldn't believe my luck when I saw a taxicab waiting in front of the mansion. My luck got even better when I observed Bubba Johnson's white maid come out the front door, lock it behind her, and literally skip down the walk to the waiting cab.

This meant there was no one home! At least not Bubba Johnson. There was no way the white maid would feel free to use the front door if he were around. Besides, if he was at home, she wouldn't have to lock it behind her. Okay, maybe she would have needed to lock it, if he was too lazy to do it or felt it was beneath him. But in any case, she wouldn't feel free to frolic down the sidewalk like an eight-year-old girl. I had a hunch, given the maid's demeanor, that she was on her way to a tryst. No woman is that happy to go grocery shopping, and since it wasn't yet noon, it couldn't already be quitting time. And if she was stealing a few minutes to be with a lover, she sure as shooting wouldn't have taken the time to set the alarm—although the odds are she didn't even know it. Even though my cleaning lady is bonded, I certainly wouldn't give her my security code.

Therefore it was with a pounding heart—but

sturdy knees—that I walked around to the back of the house and rang the bell. I rang it a couple of times, and waited a full two minutes before concluding for sure that no one was home. Most folks don't wait long enough, you know. (There is nothing worse than hearing a bell, pulling one's panties up to one's knees, waddling to the door, and peeking through the blinds, only to see the mailman walking blithely off with one's return-receipt-requested package.)

When, after this decent interval, nobody answered, I tried the door. It was locked. Then I went to collect the key from its obvious hiding place. Bingo! No, it was not under the mat; it was under a fake stone next to the fountain depicting Leda being raped by the swan. To celebrate my brilliant piece of detective work, I skipped from the fountain to the house. If the maid could do it, so could I.

Yes, I know that breaking into and entering someone's house is not only wrong, it's illegal. But I was merely entering. Besides, it's not like it was the house of a total stranger. Most importantly, let's not forget that this was for a good cause.

The door opened easily, and just as I'd guessed, the alarm had not been set. The table, however, was still covered with breakfast things. A leftover piece of cinnamon toast—completely untouched—beckoned from a fine porcelain platter. I quickly polled me, myself, and I. We unanimously agreed that the toast would only go to waste if not added to our waist, so we did the thoughtful thing and licked the plate clean.

Feeling fortified by the riboflavin, I set my purse carefully down on a clean spot, put an only slightly used starched napkin over my nose, reclaimed my purse, and headed straight for the dining room door. This time the stench was ameliorated somewhat by the cloth, but my eyes stung just as much as they did the first time they beheld Bubba Johnson's strange hobby.

Nevertheless, it was fascinating to walk leisurely between the rows of stacked cages. There were birds of all feathers surely, and just as surely they were flocked together. One section was devoted solely to canaries. Who knew there were so many different breeds? German Roller, American Singer, Waterslager, Norwich, Red Mosaic—that's just a fraction of what I saw. Next were the noncanary finches—there must have been a hundred different types of those. There were fewer parakeets—at least fewer of the little budgies that sit on one's finger— but there were plenty of their larger cousins, and when it came to parrots proper, what had once been a drawing room was filled from floor to ceiling with talking, whistling, and shrieking birds of the family *Psittacidae*.

In the downstairs powder room (the toilet wouldn't flush) I found a dozen different kinds of mynahs. That's what the plaques said at any rate. Frankly, they all looked alike to me, and not one looked exactly like Monet. What I mean is, my missing mynah had a certain *je ne sais quoi* that these bundles of feathers lacked.

But I hadn't gained entry into the mansion in order to bird-watch. My primary mission was to find Mama, or at least some clue that led to her whereabouts. I searched all the downstairs rooms, finding only more birds, or bird paraphernalia, such as seed, gravel, and stacks of newspaper to line their cages. One room, probably intended as a library, was filled with empty, and gleaming, birdcages, arranged on display. There were wooden cages that ranged from simple bamboo to elaborately carved hardwood structures—one appeared to be ebony with ivory inlay. Then there were metal cages ranging from cast iron to gold plate, and even one solid gold cage—albeit no more than three inches high, but studded with gemstones. Each cage was displayed alone on a pedestal or shelf, with a brass plate that told where and when the cage was purchased, and in some cases, the manufacturer. But none of the cages, no matter how exquisite, surpassed the Taj Mahal in beauty. It was immediately apparent why Bubba Johnson coveted this masterpiece. Of course Mama wasn't in any of these cages, and I didn't have time to tarry. Still, it was hard to tear myself away from the museum to avian imprisonment.

The runner on the broad staircase that led to the second floor was silk needlepoint and featured green acanthus leaves on a beige background. It was the only ornamentation I saw that wasn't bird related. I followed the pleasant anomaly up the stairs with a mounting sense of excitement and danger. Experience has taught me that escaping from upstairs windows can be a mite challenging.

If, after all, Bubba Johnson was in the house, he surely could not have heard me. I work hard to keep my weight down, so as a consequence, I am light enough to walk on figments of my imagination. And anyway, the racket produced by the feathered crowd was loud enough to drown out a gathering of Hell's Angels.

There were just as many birds upstairs as there were downstairs, perhaps even more, given that there wasn't space set aside for a cage museum— which is not to say the upstairs lacked a museum. The first room I came to was filled with birds; not in cages, but sitting on perches, pecking at walls, even flying through the air. It took a few seconds for it to register with my bird brain that not one of the creatures was moving, even the soaring swallows over my head. These were real birds, all right, but stuffed. The ones that appeared to be airborne were suspended by fine wires. They represented many sizes and species, but the one thing they all had in common were beady black eyes.

"Holy guacamole," I said, and backed from the room.

Why is it that every time I search for something, I find it in the last place I look? Alas, I didn't find

Mama. What I found in the last bedroom I searched was, of course, more birds, but there was also a cot and a small desk piled with papers. Parked neatly in front of the modest bed was a pair of Tweety Bird slippers.

While one might say that I rifled through the papers, I much prefer the word "sorted." I also sorted through the contents of the desk. What I found was the normal stuff of everyday living: bills, insurance papers, medical files—nothing related to his dry cleaning stores that I could see. No doubt Bubba Johnson had an office outside the home.

It is darn hard to find something when you don't know what you're looking for. If you keep at it too long, you're bound to find trouble. When I was done with Bubba's desk, I did only a cursory search of the two massive armoires that served as his closet. Neither held anything out of the ordinary for a middle-aged businessman—if you discount a red feather boa, which I did. In the absence of a pair of matching heels, size twelve, it was reasonable to assume that the boa was part of his avian collection.

Now it was time to skedaddle. The way I saw it, I had just as much chance of being caught sneaking out the rear as I did making a grand exit out the front door. Probably even more. So holding my head as high as it could go, I tugged the towering bronze door shut behind me and sashayed down the walk, from the steps to the street, like I was Mrs. Bubba Johnson, mistress of the manor.

"She doesn't look rich to me," I heard a New York woman say, in that pleasantly nasal tone that is that city's trademark.

"Maybe she's the maid," her male companion said.

I turned right on East Bay and picked up speed.

"Don't waste film on her," the woman said.

"It's the digital camera," the man said. "There's unlimited room."

"Then hurry."

And that's exactly what *I* did. I broke into a trot and didn't stop until I reached one of my favorite places in all of Charleston.

Waterfront Park is arguably the loveliest urban park in the nation, situated as it is along the harbor, and just yards from the spot where the Atlantic Ocean is born. The most famous landmark within the park is Pineapple Fountain (the very same fountain to which I'd been instructed to bring a mythical Monet). Oddly enough, the fountain is shaped like a prickly Hawaiian fruit. Another fine example of garden architecture is the gravel walk, which was the brainchild of our mayor, who collected gravel samples from around the country to find just the right grade.

A massive container ship was inching its way out of the harbor, and I sat on a bench to watch it pass. Big ships stir my blood, causing me to think of travel to exotic ports of call. One of my dreams is to shop for antiques in the Far East and ship them back to the States for resale. So far I haven't had the courage to undertake something that grand.

But dreams are the foundation of action, and I was well on my way to building my castle in the sky when something landed at my feet. For a split second I thought that a squirrel had fallen from a live oak branch overhead. When I looked down, I saw a manila envelope, a padded one, similar to the envelope that Mama's crinoline had arrived in. Yet when I glanced around, there wasn't anyone within ten feet of me. There was, however, a smattering of sweltering tourists strolling in both directions.

Perhaps it was stupid of me, but I picked up the package and held it aloft. "Did anyone drop this?" I called.

A few people turned. No one responded.

"Someone dropped a package," I shouted through cupped hands.

"Could be a bomb," a tall woman with a mop of blond curls muttered. She strode swiftly away. Thank heavens the rest of the tourists paid no attention to her.

I examined the package. It had *my* name written on it—in small block letters, written with a felt-tip pen. In fact, the letters were so tiny they ran together. But there was no mistaking that it read Abigail Washburn.

How could this be? I looked up. There was no one in the tree. I didn't for a second believe it had fallen from Heaven because, as everyone knows, that celestial city is directly above Australia. Besides, God has better penmanship than that—at least I assume She does.

I shook the package and heard a faint clink. Could I have lost some keys that were being returned? That would certainly explain how Monet's birdnapper had gained entrance to my shop. The only problem with this explanation was—I hadn't lost any keys!

Well, there was only one way to find out. With trembling fingers I ripped open the flap and peered inside. If I sat staring stupidly at the contents of the envelope, it was because I couldn't believe my eyes.

CHAPTER 20

Could those possibly be Mama's pearls? Mama *never* took them off, not even when she showered. They were the last gift Daddy gave her, and in her mind, to remove the pearls would be to fully acknowledge that Daddy was dead and it was time to move on with her life. To take the pearls off would mean it was time to leave behind the world of crinolines, full-circle skirts, and pinched waists, of *Donna Reed* and *Father Knows Best,* of cars with fins, Bryl Creem, drive-in movies, and families holding hands as they walked to church—in short, the way the world was the day Daddy died.

A gemologist who attends Mama's church once remarked to Mama that her pearls were the finest he'd ever seen. He asked her if he could have the pleasure of examining them. Mama said he could, but on the condition that the pearls remained around her neck. When he was through—the examination took place in the church kitchen—a very skeptical gemologist said that there was no way these pearls could look like that and be as old as Mama claimed. Mama didn't mind being called a liar, because she knew the truth. Except for a small nick on one pearl—thanks to my teething brother Toy—the gems were every bit as pearlescent as the day they were plucked from the sea.

I sifted the string of pearls slowly through my fingers, dreading what I might find. Sure enough, the third pearl from the center bore the telltale scar of my baby brother's tooth. With tears blurring my vision, I scanned the clumps of tourists in vain for anyone looking suspicious—well, there was one.

Out of perhaps fifty people, only one of them was dressed modestly, in a manner befitting a visit to one of the nation's most historic cities. This woman's outfit came to well below the knees, and her upper arms were covered, surely a blessing when the subject is over fifty. There was one caveat, however. The lady in question was a nun! I couldn't very well run after a nun to ask her if she'd lobbed a package into my lap. Could I?

You bet your best coon dog I could. Gripping the pearls tightly in one hand, my purse in the other, I raced after the nun like Mama's life depended on it. Just as I reached grabbing distance, I tripped on a root that extended into the gravel walk and went flying. I flew right into the nun, knocking her down. I ended up on top of her, which, I'm sure, looked to the rest of the tourists as if I'd tackled the poor woman.

I scrambled to my feet, perfectly unharmed. "I'm so sorry," I said.

The nun took longer to get up. There was the imprint of gravel on her bare shins and on the palms of her hands. Her wimple was askew and there was a look of utter terror in her eyes.

"*Que?*"

"I said 'I'm sorry.'"

"*No hablo ingles.*"

"Oh my, you don't speak English, do you?"

Despite what sounded like loud protests in Spanish, I tried to help the woman up.

But the protests grew louder, and the next thing I knew, I went sprawling again. This time the nun dodged me, and I skimmed along the surface of the gravel walk like a water ski, sending up a spray of small pebbles. I came to a gradual stop, miraculously unhurt, only to be pummeled by a thousand fists. The louder I yelled and squirmed, the harder and more frequent the blows. Finally able to twist around, I beheld five hundred angry women, each of them swinging a monstrous black purse just as easily as if it were a bag of marshmallows.

"Bully!" one of my attackers screamed.

"Pick on someone your own size!" another shouted.

"And they call this the Holy City," a third voice muttered. That comment hurt me most of all.

"So Abby," Bob said, returning with my drink, how many women were there exactly?" My drink, by the way, was a diet cola, and we were sitting in a booth of the Subway restaurant on East Bay, not far from the scene of my crime. After managing to escape from the nun's benefactors, I'd called my friends on my cell phone. They'd been incredulous at first, then nearly busted their guts laughing, but had now settled into their serious, nit-picking stage.

"There were five hundred," I said—okay, maybe minus the hundred, but they came out of nowhere. Besides, it was none of their business.

"Good for them," Rob said.

"Excuse me?"

"Hmm, let's see. A nun gets assaulted in broad daylight, in a heavily trafficked area, and no one comes to her aid—what would that say about us as a society?"

"But I wasn't assaulting her!"

"You're lucky you didn't end up in jail, Abby."

I was still clutching Mama's pearls in my left hand, which I now waved. "I thought she might have been the courier. Obviously I was wrong."

"What makes you say that?" Bob asked.

"Well, because—she, uh—didn't even speak English."

"How do you know?"

"Because she said that she didn't."

"I'm the Prime Minister of Canada," Bob said. "Do you believe that?"

"Of course not."

"Then who is?"

"I don't know," I wailed in exasperation. Sadly, I'm not alone in my ignorance.

"My point is, Abby, that saying so doesn't make it so. That nun could have been a drama student from the College of Charleston."

"Ditto for those five hundred women," Rob said.

I flashed him my tongue. "What do I do now? Go to the police with these? You know what they'll say. I don't have proof, but they'll write it up, yada yada yada."

Rob slipped into my side of the booth and started rubbing my neck. "Where's Greg?"

"Still dealing with his best friend's marital crisis. But he should be home at any time. Do you think I should call him?"

"And tell him what? That an angel dropped Mozella's pearls in your lap, which caused you to go berserk and tackle a nun?"

"Wait until he gets home," Bob said. "It will be easier telling him face-to-face."

I took a deep breath. "I suppose while I'm at it I should tell him I broke into Bubba Johnson's house and searched every room, including his armoires."

"Abby, you didn't," my friends cried in unison.

"I'm afraid I did. But it wasn't really breaking and entering, because nothing got broken. I used a key—good golly, Miss Molly! I still have the key!" I dug in my pocketbook and removed the evidence. "What do I do now?"

Rob grinned. "Let me guess. Under the mat, right?"

"Fake rock by the fountain. Come on, guys, what should I do?"

"Toss it into the harbor," Bob said.

Rob and I stared at him. Bob Steuben, the good Catholic boy from Toledo, breaks eggs, not rules. Perhaps my life of crime was rubbing off on him.

"Well, I was only an eighth grader," he said quickly. "They were my uncle's car keys, which I sort of borrowed, so that I could sort of borrow his car. Afterward I got to thinking that if he were to have them checked for prints, I could end up in big trouble, so I tossed his key ring into Lake Erie. It had all his keys on it, even his mailbox key."

"And why would he check his keys for prints? Rob asked, before I could spit the words out.

"Uncle Bob was a weird bird; you never knew what he would do. And like I said, I was just a kid. I had a right to be paranoid."

Rob winked knowingly at me. "Yup, I guess you did. But Abby, he's right about the keys. Putting them in a fake rock is just a break-in waiting to happen. If he ever finds out they're missing, maybe he'll wise up. But enough of that, what did you see in the mansion?"

"Birds."

"Besides birds."

"Just birds, I'm telling you. Maybe thousands of them. Even a collection of dead birds. It was really creepy."

"But what about furniture? Anything interesting?"

"No antiques, Rob—in fact, no furniture except for the kitchen and one bedroom."

"Wow," Bob said, "and that's a huge house. Maybe six thousand feet or more. Abby, this has got to be your guy."

"Somehow I don't think so. Bubba also has a birdcage collection. Some of them are fabulous. I think he had a legitimate reason for wanting the Taj. Whoever it is that has Monet—and Mama—obviously wants something more."

Rob patted my back. "Darling, you look like you could stand to eat something. Tell me what you want. Your wish is my command—but I recommend their wraps."

Bob reared back in his seat like he'd been slapped. "We are not going to lunch in a fast food restaurant."

"Maybe you're not, but I am. How about you, Abby?"

"No thanks, I'm really not hungry. But you go ahead."

Rob hopped to his feet. He has the metabolism of a teenager—when not faced with Bob's cooking. I could sense that Bob was both hurt and angry. But if he was hoping for an apology from me, he was out of luck. Rob put up with more of his partner's culinary nonsense than I ever could. The poor man had a right to eat what he wanted every now and then.

"I know what you're thinking," Bob suddenly boomed, almost causing me to spill my cola.

"I'm sorry, Bob—except that I'm not sorry—oh heck, I'm not sure what to say."

He grabbed my hand, the one holding the pearls. "It's all right, Abby. I know that I can be overbearing when it comes to food. There's no need to apologize—" I felt him tug gently on the pearls. "Hey, do you mind if I look at these for a minute?"

Actually, I did mind. If they couldn't be around Mama's neck, then they should be in contact with me, since I was her flesh and blood. It seemed almost sacrilegious to wear them around my neck, but I couldn't very well just carry them around in my hand, could I? Then again, I didn't want to be weird about it, either.

"Just for a minute," I said, handing them over like I was passing my firstborn to a clumsy baby-sitter.

Bob took the gems solemnly and began to slip them through his fingers as if they were worry beads. Then he frowned.

"What is it, Bob?"

"Just a second." Then, before I could utter a single word of protest, he brought the pearls up to his mouth and began to rub them against his teeth.

"Bob!" I shrieked.

Besides Rob, there were three customers and

two employees in the Subway shop. All of them stopped what they were doing to stare at me.

"They aren't real," Bob said calmly.

"What?"

"They're fakes, Abby."

I snatched back Mama's pearls and patted them gently against my blouse. "Papa loved Mama with all his heart. He never would have given her simulated pearls and then lied about it."

"I'm sure your papa didn't. I'm saying that these aren't your mama's pearls. Abby, you know as well as I do that the first test for authenticity is to rub them against your teeth. Fakes will feel smooth, but the real McCoy will feel gritty."

"But what about this nick? Mama's pearls have one in this exact spot."

"Look closely, Abby. That's a fresh nick."

"But that doesn't make a lick of sense."

"What doesn't?" Rob asked. He had two wrap sandwiches, one of which he set down in front of me. Bob looked fit to be tied.

"Bob said these pearls are fake," I said, "even though they have a nick right there. See? Why would someone send me fakes when they have Mama, who has the real thing?"

"Maybe they don't have Mozella, darling."

"Come again?"

Rob slid back in next to me. "Let's review the facts: first your bird goes missing, then Mozella, then you get her petticoats, and now this. When was the last time you got one of those bizarre calls from the bird? Before, or after, you got the petticoats?"

"They're crinolines, dear. But now that you mention it, the last time I got one of those calls was before that package arrived at the shop."

"And where was it, Abby? I mean, exactly."

"In the alley, leaning against the door."

"Don't you think it's a little odd that whoever—let's call it a guy for now—left the package outside, when he presumably has a key?"

"Yes, but—oh man, I'm so confused."

Rob began patting me on the back like I was choking, which I was, in a way; I was mentally choking on my thoughts. But just as the Heimlich maneuver, not patting, is the preferred way to alleviate choking on food, there must be some other way to clear our thought conduits.

"Please," I begged. "That hurts."

"Sorry, Abby, I was just trying to be pastoral."

"Rob wanted to be a rabbi when he was growing up," Bob said.

I looked at my handsome friend. "Is he kidding?"

"No. But it was a short-lived phase, right between cowboy and Davy Crockett."

My cell phone rang. Normally I turn it off when I'm in restaurants, and I absolutely always do when at the movies or in church, but we were originally only stopping by Subway for something cold to drink.

"It's blocked," I said.

"Answer it anyway," Bob said. "I've got a feeling

it's important." Apparently, before the days of caller ID, Bob had a reputation of being able to guess who was calling. But this supposed psychic ability of his did not apply to anything except telephones.

"Hello," I said.

"Abby?"

"Who's calling, please?"

"Pretty dish."

"Excuse me?"

"Four and twenty King."

My heart pounded. "Please—whoever you are—please don't hurt my mother. I'll give you whatever it is you want—" I got a dial tone.

"What did they say?" my friends demanded in unison.

My hand was shaking so bad I dropped my cell phone, which then skidded across the table and landed in Bob's lap. I waited until he handed it back before answering.

"It was definitely Monet again. He said 'pretty dish,' and then gave me an address on King Street. Whose shop is at 24 King?"

"Well, there's only one way to find out: let's hop in my car and take it for a spin. I'm parked in the Vendue Range garage, by the way."

"Wait a minute," Bob said. He was rubbing his temples with his index fingers. It's a habit he engages in sometimes when deep in thought, although both Rob and I think it might be contributing to his increased hair loss. "That's not an address, that's from a nursery rhyme."

"And I'm Little Bo Peep," Rob said.

Bob was clearly not amused. "I'm not joking. Who says 'four and twenty' these days, except maybe for mad dogs and Englishmen?"

Rob and I both shrugged.

"This better be good," Rob said.

"Shut up and listen," Bob said.

CHAPTER 21

"Sing a song of sixpence, pockets full of rye,
Four and twenty blackbirds baked into a pie.
When the pie was opened the birds began to
sing,
Now wasn't that a pretty dish to set before the
king."

"Bob may be on to something," Rob said.
"Yes, but—"
"Abby, tell us again what was in the other messages."

I did my best to relay the information.

Rob shook his head. "Sorry, Abby, I jumped the gun. I don't see a connection."

Bob glared at his partner. I've never seen him that angry, except once when his culinary skills were challenged.

"That doesn't mean there isn't one."

"Guys," I said, "maybe you're both right. Maybe this time it was a nursery rhyme, and it was just meant to confuse us."

Neither of them responded, which was fine with

261

me. But as they sat there sulking, a devious plan bored its way through my thick skull. As much as I appreciated the Rob-Bobs' support, they put a crimp in my style. If I wanted the freedom to do what I pleased until Greg got back, I needed to lose them.

I extracted the pearls gently from Bob's hand and put them on. "Okay," I said, drawing from my fast-depleting reservoir of false cheer, "I'm off to the ladies' room. When I return, I expect you to kiss and make up—well, maybe Charleston's not quite ready for that. But you know what I mean."

Still no response.

"Rob, darling, you're going to have to let me out."

"Sorry, Abby," he muttered, and the second I slipped around him, he threw himself back on the bench.

"Give it up y'all, it's not important who's right—"

If their eyes had been lasers, I would now look like a four-foot-nine-inch chunk of Swiss cheese. But I know from my own life that public outbursts of emotion are usually just the tip of the iceberg. If I had to wager a bet then and there, I would put my money on a chip that read: *Rob is always right and refuses to lose an argument.* Whatever their reasons for this quarrel, they needed their space.

Without further comment, I grabbed my handbag and headed toward the back of the shop where, from experience, I knew there was a ladies' room. I also knew that there was an exit door in the back, and all I had to do was wait until more customers showed up, at which point I could easily sneak out the back unseen.

And that's exactly what I did.

It wouldn't surprise me to learn that Charleston has more jewelry stores than it has churches. True, a lot of these stores carry souvenir type merchandise, such as charms and earrings shaped like palmetto trees, but there are a lot of high-end stores as well. Studs for Studs limits its merchandise to "earrings for today's discerning gentleman," but right next to it is a tiny gem of a shop called Diamonds and Pearls, which is owned by a tiny woman named Sultana Habib. Her clientele, mostly word-of-mouth customers, have to reach deep into their ostrich skin handbags, purchased on their most recent visits to the swank shops of Sandton City near Johannesburg, South Africa. Diamonds and pearls are all that Sultana sells, and truly, if you have to ask the price, the odds are you can't afford it.

I'd met Sultana socially and we hit it off immediately, in part because we are exactly the same height. Although I am well off financially, I still do need to ask prices, so I have only ever browsed in Sultana's exclusive shop. Nonetheless, when Sultana saw me peering through the glass door, she buzzed me in with a smile.

"Taking a break today, Abby?"

"Yes—actually no. The Den of Antiquity is closed."

"Oh? Not forever, I hope."

"I hope not, too. Sultana, I'm here to ask you a favor."

"Ask away, Abby, but you know the drill: if a customer rings the bell, then you're on your own."

"I wouldn't have it any other way. It's about the pearls I'm wearing. I'd like to test them, make sure they're real."

She looked me *straight* in the eyes—always a pleasure—and then burst out laughing. "Abby, how long have we known each other?"

"I don't know—a couple of years."

"And all this time I never thought you were the kind to play practical jokes. Well, I love it!"

"What practical jokes?"

"And to keep such a serious face. Really, Abby, you're a mess."

Sultana's grandparents immigrated to Charleston from someplace in the Middle East, but she is as Southern as collard greens cooked with fatback. When she uses the word "mess" in that context, she means that I'm witty and entertaining, not that I'm in need of a washcloth and comb. Alas, I'm not in the least bit amusing.

"I'm afraid you've lost me, Sultana. I haven't the foggiest what you mean."

"Those hideous pearls, where did you get them? A dollar store?"

I must have turned as red as a Cherry Smash.

"Yeah, something like that. I was feeling kind of goofy this morning when I got dressed."

She has a delightful laugh, so I waited until she was quite finished.

"Sultana, bear with me. And please keep in mind that I handle very little estate jewelry. How did you know these were fakes without touching them?"

"I didn't say they were fakes, Abby, I said they were hideous. But to be blunt—"

"That would be a refreshing change."

She laughed again. "Anyway, I've been in this business so long that I've developed this—well, I guess it's almost like an instinct. I pick up on subtle clues that are really almost impossible to explain. I don't mean to brag, but I'm usually right."

"I do know what you mean. I have a friend who collects different kinds of palm trees. They all look alike to me, but she can instantly spot a new variety when we're riding around town. 'There's just something about it,' she says."

"Exactly. Here, let me see that necklace."

She undid the clasp for me, and then did the tooth test, just as Bob had. Then she went one step further and examined them through a jeweler's loupe, which magnifies things tenfold.

"Sorry, Abby, I was wrong about these."

My heart missed a beat. "Come again?"

"These aren't from a dollar store—I'd say Target is more like it." She paused to laugh at her own joke. "But in all seriousness, they are synthetic. Pretty nice clasp, though, but it isn't gold. There isn't a stamp." She handed the fakes back to me.

"Thanks, Sultana."

"No problem. Well, as long as you're in here, can I interest you in some real pearls? Or maybe some diamonds. They're all conflict-free."

"Excuse me?"

"That means no one has died, or been maimed, over these diamonds. What most people don't seem to know—or care—is that, ironically, a large percentage of the world's precious gems come from countries where the people are very poor. Many of these countries are experiencing civil wars, and control over the mines is crucial to the rebel groups. Haven't you seen pictures of children, forced to work in the mines, who have had their arms or legs hacked off with machetes?"

I shuddered. "No."

"Well, fifteen percent of the world's diamonds come from conflict areas—places like Angola, Sierra Leone, and both Congos. Unfortunately, by the time a diamond reaches a retailer, it's hard to trace its history. That's why I sell only Canadian stones."

"Canada has a diamond mine?"

"You bet it does. The Ekati diamond mine is located two hundred miles north of the Arctic Circle. Not only does it produce gorgeous stones, but they come with proof of origin."

"Wow! Who knew?"

"I have some Russian diamonds, too, Abby, and of course the finest in the world—Golconda diamonds from India. I'm sure you're already aware that my prices reflect the rarity of my merchandise."

"Excuse me?"

"Sure, you might find better deals—or what you think are better deals—in other stores in Charleston, but I stock only—"

"Go back to the G word, please."

"I'm not sure what you mean."

"It sounded a little bit like 'anaconda,' but it started with a G."

"Oh! You mean Golconda. That's the name of an ancient fortress near Hyderabad, India. The world's best diamonds come from the surrounding hills."

"Golconda," I said slowly, then slurred it like Monet had on the phone. *Golconda*! It was the same word. A simple place name, like Charleston, or New York, or Shelby, North Carolina. No doubt that's where Monet and his beautiful palace had originated. It wasn't much to go on, but it was at least *something*.

"Abby, are you all right? You look a little pale."

"I'm fine. Sultana, what's so special about these diamonds?"

"They lack any trace of nitrogen, which makes them the clearest diamonds in the world. Some of the most famous diamonds in history have been Golcondas; the Hope, the Koh-I-Noor, and the Archduke Joseph. That one weighs over seventy-six carats. Celine Dion wore it on a CBS special. I nearly died when I saw it." She burst into laughter again.

"Sultana," I said as her peals subsided, "you wouldn't happen to know where the Taj Mahal is located, would you? Of course it's in India, but where exactly?"

She shrugged. "But you know, Golconda diamonds were used in some of the decorations—embedded in some screens, I think."

"Get out of town!"

"Abby, are you taking a trip there?"

"Heck no, I own the Taj Mahal."

Her melodious laughter was interrupted by the sound of the door buzzer. "Gotta go, Abby. You know the drill."

Indeed, I did.

I stepped into blazing sunshine, and humidity so high I wouldn't have been too surprised to see a fish swimming by. It was the kind of weather that made one gulp for air, and both hair and clothes went instantly limp. God bless Willis Haviland Carrier, the man who invented air-conditioning.

Adjusting to this abrupt climatic change took a minute or two, and as I stood outside Diamonds and Pearls, catching my breath, I felt someone touch my arm. If I hadn't been quite so sapped of energy, I might well have jumped out of my sandals.

"What the—"

"Mrs. Washburn, I didn't mean to scare you."

Certainly Charlie—a.k.a. Blackmond—Dupree was dressed for the tropics, outfitted as he was in a white linen suit, white buckskin shoes, and a white straw hat with a guinea feather tucked jauntily in the white silk band. Frankly, he looked almost handsome enough to grab and whisk off to the land of adultery and divorce. *Almost* that handsome; the dyed mustache was a deal-breaker. But if Greg didn't get his well-toned bottom home soon, and if Mr. Dupree was to shave off his dyed mustache, I might reconsider my status as a lady.

"You really shouldn't sneak up on people like that," I said.

"I apologize. Mrs. Washburn, we need to talk."

"Do we? But sir, I'm not sure we've ever met. Your English is so—well, so Lowcountry."

"Touché. Have you had lunch yet?"

"Not that it's any of your business, but no."

"May I take you to lunch?"

"Sorry, but I'm not in the mood to have someone twitch their tummy in my face while I'm eating."

"I was thinking of someplace closer, like Poogan's Porch. My treat, of course."

That was a dilemma. I didn't have time for a sit-down lunch. On the other hand, Poogan's Porch is one of my favorite restaurants. The biscuits it serves are so light that one needs to hold them down to keep them from floating off one's plate. C.J. claims that she took her Granny Ledbetter to lunch there, and that they requested an additional basket of biscuits. Granny, who liked to hoard food, filled her enormous purse with them. After lunch, as they were walking along Queen Street, a gust of breeze came along, and when coupled with the buoyancy factor of the old lady's purse, lifted her right off the sidewalk. Granny would have become entangled in the power lines, and possibly been electrocuted, had she not panicked and dropped her pocketbook. Fortunately, C.J., the big galoot, was standing under her grandmother and cushioned her fall. C.J. swears by this story, never mind that there aren't any overhead power lines on this section of Queen Street.

Willpower may have won out over biscuits had I not caught sight of the Rob-Bobs heading our way from the direction of the Market. Of course I couldn't be sure, but I didn't think they'd spotted me.

"Lunch would be fine, Mr. Dupree—since it's your treat."

Poogan's Porch, at 72 Queen Street, was built as a spacious home in 1888, surrounded by a lovely garden and enclosed by a wrought-iron fence. In 1976 the owners sold their home and moved away, leaving behind their faithful dog, Poogan. The charming Victorian structure was subsequently turned into a restaurant, but Poogan remained, claiming a perch on the front porch, from which he greeted customers until his death. The heartbreaking story alone makes it worth a visit. Throw in an Apparition American—Poogan's is haunted—and you have the perfect place to lunch on a hot summer day.

I requested that our table be in the back room, which was more than fine with Mr. Dupree. I got the impression he was no keener on being seen than I was. After we'd ordered—just a salad for me so I had room for the biscuits—and I'd had several swigs of my sweet tea, I gave the restaurateur my business smile.

"Okay, Mr. Dupree, I'm ready."

He glanced around the room before speaking. "I hear you talked with Simone."

"A beautiful woman, isn't she? Too bad you're not a single man."

"Mrs. Washburn, I can explain."

"I'm not going to stop you, but there's really no need. What you do with your life is your business."

"I'm glad you feel that way."

"But Simone is a tad young for you—seeing as how you're used to 'old bags'—and killing someone's orchids, their pride and joy, now that's a little mean-spirited, don't you think? But like I said, it's none of my business. If you want to keep on pretending you're a Moroccan of French descent, have at it, by all means. Just don't blame me if, at my next cocktail party, I forget that this is supposed to be some kind of secret."

"Mrs. Washburn! Are you trying to blackmail me?"

"Mr. Blackmond, I do not blackmail."

"It's Charlie, actually."

"Yes, I know."

271

"So you won't squeal on me?"

"Squealing is for pigs. Just try to work something out besides herbicide."

He smiled. "Sure thing. Mrs. Washburn, have I told you how pretty you are today?"

"I'm happily married to a monogamous man, Charlie."

"Point taken."

"Black—Charlie, did you really want that birdcage to decorate your restaurant?"

"Absolutely. Ever since I backpacked through India after college, I've had a thing for the Taj Mahal."

"You've seen the *real* deal?"

He nodded. "It was awesome."

"What's it like?"

"It's in India. I don't mean to be facetious, but in India it's easy to go on sensory overload. The smells—they can be pretty rugged. And the slums, the people sleeping on the sidewalks, the beggars, and then all of a sudden you look up and there she is, the most beautiful building in the world. It just lifts you up, makes your spirit want to soar. My only regret is that I was too young then to really appreciate the experience. I was twenty-one, twenty-two—something like that. Too young to have any sense of historical perspective, and far too young to appreciate a love that deep and abiding."

"The love between the Mogul emperor Shah Jahan and his wife?"

"Wow, I'm impressed."

"Did I pronounce it right?"

"Close enough."

I was starting to like the man. Maybe even believe him. I took a huge bite of warm biscuit, dripping with honey butter. It gave me an excuse to observe him without the risk of sticking my foot in my mouth. I could see how a young woman like Simone would find him devilishly attractive. His eyelashes alone could sweep away any thoughts of resistance.

"Mrs. Washburn, do I have something caught in my mustache? Maybe some biscuit crumbs?"

I swallowed hard. "No."

"I just wondered. You've been staring at me."

"Absolutely not. You see, there's this very interesting couple sitting behind you—don't turn around—and I've been watching them. People watching is so much fun, isn't it?"

"Yes, ma'am, it can be very entertaining," he said, a smile tugging at the corners of his mouth.

It was time to get back to business. "Mr. Dupree, suppose one was to build a hiding place in the Taj Mahal, where would it be?"

He looked puzzled, perhaps properly so. "Sorry, but you've lost me."

"What I mean is—well, from what I understand, the birdcage is a pretty good replica of the real thing, given that one is a building and the other a cage with bars. But the scale is the same, and some of the more important architectural elements have been included in the cage. Wouldn't you agree?"

"Certainly. That's why it would have looked so sharp in the middle of my restaurant. I was serious when I called it a work of art."

I nodded. "Now let's say you were a smuggler—or I was the smuggler—and I wanted to use the birdcage to bring in my contraband. Given your knowledge of the real Taj Mahal, where would I stash it?"

"Well, the real Taj Mahal contains a tomb, which would be the obvious hiding place. Of course the cage doesn't have a corresponding structure—"

"I apologize. That was a stupid question. You're totally right. Comparing a cage—no matter how ornate and cleverly constructed—to a building is crazy. There is no comparison."

"Actually, there is."

CHAPTER 22

"Excuse me?"

"The central dome. That's what struck me when I first saw it at the auction preview. Although the rest of the cage is filigree wire, the dome is covered with some kind of metal."

"Yes, but it's hollow inside. I've already looked up in there. But you know what, it's just as beautiful inside as it is outside. And only the bird gets to see it."

"Lucky bird." He sipped his sweet tea thoughtfully. "Mrs. Washburn," he said at last, "the real Taj Mahal has a double dome. Were you aware of that?"

I felt as if my heart was going to burst right out of my chest, like the alien offspring in some Sigourney Weaver movie. I had to recall my Lamaze breathing lessons.

"Did you say a 'double dome'? With a space between them?"

"Yes, ma'am. That allowed the architects to make the top dome any shape they wanted, and as high as they wanted, without compromising the basic structure. Pretty clever, huh?"

I tried to remember what it had looked like inside the dome of my mini-Taj. The interior space was about the size and shape of a basketball, yet when seen from the outside it was shaped more like an onion, a discrepancy that hadn't sunk into my thick Wiggins skull until now.

"Mr. Dupree, I hate to be rude, but I have to run now."

"But we haven't even been served our entrées."

I gave him what I hoped was a winsome smile. "I ordered just a salad. You're welcome to have it."

He stood, something every gentleman should do when a lady leaves the table; not just Southern gentlemen. "I hope to see you around, Mrs. Washburn. By the way, you're not a bad belly dancer. With a few lessons you might even be good."

"You *know*?"

"What is it they say? Oh yes, you can't con a con man."

"But Simone—I mean, I didn't think she knew."

"She doesn't. She still thinks you're with the IGS. That's a good one, Mrs. Washburn. How long did it take you to think that up?"

"You have your lovely paramour to thank for that, I'm afraid. Mr. Dupree, it really has been a pleasure this time. Thank you very much."

I didn't even make it to the corner when the lecherous albeit devilishly attractive restaurateur caught up with me. Again he grabbed my elbow.

"Mr. Dupree!" I whirled to give him what for

and found myself looking at my beloved's chest. I can't say who was more startled.

"Abby, hon, is that any way to greet your long-lost husband?"

"Greg! I thought it was—someone else."

"Obviously." He picked me up, kissed me like it was our last, and then set me gently down on the pavement. "So who is Mr. Dupree?"

"No one. I mean—well, he owns the Chez Fez."

"Interesting-looking place. You want to try it sometime?"

"Yeah, sure."

"How about now? It's lunchtime and I'm starving."

"I just ate, darling."

"Then come and keep me company. Needless to say, we have a lot to talk about."

"That's for sure, but you see, I'm kind of in the middle of something."

"This has to do with that damn birdcage, doesn't it?"

"Not just that—Mama, too."

A herd of tourists from one of the square states was stampeding our way (the light had turned green), so Greg, ever gallant and loving, shielded me with his body. Then, just as we resumed our conversation, a second herd, this one from that lovely city where folks say yinz instead of y'all, almost mowed us down again.

"You see," Greg said, "our lives are in danger if we stay here."

Indeed they were. It used to be that two

couples—holding hands—could pass each other on the sidewalks of Charleston and not even brush sleeves. Today I sometimes have to flatten myself against a storefront just to allow *one* person to pass. The alarming part is that our sidewalks have not gotten any smaller.

"You win," I said.

Of course Charlie (a.k.a. Blackmond) Dupree was not there to seat us. Nonetheless, we got a decent seat with a good view of the musicians performing on the dais. The belly dancers were on their break when we arrived, and I honestly think Greg was surprised by their sudden appearance. The rather hefty dancer, the one who had seen me as a threat on my first visit, was certainly surprised. I was surprised as well, as I had made sure that we were not seated at her station.

"We had a deal, missy," she hissed as she began a slow bump and grind, which I'm certain is not part of any real belly dancer's routine.

"What deal was that?" The music was steadily getting louder.

"The deal was that I got the good-looking guys. And this guy is hot. You leave him for me, you hear?"

"This hotty is my husband," I hollered over the din.

Her eyes blazed and her mouth opened wide enough to catch a mockingbird. Greg is not the type to interfere in a fight between two women, and I was not stoked enough to tussle with a tasseled hussy. I had no choice but to close the thick velvet drapes.

"What was that all about?" Greg said.

"She's husband hungry. Thinks you'll make a good catch."

"You know her?"

"I know her type." That certainly was not a lie.

"Well, I must say it is romantic in here."

Why is it that for men—at least for Greg—a romantic spot is anywhere that offers enough privacy to do what comes naturally? For my one and only, an empty refrigerator carton in a back alley is just as romantic as a canopy bed with pink satin sheets—which is *not* to say we've ever gone the pink sheet route. Greg is more the navy and brown type.

"Greg, darling," I said, in the interest of time, "I've got a lot of work to do today yet. Tell me about your adventure with your buddy, Mark, and then I'll tell you about the latest Mama news."

What happened next would have shocked the socks off me, had I been wearing any. My usually circumspect husband, who can be counted on to say less than twenty words when we dine out together, let go with a torrent of words that seemed to never stop. I got to hear every detail of Mark and Caroline Gallentree's marriage (some of the stuff was actually pretty interesting) and a step-by-step description of their failing finances, the sneaky thing Mark did to fix that, and then, of course, the dramatic aftermath.

"All's well that ends well," the bard said, but my beloved couldn't find an ending. I should have counted my blessings, I guess, but there were things I needed to say, too. Besides, he hadn't even noticed the necklace I was wearing. I interrupted him to point that out.

"It is nice," he said. "Man, Abby, who would have thought that a sensible woman like Caroline could become addicted to something as asinine as shopping?"

"An addiction is an addiction, darling. But anyway, do you recognize these pearls?"

"Am I supposed to? Give me a break, Abby. I'm trying to tell you about my buddy, and you keep changing the subject."

"That's because I have some important things to share, too. You see, these pearls—"

"Honestly, Abby, I thought we could have a meaningful conversation; not talk about jewelry."

"You're absolutely right," I said, popping out of my seat like a pastry tart. "I just thought you might be interested in knowing that these pearls—which I found in a Dumpster, by the way—have just been appraised at half a million."

That got his attention. "You're serious?"

"As serious as a hen in a den of foxes." With that I slipped between the drapes. "He's all yours," I said to the dancer with matrimonial aspirations.

She grinned happily.

★　★　★

Despite the fish tank humidity, I didn't even try to find a cab. Instead, I hoofed it to the Rob-Bobs' house. I mean that literally. Tommy (that's not his real name) is a horse-drawn carriage driver. Last year I cut him a break on a breakfront he wanted to surprise his wife with on their twentieth wedding anniversary. When Tommy saw me plodding along in the heat, he stopped his surrey and motioned for me to climb aboard.

"How far you going?"

"All the way to the Battery."

"You know," he whispered, "I'm not supposed to give rides to anyone except paying customers. They'll fire my butt if they find out, so just play along."

"Gotcha."

Tommy turned to his passengers. "Folks, we've got a real treat for you today. Melanie Bugglesbottom-Thompson, here, is a real Charlestonian. She is a direct descendant of Alfred Bugglesbottom-Thompson, the first settler in Charleston to be accused of antediluvian celibacy."

The passengers gasped their disapproval.

"What the heck does that mean?" I whispered to Tommy.

"I haven't the foggiest. Isn't this fun?" He switched to his tour guide voice. "The old families socialize only with each other. They maintain their own secret societies and traditions, but Miss Bugglesbottom-Thompson has graciously agreed to share some of this privileged information with

281

y'all. Go ahead, Miss Bugglesbottom-Thompson, it's all yours."

Many of the passengers, especially the women, buzzed with excitement. I smiled and waited until every face was turned to me in anticipation. Even then I didn't have enough time to prepare. I cleared my throat, which gave me another second.

"Well, to begin with," I said, "we are extremely inbred. Did you know that I am, in fact, my own cousin?"

Some uncharitable soul groaned. "I've heard that one before. I thought it had to do with the Amish, not Charleston."

"Oh no, that's pure Charleston. But enough genealogy. Today I'd like to teach you our secret Charleston handshake. Do I have any volunteers?"

Just about every hand shot up. Even the uncharitable soul raised his. I chose an eager young man with earphones hanging around his neck and hair the color of ripe lemons. His T-shirt read: I SURVIVED THE CICADA INVASION OF 2004.

"The handshake I'm about to demonstrate for y'all," I said, trying to sound as grave as my high school algebra teacher, "will get you admitted into all the right parties, and even into some private homes. It's called the 'esnesnon' handshake, and was invented by my illustrious ancestor, Beauregard Esnesnon Bugglesbottom-Thompson in 1868 in order to help us native Charlestonians tell ourselves apart from the carpetbaggers that invaded our fair city during the Union occupation, many of whom had taught themselves to speak in a passable Southern accent, so great was their deviousness."

While I couldn't for the life of me repeat now the complicated handshake I demonstrated for them, I'm pretty sure I displayed both dexterity and imagination. My volunteer was a quick study, and soon we had everyone in the surrey passing the secret shake.

"Now remember, folks," I said as Tommy stopped the surrey for me to disembark, "that handshake is your entrée into Charleston society. Try it on the desk clerk when you get back to your hotel. If you forget the exact moves, then just whisper 'esnesnon.'"

Everyone clapped.

"You've made my day, Abby," Tommy muttered.

I have a key to the Rob-Bobs' house, and they have keys to mine. We also know each other's security codes. I hadn't seen either of their cars in the driveway, so I assumed they weren't home, but I called out just to be safe. The next thing I knew, I was being assaulted by a yellow-haired male who wasn't wearing any pants.

"Dmitri!" I cried, and threw my arms around my ten-pound bundle of feline joy. "Did you miss Mama? Did you? Did you?"

Dmitri responded by lashing me repeatedly in the face with his bushy tail. Then he meowed long and plaintively, no doubt blaming me for everything bad that had ever happened to him, starting with me wrenching him from his mama's breast when he was a mere eight weeks old.

"Don't worry, darling," I said, trying to spit cat hair at the same time. "Tonight your daddy will be home, and you can sleep where you always do—on top of him."

After giving him another hug, which he protested loudly, I hurried to the Rob-Bobs' sunporch, where we'd stored the Taj for safekeeping. Dmitri pattered along behind me, still complaining about my shortcomings as his substitute mama, chief amongst which was the fact that I didn't give him treats every time he begged.

It's not that I expected to find anything amiss, but I breathed an enormous sigh of relief when I saw the Taj Mahal, that splendid work of art, gracing a white wicker coffee table. Dmitri, sensing my heightened emotion, took advantage of the situation to beg even harder.

"Okay, okay," I groused, and ran off to the kitchen, where my friends had stored Dmitri's food and treats. Dmitri ran with me, getting underfoot constantly, eventually tripping me. In trying to catch my balance, I accidentally stepped on his tail. You would have thought I'd done it on purpose. To placate the hairy beast, I dumped the entire contents of the treat bag on the floor and dashed back to the sunporch.

The miniature Taj was even more beautiful than I remembered. It must have taken a skilled metal worker hundreds of hours to bend the wire so it functioned both as a birdcage and a fitting homage to the real Mogul tomb—although the latter was built primarily out of white marble. The bulbous central dome of my Taj Mahal, and the smaller domes that surrounded it, were constructed of sheets of hammered metal that had been gilded and bezel-set with myriad tiny semiprecious stones. I recognized amethyst, turquoise, garnet, peridot, blue topaz, citrine, even a few opaque rubies. None of these stones were large enough, or rare enough, to be valuable in and of themselves, but together they were magnificent. Could there also be Golconda diamonds hidden between the outer and inner domes? Or did this birdcage—for that's what it really was—contain no secrets? There was only one way to find out.

CHAPTER 23

Please believe me, I wouldn't have dreamed of destroying an object so beautiful had I not been convinced Mama was in big, possibly even life-threatening, trouble. But even then, there had to be a way to access the space between the domes without causing a whole lot of damage. I began by trying to unscrew the outer dome, as I would a lightbulb—a lightbulb the size of a three-gallon jug.

Although the bezel-set gemstones gave me plenty of grip, I couldn't get the dang thing to budge. I may be small, but I'm pretty strong; moving heavy antiques around has given me a surprising amount of upper-body strength— well, surprising to strangers. At any rate, I gave up on Plan A before I burst a blood vein in my head, and scouted around for a magnifying glass. Since Rob is a few years closer to presbyopia than I am, it didn't take me long to find one. But alas, a careful examination of the central dome's base revealed no seam. Even if the outer dome had once been removable, that was no longer the case.

Then on to Plan B. That was a little trickier, since I had no one to hold a flashlight for me. Fortunately, the Rob-Bobs' sunporch really does catch the late morning, and early afternoon, sun. I removed the cleaning tray and turned the Taj over gently, so that it lay on its back. I was about to stick my head in when my cell phone rang. "Saved by the bell," I said aloud. I am, after all, not fond of tight places.

Neither am I fond of folks who block their phone numbers. I knew in my gut, however, that the caller was not a telemarketer, but the person who'd stolen my mynah, and possibly even my mama.

"Hello."

"Mrs. Washburn?"

There was something strange about the voice. It was high-pitched, but it didn't sound like a woman's voice, or even that of a little girl. Nor did it sound like a bird.

"Yes, this is she."

"Do you love your mother, Mrs. Washburn?"

The pitch was uneven, and got lower toward the end. It sounded a lot like a man who'd just sucked helium from a balloon—like Daddy used to do at my birthday parties. That was it! The birdnapper had given up on using Monet's voice—maybe the poor bird really was baked in a pie—and had resorted to renting a tank of helium from a party supply store. Now we were cooking with gas.

I made an effort to control my excitement. "Yes, of course I love her."

"Then why haven't you—" He paused to suck another mouthful from the tank. "—been following my instructions?"

"Because there is no Monet painting."

The caller was silent for a moment.

"Monet is just the bird's name," I said. "If you really want him, you can have him. Please, just let my mama go."

"I don't want the damn bird. I want the Monet."

"There isn't any!" I screamed.

"The hell, you say, Abby!" The caller hadn't taken the time to inhale more helium. That definitely wasn't Mickey Mouse on the phone, but someone I knew quite well.

I gasped. "Martin Gibble, is that you?"

"You see what you made me do?"

"I didn't make you do anything, you blithering idiot."

"I'm afraid I'm going to have to kill her now, Abby."

"Mama?"

"She hasn't been anything but trouble. Hell, you should see the bruises on my shins."

I was trembling with fear. Martin makes a bad enemy in the best of times; I had no trouble believing that he would kill Mama if he was desperate. The trick now was to make him believe that he had a way out of the hole he had apparently dug for himself.

"What can I do to fix this, Martin?"

"The courier said the stupid bird had the info. But he was lying, Abby, wasn't he?"

"What courier?"

"Don't play games with me, Abby."

"I'm not. Look, Martin, all I know is that I bought this beautiful cage at auction, and that it came with a bird. Whatever secrets came with it— I really don't know."

"Is that how much you care about her, Abby? Because I'm not bluffing. I've got nothing to lose now, do I? Either you tell me, or she dies."

My legs gave out and I sat on the floor beside the wicker coffee table. My chest felt like there was an elephant sitting on it, maybe even a tourist from Nebraska.

"Martin, listen to me. I don't know about any Monet painting, but I think there might be diamonds."

"Speak louder, Abby. I can barely hear you."

"Diamonds," I yelled. "Little bits of pressurized carbon."

"What about diamonds?"

"I think there may be some very special ones hidden inside the birdcage."

"There's nothing hidden inside that damn cage. I already checked. I didn't just twiddle my thumbs the night I took this sorry excuse for a bird."

"Why didn't you just take the cage as well? Wouldn't that have been a whole lot easier? And if you wanted either of them so bad, why didn't you simply outbid me at the auction?"

"Shut up and listen, Abby."

"I'm all ears."

"I mean it. Don't piss me off. You do it again and your precious mama gets one chance to fly like a bird. If she can't do that—splat. All the king's horses and all the king's men aren't going to be able to put together Abby's mama again."

"I'm listening. I really am."

"Where was I—oh yeah, I was working late one night, doing inventory in my shop, and this guy knocks on the door. I point to the hours posted on my door, but he doesn't pay attention. Then I notice that there's something on the sidewalk behind him, something in a blanket. Maybe it's the family silver he wants to sell. That's happened before. What the heck, I think, I've got a gun in my desk drawer, so I let him in. When he schleps in the thing and uncovers it, I can hardly believe my eyes. It's a damn birdcage."

Sometimes one can't help but interrupt. "But that day in your shop you told me to make sure Monet didn't poop in the cage. You made it sound like you thought it was the most beautiful thing to be created since a sunset."

"Abby, Abby. You don't shut up, and you don't use what little brain you have, either. I wanted you to think it was the cage I was interested in, not the stupid bird. Now, if you don't do as I say and shut up, your precious mama will fall down and break her crown, and you'll be tumbling after."

"I'm locking my lips and tossing away the key—uh, you didn't hear a thing; zilch, zip, nada."

"Anyway, I ask this guy why he's trying to sell me some kitsch birdcage. First he tells me it's solid gold, but I prove right there on the spot that it isn't. Then he tells me that it's really old, and that it belonged to his grandma. But I tell him that I'm sure his grandma had bunions, too, but I'm not interested in buying them, either. So finally he says he's going to tell me the truth. I tell him it's about time, because I was fixing to call the police if he didn't get around to it real soon.

"'No, no,' he says. 'No police.' But I got to swear to secrecy. I tell him nothing doing. It's no skin off my back what happens. 'Okay,' he says, and tells me that he's a courier. It's his job to smuggle things to and from the big container ships that come into harbor. I ask him how that can be, with security as tight as it is these days. He says it's not that kind of smuggling. Yeah, sure, the stuff he carries is illegal, but it's not the kind of stuff that endangers national security. In fact, most of the time he has to go through security—*most* of the time.

"So then one day he has to get this bird and its cage past customs, otherwise the bird will be quarantined, maybe even confiscated. He's supposed to take them to this address in Summerville, collect his fee, and that's it. But he can't find the address, see. So he takes the bird home with him, and keeps looking—for a month. But he still can't find the address. So that's when he brings it to me. Thinks I might buy it because of the cage."

"Which you didn't," I said. "Oops! Sorry, Martin."

"Yeah, but that's not all. This courier guy said he overheard the guy from the ship talking on the phone. Something about the bird being the *real* courier. There's this stolen Monet, you see, and the bird, which can talk, has the information. The painting is sitting in a warehouse someplace just waiting for someone to pick it up. All you have to do is get the bird to talk and you're worth millions.

"Of course I didn't believe any of that crap. I told the guy to get lost. Then about a year later the damn birdcage comes up for auction. Next thing I know you're bidding like there's no tomorrow. At first I'm as confused as a rubber-nosed woodpecker in the Petrified Forest. Then I put two and two together. You've heard the Monet story, too, and you believe it. Well, you outsmarted me once before, Abby. But not this time; this time I outsmarted you. I let you pay for that monstrosity of a cage. All I had to do was take the bird home with me. You do remember that it was your idea that we give each other keys, like good neighbors should, don't you?"

"I didn't intend for us to steal—"

The cell connection was interrupted by a blast of sound that made me drop the phone. I scrambled for it, but when I put the phone to my ear again there were bells. Church bells! But bells ringing at intolerable decibels, so loud that listening to them hurt my ears, forcing me to turn off my phone.

What was I to do now? Martin wanted only one thing in exchange for Mama, and that was a Monet—which I did not have. Surely he'd settle for diamonds.

I dashed back to the kitchen, where Dmitri was still chowing down on the kitty treats. The Rob-Bobs eschew everyday flatware, so it really wasn't my fault that I had to grab a sterling silver dinner knife. Besides, I was more concerned about damaging the Taj than I was about ruining a piece of Sir Christopher.

My intent was to pry the inner dome loose from the inside. To do so meant removing the bottom tray and sticking my head and shoulders into the cage. This wasn't as easy as it sounds. I may be small, but I'm a lot larger than a mynah. Plus there were three perches to contend with, only one of which was removable. That meant weaving my body around the two remaining perches, with my arm extended above my head, knife in hand.

C.J. and I took turns keeping the Taj as clean as one of Monet's whistles. Nonetheless, the inside of the cage smelled strongly of the wrong end of a bird, and the ammonia stung my eyes. It was hard to see what I was doing, which, frankly, wasn't that much. With my free hand I felt around the base of the dome for a seam, but could find none. If I didn't find something soon, I was going to have to resort to mankind's favorite tool: the hammer.

Engrossed as I was in the task at hand, I came late to the realization that there was someone else in the room with me. In fact, I wasn't aware of that important detail until my world went black—I mean that literally. My first thought was that I'd somehow managed to hit my head hard enough to knock me out. It took me a couple of seconds to realize that something had been thrown over me. Since Dmitri has little practice throwing blankets, I jumped straight to the conclusion that Martin Gibble was the culprit.

I was not about to go peacefully into that good night, blanket or not. Martin, curse his evil little heart, was going to get the fight of his life. My first order of business was to extricate myself from the cage. This was by no means a straightforward task, as both my clothes and my hair had become enmeshed in the fine filigree of the cage. While I struggled to free myself, I thrashed my legs and screamed at the top of my lungs.

But I was no match for Martin, who grabbed my legs and pinned them down by sitting on them. He then threw the weight of his upper body against the cage, effectively immobilizing me. Strangely, he smelled of a women's perfume.

"Get off of me you glob of glutinous guano!"

"Abby, is that you?"

"*C.J.?*"

"Ooh, Abby, I thought that was you, but I

couldn't be sure on account of I only saw the back of your head. So I got this comforter from the master bedroom and—"

"C.J.! Off of me—*now*! And get that comforter off me, too."

Daylight returned. "All right, but you don't have to get so huffy."

Irritation and relief battled for my emotions, relief winning by just a hair. "C.J., help me out of this thing, will you?"

"Sure thing, Abby."

I got exactly what I asked for. The big galoot made short shrift of the task by virtually yanking the Taj off over my head. Bits of DNA and fiber samples remained, intriguing clues for future generations of anthropologists.

"C.J.," I said when I was through moaning, "what are you doing here?"

"I just got back from seeing your brother, Abby. I was driving down King Street headed for the shop, and I saw the Rob-Bobs walking. They never walk anywhere, Abby, so I stopped and asked them what they were doing. They said they were looking for you. Why are you missing, Abby?"

"I'm not—I'm here."

"Right. So anyway, I volunteer to go to your house to look for you, and Rob asks me to swing by here and put a roast beef sandwich from Subway in the refrigerator for him. Boy, did that make Bob mad. He went on and on about how restaurant food didn't deserve a place next to his rhea roulade. Finally, I just took off, but I had to backtrack on account of there's a big wedding at St. Philip's. Ooh, Abby, you should have heard those bells."

The hairs on the back of my neck stood up. I stood up to keep them company.

"Maybe I did."

"Abby, you might have seen stars when I tackled you, but I don't think you heard any bells. What were you doing inside the birdcage anyway?"

Maybe I did hear bells—the bells of St. Philip's! Those references to Mama falling down and breaking her crown, and having one chance to fly like a bird . . . St. Philip's Episcopal Church was only a hop, skip, and a jump from the spot where Mama had disappeared. And its steeple was a real cloud-poker. It was only a hunch, but as my friend Magdalena is fond of saying, "a hunch from a woman is worth two facts from a man."

"C.J., give me fifteen minutes—no, make that half an hour—at which time if I haven't called you, call the police and tell them to look for my body at the base of St. Philip's bell tower."

She looked alarmed, as only a dear friend can. "Abby, you're not going to run in front of the wedding guests, are you?"

"I beg your pardon?"

"Like they do in Pamplona."

"Those are bulls, darling, not wedding guests."

"Are you sure?"

"Positive."

"Abby, I'm not trying to argue, but Cousin Leonardo Ledbetter—"

"Later, C.J." I took off like a bat headed toward its belfry.

CHAPTER 24

The crowd of wedding guests was thinning when I arrived, enabling me to slip into the church without garnering a lot of attention. Because I was casually dressed—at least by wedding standards—some folks probably thought I was a florist, or a caterer, attending to postnuptial details. And since I'd actually been in the bell tower once, on a guided tour of the church, I knew exactly where to go.

There are slightly less than a million steep steps that lead to the top of St. Philip's steeple, and I'm not in the best of shape. However, the imminent murder of one's mama can be a powerful motivator. I removed my shoes, so as to make as little noise as possible, and paused frequently to listen for any sounds coming from the top. At one point I thought I heard voices, but then realized they were coming from outside.

Perhaps I was totally off base and would find nothing at the top except for bird droppings and deaf pigeons. But if that was the case, there would be no harm done—except to my calf muscles. I just hoped that the sextant didn't lock me in the tower. St. Philip's Episcopal Church has one of the most historical cemeteries in the nation, and no doubt there are a few Apparition Americans who have taken residence in the bell tower.

But I got barely more than halfway to the top when I heard Martin Gibble shouting down to me. His voice echoed in the tower, and it was hard to sort out the words.

"Come on up, Abby, the view from up here is a killer." At least that's what I thought he said.

"Martin," I shouted back through cupped hands, "if you let my mother go, you can have the Monet, and anything else you want."

"I want you to come up here, Abby."

Strange that Martin wanted me to come there, to confirm with my eyes what my heart already knew. But maybe not so strange after all. If I got close enough so he could shoot me, or push me off the tower, or snuff me out in any number of ways, he might still be able to escape scot-free. Of course he'd have to kill Mama, too—if she wasn't already resting comfortably with Daddy on the Wiggins family cloud. But as long as I stayed out of Martin's reach, I remained a threat.

"I'm not coming up there, Martin. I sprained my ankle yesterday; I can barely walk."

"Don't lie to me, Abby. There was nothing wrong with your ankle a few minutes ago. You were practically running down the street."

"But I am afraid of heights, Martin. Honest. Tell you what: I'm going to leave the key to a storage unit on the ledge of this little fake window next to me. The name of the storage company is—"

"Acme?"

That's exactly what I was going to say—but I was just making that up. I had no idea if there really was an Acme Storage in Charleston. Maybe there wasn't, and this was a test.

"Actually, Martin, the storage company is in Orangeburg, South Carolina. It's called Treasure Keepers. The number of the unit is tied to the key."

"You're lying, again. Why do you lie to me, Abby? Don't you love your mama?"

The man was brighter than I gave him credit for, and a whole lot more intuitive. His hunches were worth every bit as much as a woman's. It was time to switch tactics.

"Come to think of it, Martin, my mother has always been a pain in the butt. 'Abby, do this, Abby do that'; she never shuts her trap. Not to mention that she's always loved my brother more. The Monet—oh, you should see it, Martin—is worth a cool three million. Even more, if the Saudis are in the right mood. No, Martin, you keep Mama, and I'll keep the painting."

"Why, Abigail Louise Wiggins Timberlake Washburn!" Mama's voice was clear as a bell. But Martin was fond of playing around with voices. For all I knew, that was a recording. Or maybe even Monet. "How dare you choose a painting over your mama. I'll have you know I endured thirty-six hours of excruciating labor—"

"Mama!" I screamed. "It really is you."

"He doesn't have a gun!" Mama screamed back.

"Shut up, bitch."

I heard scuffling overheard, the clank of a bell hitting something—or someone—and another scream. It is easier, and quicker, to run down a zillion steps than it is to run up. I took the path of least resistance.

The body was lying on the sidewalk, faceup. I expected it to look worse, perhaps because I'd seen so many gruesome scenes on television and in the movies. Martin Gibble, on the other hand, looked for all the world like he'd decided to take a nap—with his eyes open.

"Who is it?" The question was on a dozen pairs of lips.

"I'm not sure of his name," a matron in wedding guest attire said, "but his face rings a bell."

Her husband nodded gravely. "That's because this fellow's a dead ringer for that antique dealer over on King Street. You know, the one who sold us that Napoleon love seat you like so well."

"Probably a suicide," a second matron opined. "People who commit suicide are so inconsiderate. He landed on our cousins from Missouri. Fortunately, they're a hard-headed bunch and no one was hurt."

That explained the condition of Martin's corpse. Mama, however, was nowhere to be seen. I ran back into the bell tower and climbed all zillion steps without pausing to catch my breath.

CHAPTER 25

I called my brother, Toy, from the emergency waiting room at Roper Hospital. "I found Mama."

"Yeah? Where was she? No, let me guess . . . she was working as the entertainment director on a Club Med cruise."

"Not even close. She was bound with duct tape and stashed in the bell tower of St. Philip's Episcopal Church."

"Sorry sis, but I like my scenario better. It's more realistic. Can't you just see Mama trying to organize a game of bingo—"

"Toy, I'm not kidding."

"Yeah, right. Who put you up to this? C.J.?"

"Shut up, Toy—please. I really did find Mama in the bell tower. She's dehydrated, and her ears hurt, but the doctor says she's doing pretty good for a woman in her late sixties—considering."

"Jeez, Abby, you're for real?"

"As real as your engagement to C.J."

"Shoot. Give me a second while I sit down."

I counted to thirty by tens. "It's a long story,

Toy, that involves a gilded birdcage and a mynah named Monet—"

"C.J. told me about that. Said the bird was a hoot, and that his cage was awesome."

I rolled my eyes. Was the world really ready for an Episcopal priest who said "awesome"? Just a few months ago Toy had been parking cars for stars in California. Maybe this seminary phase was just that: a phase that would pass, leaving us the irresponsible Toy we all knew, and some of us loved. That Toy was easy to compete with—it wasn't even a contest. But Lord knows, if he really was getting his act together, I was going to have to pedal hard just to keep up.

"Speaking of your fiancée," I said, "here she comes now. I'm going to put her on the phone and let her tell you the rest."

"Thanks, Abby. And sis?"

"Yes?"

"I love you."

"Excuse me?"

"I love you."

"Uh—me too. What brought that on?"

"I've been kind of a jerk my whole life, Abby. I want things to be different from now on."

I crossed my fingers. Yeah, me too."

Mama reigned majestically from her hospital bed. Yes, she was traumatized by her experiences in the bell tower, but that didn't stop her from milking those who loved her for all the sympathy she could get. As her strength and confidence returned, she turned her milking skills on the public. The woman was brilliant at PR.

The three major networks did live remotes from her hospital room, which Mama had us record and play back to her ad nauseum. She was a natural-born performer, with impeccable timing. She flirted with Charley Gibson, complimented Al Roker on his weight loss, and told Julie Chen she wished she had a daughter just like her. Mama's only gaffe was to tell Katie Couric that she really preferred to be interviewed by Matt Lauer, who happened to be on vacation that week.

In addition to the electronic media, Mama gave interviews to dozens of journalists, including a few of the less scrupulous. It was her own fault, therefore, when headlines on a supermarket rag read: SIXTY-NINE-YEAR-OLD GRANDMOTHER HAS MICHAEL JACKSON'S BABY." Mama was incensed and demanded a rebuttal. "I'm only sixty-eight," she said angrily on *Larry King Live*.

Even when not embellishing the truth, details of her captivity made for fascinating copy. Martin Gibble, it would appear, had been petrified by my half-pint parent. Her wish was his command— except, of course, her wish to go free. Martin had come every evening to feed her and let her use the comfort room. For the latter, the nasty napper had to carry Mama down and up the zillion steps. And on two occasions she sent him back to a restaurant to get new meals, complaining that the ones he'd brought were too cold. During the day, she slept on a goose down comforter, folded to make a bed, or watched a battery-powered television, which she listened to through headphones.

Just because Martin jumped when Mama told him to didn't make him a good guy. He'd wanted, of course, to frighten me with the parcels containing her crinoline and pearls, respectively, but Mama had refused to part with them—even when staring down the barrel of his gun. Martin had to settle for a secondhand crinoline from Granny's Goodies on King Street and "pearls" from a discount department store.

Monet was almost as difficult to deal with as Mama. He talked up a storm, but said nothing revelatory about a stolen painting. Then Martin, who was convinced I knew something about the theft—thus my fierce bidding—tried to get Monet to talk into a tape recorder. Martin would then use the bird's voice when he made his ransom calls. It was, at least in theory, a brilliant plan: the FBI would be stumped, unable to match the mynah's voice to any human voice pattern. But the black bird from India would not cooperate. Instead, he got into a rut, reciting nursery rhymes he'd learned from a previous owner.

Although it was the Charleston police who rescued Monet from Martin Gibble's house, he was put in the temporary custody of the Feds, as was the Taj Mahal. I would like to say that I stewed and fussed about Monet's welfare, but the truth is, Mama demanded, and received, almost all of my attention. The rest of my energy went to Greg.

My darling husband had made a convincing show of remorse upon his return from McClellanville. When he wasn't with me at the hospital, he was home burning supper or trying to master the great mysteries of vacuum cleaners and washing machines. The man certainly gets an E for effort.

I returned from the hospital one evening to find Greg entertaining a beautiful young woman with legs up to her armpits. Before I could jump to conclusions, my beloved jumped to his feet.

"Hon," Greg said, "this is Agent Krukowski. She wants to talk to you about Monet."

I shook the proffered hand. "I'm afraid you've wasted your time, Agent Krukowski. I know very little about the artist—or his work."

"Mrs. Washburn, it's the bird I want to talk about, not the painter."

I was suddenly overcome by a wave of emotion. It was as if she had come to deliver bad news about a loved one.

"What happened?" I demanded.

"Relax, Mrs. Washburn, he's fine. He came through the surgery with flying colors."

"Surgery?"

"Yes. We gave the bird an ultrasound—to see if perhaps he'd been embedded with a chip of some sort, or surgically implanted with a key. What we found was rather startling."

"Go on!" I wanted to yank the words out of her with a tongs.

Agent Krukowski reached into a scuffed leather briefcase and took out a small envelope, the size of a seed packet. She dumped the contents into her hand.

Greg reacted first. "Wow! Is that a diamond?"

Agent Krukowski nodded briskly. "Not just any diamond. The finest in the world."

"A Golconda diamond from India," I said, which startled the agent, but caused my husband to smile proudly.

"That's right, Mrs. Washburn. Once we had the diamond, we were able to trace its provenance, due to its rarity and size. As you can see, it's heart-shaped. This diamond is, in fact, named the Heart. In Hindi, the word heart is *mun*. We believe that 'Monet' may have been a corruption of *mun*. The courier on this end may well have misunderstood what he was told during the handover. At any rate, it is absolutely flawless and weighs 47.5 carats, with an insured value of five and a half million dollars."

Greg whistled. "That's a lot of moolah."

"Indeed it is."

"Wait just a cotton-picking minute," I said. "Are you saying that this was *inside* Monet?"

"I am. But don't worry, Mrs. Washburn. We've learned that it was placed in his gizzard by laparoscopic surgery, and that's how we removed it. Because birds lack teeth, they normally eat small stones to help them grind their food. This is, of course, much larger than any gravel he would eat on his own, but I can assure you it caused him minimal discomfort."

"What happens to Monet now?"

"That's why I'm here. To put it crudely, we're through with him. Legally he is yours, and you may have him back. I just wanted you to know that another party is interested in acquiring him, if only to nurse him back to health."

"Another party?"

"A Mr. Bubba Johnson. He's been following the story on the news. Just so you know, Mrs. Washburn, we've checked him out, and he seems to be quite an expert on birds."

"Tell me about it." I clamped a hand over my mouth.

Greg was too busy planning his next question to notice. "What happens to the diamond?"

"I was waiting for someone to ask that. Its rightful owner is an Englishwoman, the widow of a former rajah, living in Agra."

"That's the city where the Taj Mahal is," I said.

Agent Krukowski's brow furrowed slightly. "You certainly are well-informed, Mrs. Washburn. As I was about to say, we will be returning both the cage and the jewel to their rightful owner." She slipped the diamond back into the envelope, which she tucked deep into her briefcase. "Well, I think that's all. Here's my card. Let me know what you decide about the bird as soon as possible. By tomorrow if you can."

We walked her to the door. It was only then that I noticed a car idling across the street. The uniformed man sitting in it was undoubtedly her security guard.

"Agent Krukowski," I said as we shook hands again, "what is Monet's real name?"

"Blackie."

"Excuse me?"

She smiled for the first time. "Not very imaginative, is it?"